AN UNFAMILIAR MURDER

JANE ISAAC

W**O**RLDWIDE

TORONTO • NEW YORK • LONDON
AMSTERDAM • PARIS • SYDNEY • HAMBURG
STOCKHOLM • ATHENS • TOKYO • MILAN
MADRID • WARSAW • BUDAPEST • AUCKLAND

W🌐RLDWIDE™

ISBN-13: 978-1-335-41873-9

An Unfamiliar Murder

First published in 2012 by Rainstorm Press.
This edition published in 2022.

Harlequin Enterprises ULC
22 Adelaide St. West, 41st Floor
Toronto, Ontario M5H 4E3, Canada
www.ReaderService.com

Printed in U.S.A.

AN UNFAMILIAR MURDER

To David and Ella

ONE

THE WALLS WERE closing in on Anna. Her chest tightened.

A loud, chilling wail rose up from beyond. She closed her eyes, pressed her palms to her ears to shut out the intermittent screams.

"Shut it!" yelled a voice in the distance.

"Can it!" growled another. "Before I make you."

"Like to see that," responded the first one. Raucous laughter filled the air.

Anna sat on the hard bench and shuddered, hugging her knees into her stomach, coiling her body to protect it. As the last decibels of laughter abated, her eyes focused on the graffiti scratched on to the wall beside her. *Read this and weep.* She stared at it for a moment then slowly, gradually, her body started to rock, forwards and backwards.

The sound of a door banging in a distant corridor reverberated around the building, breaking her abstraction. She looked around at the windowless room, the empty, off-white walls; the grey metal door; the dazzling light bulb in the middle of the ceiling that made her eyes ache; the grey flecked 'easy clean' flooring. A smell of bleach pervaded the air.

Anna felt a pang in her bladder as her eyes focused on the small cubicle in the corner. She quivered, wrinkled her nose. The thought of using what was inside didn't appeal.

Footsteps and the jingle of metal brought her attention back to the door, her nemesis and barrier to the outside world. She held her breath as they halted for a second, before moving on, fading into the distance. It wasn't her turn yet.

Anna massaged her shins gently through the navy jogging suit that hung off her tiny frame. She wriggled uncomfortably as the folds of material rubbed against the bare skin beneath, resenting being ordered to wear it, like a young child whose mother chooses their wardrobe.

Thoughts of her own mum made her shudder. She closed her eyes and imagined the scene at her parents' home right now. This was supposed to be their special evening, their 30th wedding anniversary celebration. The invitations had been sent out weeks ago. She could see their friends arriving all smiles and congratulations, only to be turned away, only to be disappointed...

The camera in the far corner of the room faced her disconcertingly. Her bladder bounced in her stomach again and she scowled at the thought of them watching her, clenching her teeth in an effort to fight away the tears, cursing her tendency to cry when angry. Were they watching her body language?

Another distant noise in the corridor outside. Thud, thud, thud, at regular intervals. She clutched her stomach. She really needed the toilet. The footsteps were measured, precise and getting louder. She listened intently, trying to block out the other noises: the whir of the camera, the jangle of metal, the voices in the background, which all conspired to dull her hearing. The sound of a key being inserted into the lock followed. The door opened to reveal a man in a black uniform looking slightly dishevelled. His hair was in dire need of a cut, his nose flattened as if, in the distant past, it had been on the receiving end of a good, hard punch.

"Anna Cottrell?" he asked. "Yes?"

"Your solicitor is on the phone for you." He held out a cordless telephone. Anna jumped off the bed, tripping over her own feet in her haste to reach it.

"Will, is that you?"

"It's me. Are you OK?"

"No, I need help." She failed to draw breath, speaking quickly, as if the call would be ended at any moment.

"I'm on my way. Do you need anything?" he asked gently.

"Just you to get me out of here."

"Sit tight. I'll be there in twenty minutes…"

TWO HOURS EARLIER, Anna switched to second gear as she free-wheeled down the hill and past the wrought iron sign indicating the entrance to Little Hampstead, completing her three mile journey home from work in the nearby midlands city of Hampton.

Due to its close proximity to the city, the small village of Little Hampstead was rapidly losing its sense of community. As long-standing residents died or moved into care, their properties were snatched up at over-inflated prices by professional people seeking the refuge of a rural, countryside setting. The school had closed two years ago, the post office six months later. Even the old village shop building was covered in tarpaulin, as builders worked steadfastly to turn it into the next hot residential property. What was left was a ghost village, the presence of the majority of its 400 inhabitants only noticeable by their wheelie bins on collection day. This suited Anna, she much preferred this environment to the goldfish bowl community where her parents lived.

Dark rain clouds, swept along by a bustling wind, threatened the November sky. Thankful for the assistance of bright street lighting as she entered the village, she slowed at the crossroads and turned right into Flax Street.

The familiar hum of her mobile phone started as she arrived outside number 22. She braked, fished her phone out of her pocket. "Mum" flashed on the screen. Manoeuvring herself off her bike, she sighed and pressed the answer button. "Hi, Mum."

"Anna. Where are you?" The voice was brittle with panic.

"Calm down, I'm outside the flat. I just need to get changed and I'll be over," Anna said.

"Did you pick up the serviettes?"

"Yes, I have them. I'll see you in an hour."

"Make it half an hour." The call was ended. Anna sighed again and raised her eyes skywards. She put her phone back in her pocket and wheeled her bicycle towards the opening that divided the cluster of terraces, sympathetically converted into apartments, and stopped, waiting expectantly.

"Damn that light," she muttered and gave up the wait, proceeding to wheel her bicycle through the aperture between the houses, which was bathed in darkness.

As she reached the rear of the property she was grateful for the slice of natural light the moon supplied as it broke out between the clouds, enabling her to see clearly enough to climb the steps to the entrance of her home.

Using all the might in her slender body she lifted her bicycle, carrying it up to the door of Flat 22a.

It wasn't until she reached the top stair, placed her bike down against the wall and fumbled in her bag for her keys, that she realised something was wrong. The door was ajar.

Anna stared at the open door for a moment, nonplussed. *Did I close it this morning?* She thought. She couldn't remember locking it. *Surely, I didn't leave it open?* Aware of the habitual rush that dictated her morning routine, she let her mind ponder these questions as her eyes searched around.

And then they found it, as they would a small crack in a windscreen: splinters down the side of the door, close to the Yale lock, chips that exposed the bare wood underneath the red paint, indicating that the door had been forced. Her body froze. A shiver rolled down the back of her head, gathering momentum as it descended, like an icy, cold waterfall.

She stood for a moment, glued to the spot, glancing around at the neighbouring terraces, praying for some sign of life.

Her senses heightened. She became aware of her own shallow breathing, the noise exacerbated by the growing darkness, and the knowledge that she was alone. On this side of the door at least.

With a sudden movement, she pushed the door with her fingertips. "Who's there?" she called out, trying to hide the panic threatening to break her pitch. Her voice disappeared into the silence of the night.

Anna sucked a deep breath and closed her eyes for a second as she held it, a gesture intended to muster any remaining courage, before she pushed the door open further to expose an empty hallway. Relief squashed the air out of her lungs. This part of the house, in any event, was empty. Her shoulders relaxed and she reached around the left hand side of the doorframe, fingertips searching for the light switch. Finally they found it and with a short click, bathed the hallway in the poor, limited light of a low energy light bulb.

The light revealed very little: a small shoe rack containing a pair of black ankle boots next to muddy trainers to the left; four coat hooks above, upon which hung a single, black fleece jacket; a quarry tiled floor, covered for the most part by a colourful Turkish rug her parents had brought her back from a holiday.

Anna paused for a moment, her eyes darting around. There were only two doors off the hallway. The first on the right led to the kitchen and was ajar, the second directly opposite led initially to the lounge, following on to a double bedroom and small bathroom. This door was closed. The main entrance provided the only access to the flat, which occupied the first floor of the old house. The only access, she thought to herself. Whoever had forced this door would have also left this way. *If they have left.*

A tremble rippled through her body. Her hands shook as she parked her bicycle outside against the wall, removed the rucksack and rummaged in her pocket for her mobile phone. One bar of charge showed up on the lit panel. She gently pressed a button, switching the sound to silent, pressed three nines consecutively and placed it back in her pocket, her thumb perched over the call button, before stepping into the hallway.

Silence saturated the flat. She stood still for some time listening for any little sound, before gingerly placing her hand against the kitchen door. Deftly, she put one foot inside and peered behind the doorway. Relief again flooded her veins. It was clear.

Bizarrely, Anna felt an adrenalin rush at this point. This extraordinary turn of events felt like an out-of-body experience, the scene of a film set, where her alter ego was on an escapade of discovery. It was the kind of story that one would relate later at dinner parties to friends who would hang on every word. *But this is no film, no story*, thought Anna. Another shiver. It shot down her back this time, making her tremble again. *This is right here, right now. This is real.*

Reaching for the second drawer on the left, the kitchen light still off, she opened it and slowly felt around, eventually drawing out a long, sharp carving knife. Armed with mobile phone and knife, her confidence rose as she approached the lounge door. A strong metallic smell filled the air.

Holding the knife firmly between her thumb and forefinger, she pushed hard. It swung open to reveal a large room, which the small streak of light seeping through from the hallway had little effect on illuminating. Just as she was cursing her laziness at leaving the long, heavily lined curtains drawn that same morning, she stopped. *What was that?* She shrank back into the hallway. *There it is again.* Tap, tap, tap. So quiet she could barely hear it. She allowed only very short, controlled breaths—as if it would impede her hearing. Nothing. Were her ears playing tricks on her? *No, there it is again.*

Anna retreated through the hallway and turned around, following the sound. There it was—the chain on the back of the door was hanging down, tapping against the back of the wood in the wind. She sighed heavily, relaxed her shoulders and turned back towards the lounge.

She repeated her earlier actions, this time reaching around the right hand side of the doorframe, a few fingers freed from the knife to search for the switch. Suddenly, the room was immersed in light. But her fingers felt soft and sticky this time and, as she drew her hand back into view, she noticed they were covered in a red liquid. It was then that she raised her eyes.

Anna gasped, dropping the knife. Panic surged through her body like a tidal wave. Her right hand clasped the doorframe tightly to prevent herself from falling as her legs weakened. She felt as if she was drowning, fiercely battling against a weight of water that was rapidly pushing her down. The room started to spin, mixing up colours, until everything was a blur. The heat in her head rose as she fought the urge to faint.

Acid rose in her throat and for a moment Anna stood there, head hung, sickly tears running down her face. Finally she turned back to face the horror of the room's contents, opened her mouth but her voice caught, suppressing any sound as she pressed the ring button on her mobile phone.

TWO

DETECTIVE CHIEF INSPECTOR Helen Lavery was standing beside the toilet, watching her fifteen-year-old son retch and cast out the poisoned contents of his stomach like an overflowing drainage pipe, when her mobile phone rang.

"Damn! Hold on a minute, Matthew," she said, patting his shoulder before walking out of the room. He looked up helplessly. The truth was that he couldn't hold on even if he had wanted to.

She reached into her pocket as she crossed the landing and answered on the fifth ring, just before the voicemail kicked in.

"Yes?"

"Ma'am, this is Inspector Henton. I'm sorry to bother you this evening, but you are the Duty SIO." It was a statement more than a question, as if he sensed her irritation, the intrusion into her evening.

"Yes, I believe so," she replied, reaching down to grab a notebook and pen from her bedside table. "What do you have for me?"

"Uniform were called to a flat in Little Hampstead at 6pm this evening, where they found a body with multiple stab wounds. Paramedics have certified it dead and the Duty DI is on the scene." The control room Inspector's voice was rushed, keen to pass on this information, as if the end of his shift were approaching.

"Any suspects?" Helen asked as she opened her wardrobe, her fingers flicking through the endless hanging clothes, most of which hadn't been worn in years.

"Only the informant, an Anna Cottrell, who claims she arrived home from work to find the body of a stranger in her flat."

"Who is the inspector at the scene?" she said, as she crossed the room and rummaged through the washing basket, pulling out a white, jersey shirt.

"Acting DI Townsend." Helen closed her eyes and sat down on the edge of the bed, tucking a stray strand of her dark, bobbed hair behind her left ear as she dug through the archives of her brain, recalling her memories of Simon Townsend.

During her first year in the force they had worked on the same shift. His nickname was "Cuff" because he was known for cuffing off jobs, choosing to do as little as possible. His reputation for being lecherous was legendary and none of the female officers liked to be crewed up with him. But there was one incident that was soldered on to her brain cells.

On one particular night shift he was paired with a junior PC, Janet Bland, a new recruit just out of training. They were tasked with staking out an industrial estate that had experienced a number of burglaries in recent months. They arrived by car and were required to patrol the area on foot every couple of hours.

Whilst alone on patrol PC Bland was accosted by three male assailants. Although she managed to shout for assistance on her radio, by the time emergency support arrived, she had been badly beaten. Townsend claimed that it had happened while he had momentarily broken contact to relieve his bladder nearby.

Bland was in hospital for six weeks afterwards, and did not return to the force. Helen never found out whether this was due to the extent of her injuries (which included cracked ribs, a broken femur and a detached retina), or as a result of the mental trauma the incident had caused. Janet, while refusing to make a formal complaint, later confided to her colleagues that Townsend had chosen to sleep in the car, rather than accompany her on patrol. The episode cast a shadow over the whole station for many months afterwards.

Whether or not Townsend was disciplined, Helen was too junior in rank at the time to know. He transferred to the Metropolitan police shortly afterwards. She'd heard that he had been promoted to Sergeant a couple of years ago and returned to the Hamptonshire force last year when his marriage broke up, but their paths had not crossed. Until now. She wondered how anybody, even a reformed character, with Townsend's background could rise through the ranks to Acting Inspector.

"Ma'am?" The voice at the other end of the line jolted her back to the present. "Would you like his mobile number?"

"No, I have it," she lied. "Is there a Duty DS on scene?"

"Yes, DS Pemberton." Helen cast her eyes to the ceiling in relief. "I will take his mobile number please." She scribbled down the digits, clicked to end the call and quickly changed out of her jeans and sweater into the tired looking suit she'd picked out, breathing in to fasten the size twelve trousers. She threw the shirt over her head, donned the jacket and reached over to grab her mobile phone, punching in DS Pemberton's number. He answered on the second ring.

"DS Pemberton." The thick, Northern accent disclosed his Yorkshire roots.

"Sergeant, this is DCI Lavery. I'm the Duty SIO this evening. What do we have?" she said as she scrambled around the bedroom, lifting the remote, moving books off the bedside table, in search of her watch.

"Have the control room not briefed you?" he asked, an indication of surprise in his voice.

"In your own words, Sergeant."

"Certainly… Well, control room were called to 22a Flax Street, Little Hampstead at six o'clock this evening by a twenty-four-year old female who claimed she'd returned home from work to find the door forced and the stabbed body of a white male, approximately fifty years old, in her flat. An ambulance was called who certified death at six-fifteen, and I arrived while the paramedics were on site." He articulated these facts efficiently and she was impressed by his competence, as always. Helen had worked with DS Pemberton for a couple of months on "Operation Sandy" the previous year, where she had led a team seeking to reduce the number of distraction burglaries in Hamptonshire. He was an old school detective with plenty of experience.

"What action has been taken, so far?" she asked, as her eyes found her watch, laid on top of the bookcase.

"DI Townsend is with me. Would you like a word?"

"In a moment. Please continue." Helen reached over and grabbed her watch, precariously balancing the phone between her chin and neck whilst fastening the catch.

"Errr… Of course." There was a trace of perception in his voice, betraying his awareness of the inspector's reputation. "Uniform cordoned off the area, preserving the crime scene. They called out the Force Medical Examiner who is here now and the CSIs, who have just arrived, and took an initial account of events from the suspect. We've started house-to-house within the vicinity. Just waiting for the pathologist."

"What do we know about the suspect?"

"Very little. No previous record. She works as a teacher in a local school, has lived in the flat for two years. Claims the victim is a complete stranger to her."

"Any weapon?"

"A carving knife was found at the scene."

Helen narrowed her eyes as she scribbled down the details. "Where is the suspect now?"

"She has been arrested and escorted to the station. She was found by the entrance to the room where the body was found, knife beside her."

"OK. I'll be there in twenty minutes. Don't let anybody move anything and make sure the Crime Scene Manager logs every movement, both into and out of the house." Helen cringed as the words flew out of her mouth before she was able to stop them. DS Pemberton would be well aware that this was the first time she had headed a murder investigation. Coupled with the fact that she had only served a short spate in CID as a Detective Sergeant during her ten-year service (a constraint of the accelerated promotion scheme), she knew that she had a lot to prove. And she also knew that her every move would be scrutinised not only by her superiors, but also by her own team.

She took a deep breath. "Thank you, Sergeant. I'll speak to Inspector Townsend now."

She could hear a momentary shuffle in the background as the phone was handed over. Townsend must have been standing right next to him.

"Good evening, ma'am. I…"

Helen cut in. "Good evening, Inspector," she said and, not wishing to invite conversation, quickly continued, "When you have familiarised yourself with the crime scene can you please get back and secure us an incident room? I believe Cross Keys is the nearest station to Flax Street?"

"It is," he replied.

"Good. Then I'll leave it to you to set things up. The press will be crawling all over this very soon and we need to be prepared. And start calling in the DCs," she paused for a moment, rubbing her forehead. "I'll call you back before you do that. OK?"

"Yes, ma'am."

"Thank you. I'll see you at the station." She clicked the button to end the call and started jotting down names of particular detectives for her homicide team.

JUST OVER TWENTY minutes later Helen flashed her badge at the PC who was blowing hot air into his hands, rubbing them together and stamping his feet in an effort to keep warm. He moved aside, allowing her to walk through the gap between the houses and climb the rear steps which led to the entrance of Flat 22a. As she arrived at the entrance hall she could see DS Pemberton, talking to a man in a long, black coat with his back to her.

"Detective." She nodded to DS Pemberton and immediately the black-coated figure turned to face her.

"Good Lord!" he exclaimed.

"Good evening, Charles," she said, relieved that, out

of the limited number of pathologists that serviced their area, she had struck gold. Dr Charles Burlington was captivated by his work, his lengthy career providing him with a wealth of experience.

"Helen, how lovely to see you!" His face lit up as he extended his hand, but she didn't miss the glint of surprise in his eyes. She shook his hand warmly and smiled.

"How are those little boys?" he asked, as he recovered himself and stood back to survey her fully.

"Oh, you know, teenagers," she replied, the smile still playing on her lips.

"Teenagers. Really?" He raised his eyebrows. "Then it really must be quite a few years since we saw each other. Do give them a slap on the back from their uncle Charles. I'm sure I must owe them both a rugby tackle."

"I think Matthew would give you a run for your money these days. He must be six inches taller than you." She laughed. It was good to see Charles. He'd been a great friend to her late father, and the family. They resolved to stay in touch after the funeral though work, family routine and moving house had restricted their contact for many years to Christmas cards. She noticed his thick, curly brown hair had transformed to white and crows' feet had crept in around the eyes, but in spite of his age he still kept himself trim.

"How is Sarah?" she asked, creasing her forehead, trying to think when she had last seen her. *It must have been John's funeral*, she thought to herself. John, Helen's husband, had died suddenly in 2000. Helen remembered Charles' devoted wife fondly. She was one of those women who had given up her job as soon as their first child had been born, and once they had grown up and left home, dedicated her life to gardening, home cooking and exercising the family collie.

"Running around after the grandchildren these days, reliving her childhood," he replied. Silence followed as he started to look around the blood-bathed room. "And what do we have here?" He was focusing on the corpse now, sat up against the large sofa that dominated the room. "Are you working on this one?" he added, turning his attention back to her.

"Heading the investigation actually," she replied, watching the surprise in his eyes warm to comprehension. "So, I'm going to need your help Charles."

"Well, well. Following in your father's footsteps, I see?" James Lavery had dedicated the majority of his career to the Homicide Team in Hamptonshire. It was his stories, his enthusiasm for the job, sheer tenacity and desire to make a difference that had rubbed off on Helen during her formative years. Leading the Homicide Team had been her ambition for as long as she could remember.

He looked back into the room. "We'd better get started then." She watched him move over towards the body, encased in his own world of forensic pathology and turned back to face the sergeant.

DS Pemberton was an imposing sight, a bear of a man in height and width with a shiny, bald head. The last ten of his twenty years in the force had been served as a detective and, having worked on the homicide team for five years before moving out to Area, he was completely comfortable in this environment.

"Good evening, ma'am," he said, his voice so deep it sounded as though it had been lifted from the pit of his stomach. "How are you?"

"Fine, thank you, Sean. And you?"

He nodded. "Can't grumble."

Helen turned and looked over the scene properly for the first time. "So, what do we know about this chap?" Pemberton started shaking his head before she'd even completed her sentence. "No wallet? Doesn't anybody recognise him?" she asked. With the amount of police staff and civilians that had passed through this room in the last hour, it was very possible that somebody might have recognised him.

"Nothing. We've checked his pockets. There's nothing on him that indicates his identity."

"Can I move him?" Helen turned around, following the voice. It was Charles, bent over the body, calling to one of the Scenes of Crime officers.

"Yes, we're done in that area," he called back.

"Excellent," Charles replied, shuffling around the corpse, absorbed in his work.

Helen looked back at Pemberton, her thoughts racing. "Has anyone taken prints?" she asked.

"Not yet, as far as I'm aware."

"Get somebody to bring down a mobile fingerprint machine, would you?" she said. "At least then we could get the prints run through the system to see if he is known to us. We could do with identifying him as soon as possible."

Pemberton nodded and reached into his pocket, pulling out a mobile phone. He turned and walked into the hallway as he made the call.

Helen stood and surveyed the walls showered in blood, looked across the floor. Finally her gaze rested on the corpse. Male, aged around mid-fifties she guessed, with grey, thinning hair. She tried to look beyond the blood wounds and extensive stains on his body. His appearance was generally unkempt, his hair greasy, his clothes ragged, as if they had seen better days. Yet he didn't look like a tramp. He wasn't dirty enough for that.

She glanced over at Pemberton as he strode back into the room. "What did the FME say about time of death?" The Force Medical Examiner, or FME, was a local GP who attended murder scenes to certify time of death.

Pemberton stifled a chuckle. "Sometime within the last four hours," he replied, raising his eyebrows.

"What?" Helen said incredulous. "What good is that?"

"Let's hope *he* comes up with something more accurate." Pemberton nodded towards Charles who was now on his knees, suitcase opened, hard at work. Helen walked over to him.

"What do you have for me, Charles?" she asked.

"Well, of course it's very early to say," he replied, as he turned his head sideways to look up at her, "but I would say that this killer knew exactly what he was doing."

"How do you mean?" She bent over to look as he turned the body over on to its back.

"Look here, and here." He pointed out two large stab wounds surrounded by congealed blood. "The knife was inserted from the front on all the wounds. He was facing his assailant the whole time."

"Interesting." Helen knitted her brows.

"And look where the wounds are placed. In my experience of stabbings, the assailant is almost whipped into a frenzy, providing far too many wounds because they panic and don't know when to stop. This is not the frenzied attack it initially appears. It looks as though our killer was going for main arteries and organs, hence the blood spatter," he gesticulated to the walls adding, "I would say that this was probably his first blow." He leant over and pointed at the heart. "The first and the fatal blow. Nobody could put up much resistance to that."

"Are you saying it was somebody skilled, a doctor perhaps?"

"Not necessarily, you don't even need A level biology to work out where the major arteries and organs are placed. All you'd have to do is read a few books. You could get it all on the Internet these days. No. What I'm saying is that he went for a quick death. He wanted him dead quickly and only continued to wound to make sure he was dead." DS Pemberton had joined them now and they were all staring at the victim, wide-eyed. It felt as though they were the only three living people in the whole room.

"And look at the smear marks over there." Charles pointed across the floor. "The victim would probably have crumpled and fallen face down, in a ball like configuration, from these wounds. But the killer didn't leave him there. He dragged him over to the sofa and sat him up against it, to face whoever walked through that door," he said, lifting his head to look over at the entrance adding, "eyes open deliberately, for maximum effect. He was intent on creating quite a show."

Helen stared at Pemberton and then back at the body, "What about time of death?" she asked eventually, breaking the silence.

"Difficult to be exact," Charles said, shrugging apologetically.

"Some indication would be useful."

"Well, he's pretty much bled out. Considering the

cold weather conditions and the lack of heating in here, his size and the pooling of the blood…" He looked at his notes, "body temperature and rigor mortis just setting in around the neck and shoulders…" He appeared to be talking to himself at this point. "I would say he has been dead for about three hours, estimating time of death at any time before five o'clock. But that is only an estimation," he looked up at Helen, as if to confirm this statement, "I'll be more sure when I open him up tomorrow."

"OK, thank you," she said.

"I understand from your officer here that you possibly have the murder weapon?" Charles asked as he carefully packed the last remaining items into his briefcase.

"Yes, a carving knife was found next to the suspect," DS Pemberton broke in.

Charles fastened his briefcase and rose to standing. "A kitchen carving knife? Are you sure?" He stared at the sergeant, perplexed.

"I believe so. That's what it looked like to me. We've had it measured and sent it back to the station for examination."

"What's the matter, Charles?" Helen asked.

"Well, I can't be sure until I perform the autopsy tomorrow, but I'd say that the blade that caused these wounds was rougher than a mere kitchen carving knife. More like that of a hunting knife." He stood up as he spoke, pulled the rubber glove off his right hand and held it out. As Helen reached to shake it he added, "I guess I'll see you at the autopsy in the morning. We'll firm everything up then." He nodded at Pemberton and waved to the CSI team, before exiting the flat.

Later, Helen pulled her jacket around her to prevent

the chilly air from biting into her chest as she crossed
Flax Street and walked around the corner. The wind
had died down now, but not before it cleared the sky of
clouds, leaving way for a heavily frosty night. When
she reached her car she pulled her mobile phone out of
her pocket, flicked through the contacts until she located home and pressed the dial. The call was answered
on the second ring.

"Hello?" a voice whispered.

"Hi, it's me. How's Matthew?" she asked, as she
climbed into her car.

"He's OK. Don't worry. He's sleeping now. How
about you?"

"Will you make sure he's laid on his side?"

"He's fine, really. I'll go check on him again in a
moment. How's it going?"

"Yeah, fine thanks. Looks like I'm going to be late
though, and probably in for most of the weekend."

"I kind of guessed that. Look, don't worry, I can
handle things here. You just do whatever you need to
and I'll see you later."

"Thanks, I really appreciate it. See you later." Helen
ended the call, ignited the engine and rested back into
her seat as she pulled out into the darkness. It was going
to be a long night...

PEOPLE SHOW AN amazing array of different reactions to
a dead body. Some are frightened, afraid that the corpse
will return to life and try to avenge their attacker, like
in a film; some are horrified at the scene, the circumstances in which a person lost their life; some are sad,
they grieve for the victim, think of their friends, their
family, the lost years of life and opportunity; others

are matter-of-fact, like the emergency services who are more accustomed to such sights and whose senses have numbed over the years as a result. Anna hadn't felt any of these emotions. In fact, she hadn't thought about the body at all. Until now.

As she finished talking to her solicitor and watched the cell door bang closed, she realised that, so far, her mind had focused on her incarceration, consuming her with anger tainted by the fear of being imprisoned. It had blocked out all earlier events, which felt like a blur, a whirlwind. An extraordinary out-of-body experience.

She recalled the blood splattered over her lounge, like a scene from a horror film. *Who would have thought that one person's body could contain so much blood?* She thought for a moment—a person. This blood had belonged to somebody. An overwhelming feeling of shame engulfed her. She had been consumed with the incomprehensible inconvenience to her life. He had lost his... Her stomach churned, but this time her bladder did not call out to her—it seemed to have frozen.

Anna forced her mind to push further into its depths. A lacerated body sat facing her on the floor. *The eyes...* She shuddered, shaking as she recalled the eyes open wide, staring at her. Eyes that had belonged to someone. Panic pulsed through her veins as realisation set in. The victim of this atrocity belonged to someone. The brutal truth of this fact made the pain in her head sear until her brain felt as if it were splitting in two. This was somebody's father, brother, husband, son...

Somewhere, some family would be disturbed this evening. Possibly watching a film, or putting the kids to bed, or maybe sitting down to dinner—a normal routine family evening, ruined by a knock at the door.

As they answered the door and saw the police officers wearing their hats, speaking in a solemn tone—"May we come in?"—their minds would race, overwhelmed with questions. Who was it? What has happened? They would brace themselves for bad news. Maybe they would think that their car had been stolen? But the police officers' tone would be too serious, their manner too empathetic and, once invited into the sitting room, they would ask them to sit down. Then, they knew it was serious—an accident, maybe even a death. Anna shuddered…

She imagined then that the questions would start. "Was your husband wearing a certain colour jacket when he left home today? Did he leave the house wearing grey trousers?" And this may instil an element of hope in the victim's family. Anyone could match that description, it was nothing significant. But then the mention of something personal like a white gold, engraved wedding ring would crush all ambiguity—and they would know, there would be no doubt.

The breathing would stop, they would clutch their head and in one moment their world would be shattered—all because of that knock at the door. And they would gaze up at the clock, reading the time when their life had changed irrevocably.

Tears streamed down Anna's face. Would they think it was her? That she could even be capable of causing such pain, such devastation? The thoughts made her head go hot and dizzy. Sweat coursed down the back of her neck as she jumped off the bed and rushed to the toilet in the corner, pushing strands of hair out of her face as she retched.

THREE

HELEN CLOSED THE door to her office and scanned the room, surveying her team. Most of them were enthusiastic detectives with a wealth of experience between them, although this didn't prevent the dark shadows that hung under many a pair of eyes and the odd stifled yawn. They had been called in from not only the end of their shift, but the end of their working week, acutely aware they faced a long night and the weekend was likely to offer little respite.

"Good evening, everyone." Helen spoke loudly, looking around at her team, some of whom were seated, others perched on the edge of desks, a couple standing at the back. "First, thank you very much for giving up your weekend. I really appreciate your help." Twelve pairs of eyes focused on her.

She moved across to the whiteboard and methodically summarised the evening's events, jotting down key points. Once complete she turned to face them, "Any questions?" The room was silent. She could almost feel them digesting the facts so far. "I want you all to know that I value each and everybody's opinion, so if anyone has any theories or information that might help, then please speak up."

"Ma'am," the soft voice came from a short, middle-aged Detective Constable at the back of the room whom she recognised as DC Steve Spencer, "Is there any evidence that this was a burglary that went wrong? Maybe she came home and found him?"

"It's possible," she said. "The front door is damaged, looks like it had been forced using something like a crowbar. There was only an old-fashioned Yale lock, so it wouldn't have been that difficult. Forensics should be able to clarify that. No sign of the tool though."

"Was there a bag left there?" A female detective, Rosa Dark, piped up.

"No, I'm afraid not."

"It does seem unlikely that somebody would break in without some sort of bag—something to carry any stolen goods. Perhaps it was a druggie, looking for cash or jewellery to sell?" Rosa continued. Helen looked across at her and smiled inwardly. She was barely out of probation a year and the youngest detective on the team, having only recently passed her exams. But any shortage of experience was compensated in abundance by her overwhelming enthusiasm.

At this moment DS Pemberton walked into the room. Helen nodded to him. "Evening. I've just been briefing everyone on the evening's events. Anything to add?" Pemberton glanced at the whiteboard and was silent momentarily as he considered the bullet points.

"Yes, ma'am," he said and turned to address the room. "I arrived just as the suspect was being led down to the car and something struck me." He frowned.

"Yes, Sergeant?" Helen prompted.

"Well, she didn't have much blood on her clothing. A few smudges, that's all." He looked over at Helen. "You saw the crime scene. It was like a blood bath. You would expect her to be covered from head to toe."

"Could she have changed?" DC Spencer asked.

"If she did, then we didn't find any blood stained clothing at the address. She must have got rid of it pretty quickly."

"Interesting. Get uniform to do a thorough search of the area. We'll find them if they are still there. And make sure they check the drains too, with any luck they might even locate the murder weapon." She nodded. "Thank you. Anything else?"

"Yes, we have an ID on the body. I tried to call your mobile, but you must have already started your briefing. His name was Jim McCafferty."

"Excellent. Is he known to us?"

"I've only had a chance to check very quickly, and yes he is known but only for petty stuff—shoplifting, theft, drunk and disorderly—that sort of thing."

"Good work, thanks Sergeant. Right then, guys," Helen addressed the whole room now, "we need to find out all the background we can on Jim McCafferty— where he lived, who his friends were, where he worked and what he does in his spare time—let's build up a picture of him. We also need to find out what we can about Anna Cottrell. She has no previous and we know very little about her."

"DS Carter will coordinate events in here and get us set up on the HOLMES system so that we can collate our findings." The Home Office Large Major Enquiry System derived from complex cases such as that of the Yorkshire Ripper in the 1970s, when mounds of paperwork had made the investigation difficult to manage. Information was collated by HOLMES software which cross-referenced all data input and Helen was keen to get started on it at the earliest opportunity.

"DS Pemberton and DC Spencer will interview the

suspect and Inspector Townsend and I will be watching from the room next door. Right, that's all for now."
Helen glanced around the room as the bodies around
her dispersed. Where was Townsend? She was sure she
had seen him at the beginning of the briefing—yes he
had been standing at the back. She looked over at Pemberton. "Sean, can I have a minute please?"

"Sure." Sean Pemberton followed her into her office,
closing the door behind him.

"Have you seen Inspector Townsend?" she asked,
sitting on the edge of her desk to face him.

"Yes. He was outside having a cigarette when I came
back."

"During briefing?"

"Well, unless you had just started, then…"

Helen spotted Townsend waltzing back into the main
office casually and cut in, "Looks like he's back now."
Pemberton turned around and looked through the open
blinds, following her gaze. "Tell him I'd like a word,
would you?"

"Of course," he replied. She didn't miss the rolling of
his eyes as he turned to leave the office, even if he did
drop his head discreetly to do so. It seemed she wasn't
the only one on the team disappointed in the inspector's behaviour.

Moments later Townsend walked through the open
door. "You wanted to see me?" Helen was looking out
of the window behind the desk, at the lit car park below.
A man and woman were laughing together, walking towards a red Toyota. His arm was stretched around her
shoulders. Helen felt a twinge of envy. They looked totally relaxed as if they had a whole weekend of fun to
look forward to. She turned to face Townsend, placing

one hand on the back of her chair, the other loosely on her hip. Was she imagining the sneer on his lip?

"Yes, close the door please Inspector and take a seat," she said curtly. He followed her words and sat opposite. In spite of the desk between them obstructing her vision slightly, she couldn't fail to notice how he slung himself over the chair opposite her.

"Inspector, do you have a problem with this investigation?" she asked.

"No."

"Is there somewhere else you would rather be?"

"Well the Coach and Horses is my usual haunt at the end of a busy week."

She stared at him for a moment, her eyes hard, boring into him.

He put up his hand. "Look, I'm only joking," he replied, a conciliatory note in his voice.

She pulled out her chair and sat down before continuing, "Would you like to tell me your take on the investigation? What are your theories?"

"Well it all seems pretty obvious to me. She arrived home and apprehended a burglar, they had a tussle and she stabbed him to death. Pretty straightforward. We just need to charge her so that we can all go and start the weekend."

"What about the murder weapon?"

"It was found at the scene, next to her body." He sighed and sunk back further down into his chair, a conceited look of triumph on his face.

"Would you like to tell me why the carving knife found at the scene is not a match for the victim's wounds?"

"What?" A look of bewilderment spread across his

face. He looked her up and down, as if they were meeting for the first time. "What are you talking about?"

"If you had been present at the briefing you would be aware of all the facts and information we have so far," she said, holding eye contact.

"When was this discovered?"

"The pathologist revealed it at the scene, in his initial findings. It appears the actual murder weapon was more akin to a hunting knife." He continued to stare at her.

"I only went for a smoke while you updated the troops," he said, defensively.

"Inspector, you are my deputy here. I need your support at every stage of the investigation."

He glanced away and mumbled something quietly under his breath.

Helen felt the heat rise in her blood. She stood, resting her hands on the edge of the desk, fingers splayed. This was probably the only time that she would ever be able to tower over him. "What did you say?"

Townsend's eyes met hers. "Nothing."

There was something in his gaze, behind his eyes, that she couldn't make out. "Listen, if you don't wish to work with me on this investigation then I'll call Superintendent Jenkins and get him to send a replacement immediately."

"There's no need for that." Townsend continued to stare at her, but sat up in his seat. The mere mention of the superintendent wiped the smile right off his face.

Her eyes were still glued to him. She took a deep breath, exhaled slowly in an effort to control her racing heartbeat. When she finally spoke her tone was measured. "Then pull yourself together. Make sure you are fully up to date with where we are and get yourself ready for the interview."

He looked up surprised, "You want me to conduct the interview?"

Helen raised her eyes to the ceiling, wondering if he was being deliberately obtuse. "No, Inspector," she replied, enunciating every syllable. "You and I will be listening next door." Did she have to explain everything? He nodded his understanding. "But, be clear on this," she added fighting to keep her composure, "I want all or nothing on this investigation. You need to show me that you can contribute and give full commitment, or you are off!" Townsend looked away and nodded. "That will be all."

As he stood and walked out of the room, closing the door behind him, Helen gripped the edge of the desk and clenched her teeth. She made a mental note to speak to Superintendent Jenkins at the earliest opportunity. She sighed out loud as her blood pressure started to drop and looked down absent-mindedly at her notes. That would be Monday—superintendents rarely worked weekends...

ANNA HAD ALWAYS felt uncomfortable in the presence of police officers. Even watching them work from afar, they always managed to make her feel guilty. It was as if she could be breaking the law without even realising it. On the odd occasion that she had borrowed her father's car she had slowed down deliberately when approaching a police vehicle, even if she wasn't exceeding the speed limit. Perhaps it was the thought of being restrained, locked away behind all those closed doors which made her so nervous?

"Let's go over this again." Anna stared at the detective opposite her aghast as he looked down at his notes. She guessed they must have been in the interview room for around an hour now, and they had spent the entire time asking her useless questions. How long she had lived in the flat in Little Hampstead? How long her lease was due to run? What her neighbours were like? Where she worked? Her morning routine? One question kept screaming in her head: *Why don't they ask me about the murder?*

The broad-set detective sat directly opposite was as bald as a light bulb, towering above her, even though they were both seated. His colleague next to him had a thick head of short, wavy hair, dark brown streaked with grey, dandruff peppering his shoulders. He was a short, slender man with dark, pointy features. In different circumstances the contrast between them would have been comical.

Anna fidgeted with the zip buckle of her jogging suit jacket, already feeling at a disadvantage opposite the two black suits. She glanced up at the camera in the corner of the room. A rush of emotion pulsed through her. Were they watching her now? Were they scrutinising her body language, looking for clues that may betray guilt? The thought made her sit bolt upright in her chair.

She glanced sideways at her solicitor who was staring at the DS thoughtfully and recalled how relieved she had been when he arrived earlier, how she thought he would resolve everything, put them right and she would be released. But as he had walked into the cell she caught the stern look on his face and her dream of a quick release immediately shattered. Although Will Southwold had been a family friend for many years, she fought the temptation to hug him as usual. It hadn't seemed appropriate and his expression certainly hadn't invited it. He had just stared at her through bespectacled eyes and said, "I have spoken with an officer in the case and I cannot pretend to you, Anna. This is serious. Now, let's start from the beginning, shall we?"

And despite them drafting a statement together, outlining her movements earlier in the evening, an alibi which didn't allow time to commit murder, she still found herself in this small, airless room, two tapes simultaneously recording her every word. She pondered at how she had woken up this morning and begun a perfectly normal, routine day. How could she have gone from sublime living to a state of ridicule in a matter of twelve hours?

The detective spoke again, breaking through her thoughts. "What time did you leave work this evening?"

Anna took a deep breath. "I've already said this in my statement," she said, exhaling with her response in an effort to give a definitive answer. Will had presented her statement to the detectives at the beginning of the interview. The larger detective read it out for the purpose of the tape and suspended the interview for a few minutes whilst he had taken it out, she presumed to his superiors. When he returned he said that the matters raised would be investigated and then, instead of releasing Anna, returning her clothes, apologising for the inconvenience to her evening, allowing her to go home, he had commenced the interview, questioning in his own way.

"In your own words please," he said, solemnly.

"I left work at four-thirty. You can check with my colleagues. I…"

"Names?"

She looked up as he interrupted. "Erica Smith was in the staffroom when I left. My boss, the headmaster, is Jason Randle." The smaller detective was scribbling down the names on his pad.

"OK, and where did you go at four-thirty?"

"I retrieved my bike from the back of the building and rode it to the Tesco store on Cross Keys roundabout."

"What time did you arrive at the supermarket?"

"I'm not completely sure, but I think it was around a quarter to five. I locked my bike and went into the shop to get some serviettes for my mother's dinner party."

"How long were you in the shop?"

"Again, I'm not exactly sure, but it was probably around three quarters of an hour. As I told you, the till receipt is in my rucksack. That should give you the time I reached the checkout."

The detective raised his eyebrows. "That's rather a long time to shop for some serviettes."

"Well, as I said in my statement," she enunciated every syllable here, nodding at the detective as she spoke, "I saw an old school friend in there."

"Yes," the detective now referred to a copy of the statement, which he held out in front of him, "a girl named Charlotte?"

"Yes."

"But you don't know her surname?"

"No, she's married now and I didn't think to ask it."

"Maiden name?"

"I can't remember."

"And you can't recall what she was wearing?"

"No," Anna said weakly. For the first time she realised how unreal this might sound, as if she were trying to dig herself out of a hole.

"Did she give you her number?" the detective asked.

Anna closed her eyes and rested her fingers on her temples. She couldn't afford to lose it now. She kept her eyes closed as she answered the question, "I haven't seen Charlotte since we were in sixth form together, six years ago. It was a chance meeting. I didn't have a pen, so she punched my number into her phone. She kept me talking for ages, catching up, and that's why I was so late leaving the store." When she opened her eyes the smaller detective was staring at her as if she were an obscure painting in a gallery.

"How did you pay?" the larger detective asked finally.

"By cash." She realised the reason for his request immediately, guessing they would probably be able to trace a credit card purchase. But there would be no way of tracing a cash transaction. "They were only a couple of pounds," she added, as if to justify her actions.

"Which till did you use?"

"One near the main entrance." Anna cringed at her response, frustrated at her inability to remember minutiae. She had never possessed that gift of recalling particular items to memory like what somebody was wearing, what time she had seen them, what make of car they drove. It always amazed her how witnesses to crimes would remember those details. Her friends often teased her at her lack of observation. A work colleague had recently given birth and, having been one of the first friends to visit, other colleagues had asked her if the baby had hair. She couldn't remember.

Anna looked up and met the detective's eyes as he

spoke. "Anna, are you sure that there isn't anything else you would like to tell me?"

She stared at him, puzzled. "What do you mean?"

"You are telling us you left work at four-thirty, went to the supermarket until five-thirty, and arrived home at six o'clock to find the stabbed body of a complete stranger in your flat. Is this right?"

"Yes," she replied, weakly. She was starting to doubt herself.

"Are you sure you didn't recognise the dead man?"

"No, I told you so," she said, quietly. The detective glared at her, as if she were hiding something. She fidgeted in her chair uncomfortably.

"Do you know a man named Jim McCafferty?"

Anna was silent for a moment, as a shiver rippled down her spine. "No." Both detectives continued to stare at her in silence. As she looked back at them a chord struck in her brain. "Was that him?" she asked, her voice barely a whisper.

"The dead man? Yes. His name was Jim McCafferty." The name made him sound so real, so alive.

At this point Will interrupted. "Look, my client has co-operated fully and given you an alibi for her movements this evening which, I'm sure you can see, demonstrates that she could not have committed this murder." He paused for a moment. "Unless you have anything new, I think it's time for her to be released."

"That's my problem," said the larger detective, ignoring the solicitor, addressing Anna direct. "Your alibi is not straightforward."

"What do you mean?" Anna gasped. Fear rose within her.

"We have checked your personal belongings and,

while there is a packet of serviettes in your bag, there is no receipt indicating when and where you bought them." She stared at him wide eyed. "With respect Miss Cottrell, we need to investigate your alibi thoroughly before it can be substantiated. You have told us that you met an old school friend in the store but cannot even remember what she was wearing or what her surname is. You have also told us that you do not know the victim. Unless you can tell us anything else, anything that can be confirmed this evening, then we will be forced to detain you overnight while we continue with our enquiries."

Anna could feel her hands tremble, her body start to shake all over. When she finally spoke her voice was barely audible, "I haven't done anything wrong. Please?" She turned to face her solicitor. "Will, I can't go back into that room. Do something." The words caught in her mouth.

She could see movement around her, smell the familiar bleach in the air, hear voices in the background, but couldn't decipher the words. It was as if they were speaking in a foreign language. Doors were banged shut, walls closing in. She was confined in an ever-decreasing space, choking behind all those closed doors...

Finally, she felt a hand on her shoulder, heard Will's words as he slowly spoke, "Anna, breathe. Try to be calm." She gulped in huge mounds of air, staring into space as the oxygen filled her lungs and fed her brain, allowing the panic attack to pass. As the colour returned to her face he asked, "Can I get you anything?"

"Some fresh air," she said, looking up at him longingly.

"Unfortunately, that is the one thing I cannot help you with at the moment..."

HE DROVE SLOWLY down the dirt track towards the edge of the lake. With headlights extinguished, the ride was tricky, but thankfully the recent icy weather meant the ground was packed hard. He pulled up at the end, got out of the car and stood, listening for any sound in the darkness. All was silent. He had chosen this area because the water was deep from within a couple of metres from the edge.

Quietly, he opened the boot and, as he lifted the dirty holdall, winced slightly. The bricks inside made it heavy and he congratulated himself for deciding to drive down. It would have been cumbersome to carry any distance. Walking towards the water's edge he started swinging the bag, gently at first and then faster and faster until he eventually swung it out into the water. It sat there for a split second, the surrounding water bubbling at its side, examining its new gift, before encasing it, pulling it from sight.

Breathing a sigh of relief he stood there momentarily, again listening for any sound of life. He heard a rustle in a nearby tree. A bird emerged, disturbed on its roost by the splash of water. Then nothing. Walking back to the car, he placed a hand in his trouser pocket and pulled out a box. Removing a short stalk of wood, he struck it and threw it on to the back seat. Hovering a few feet away, he watched as the flames licked through the interior, fascinated by the power and destruction contained within one match. Finally, satisfied, he turned up his collar and started walking back up the track. Round one complete. Now for round two.

FOUR

KILLERS NEVER LOOKED as you expected them to. The job had taught Helen to be non-judgemental. There is no stereotype in murder. She knew that most victims were actually killed by someone they knew but it never ceased to amaze her what could lurk beneath a normal, healthy skin.

As she lay in bed the following morning, these thoughts occupied her mind. She methodically considered the limited evidence before her. It was fraught with difficulties, little holes that prevented one piece linking to another. Anna was a size eight, ten at most—how would she be able to move a middle-aged man almost twice her weight? Also, the knife on scene didn't appear to match with the wounds applied to the victim, so where was the original murder weapon? And, if Anna had committed this crime she should be drenched in blood from head to foot, so why did her clothes only show small traces? Then there was her alibi—why hadn't she told the police at Flax Street about leaving work early, going to the supermarket, seeing a friend? Was it because she was in shock, or did she later realise that it deliberately put her away from the scene?

She tried to turn the evidence around, to look at the flip side. Perhaps Anna didn't arrive home and encounter a burglar, maybe she had an accomplice? She knew that the murder took place in her flat, in the afternoon, and a man was stabbed, possibly with a hunting knife. Why her flat? What was her link to this man? Was Anna mixed up in something and somebody was sending her a message? She wasn't known to the police and her background and profile certainly didn't fit this explanation. It didn't add up.

Helen sighed. Was she missing something? Her brain was starting to feel like it had been bashed about like mashed potato. She opened her mouth and yawned deeply then raised her hands, allowing her fingers to massage her temples. As she rested her arms down she glanced at the empty bed next to her: the crisp clean, creaseless pillows, the undisturbed duvet. A pang of loneliness shot through her chest.

She turned over, pulled back the bedclothes and climbed out, reaching for her dressing gown and pulling it around her shoulders as she crossed the landing, her slippers softly creeping over the carpet. She peered around Robert's bedroom door. He was fast asleep, his body completely still. She marvelled at how his face looked astonishingly childlike whilst sleeping.

Matthew had taken to closing his bedroom door in recent months. She opened it gently, just enough to squeeze her body through. The room was dark, forcing her to blink twice to allow time for her vision to adjust before bending down beside his bed. Drawing a deep breath in relief, she saw that he lay on his side, his breathing slow and regular.

Many years ago she had been on holiday in Spain when a teenager in the hotel next door had choked to death on his own vomit. The memory made her shudder. If she closed her eyes she could still see the despair in his mother's face. Your children weren't meant to die before you, even the thought was inconceivable. Perhaps the hangover would teach him a lesson against future bouts of binge drinking? Resisting the huge temptation to lean down and kiss his forehead she made her way back to the door. He wouldn't welcome the intrusion into his room or the interruption to his sleep.

Helen walked downstairs, gingerly lifting her feet as if they were crossing hot coals. Although they had lived in this new-build for almost twelve months, she still half expected the odd squeaky floorboard or creaking door and moved around the house softly, as if to avoid them. When she finally reached the kitchen, she flicked the light switch, turned and instantly gasped, lifting her hand to her mouth.

"You startled me!"

Jane Lavery sat at the kitchen table, cradling an almost empty mug of warm milk. She looked up at her daughter. "Sorry."

"What are you doing, sitting in the dark?"

"Can't sleep, legacy of old age," she replied, staring into space.

"Why didn't you put the light on?"

"Didn't want to disturb the boys." That was just like her, not wanting to disturb the children. Both boys slept at the back of the house, directly above the kitchen. Whilst Matthew would need to be physically roused in the middle of an earthquake reaching eight plus on the Richter scale, Robert was a light sleeper and easily disturbed.

Helen cocked her head to read the station clock on the kitchen wall. It was six-thirty. She turned and flicked the kettle switch. "Want some coffee?"

"No thanks," her mother replied, removing her hands

from the mug to rub her eyes and smooth back her grey hair. Jane Lavery had a classic appearance, one of those few women who could still wear their hair pulled off their face at sixty-five and look attractive. She was blessed with kind, grey eyes and softly defined cheekbones. "What time did you get in?"

Helen turned to look at her. "Just after midnight."

"How are things?"

"A bit manic. Lots of work to do."

"I've ironed you some shirts and aired you a couple of suits. They're hanging in the utility." She nodded towards a door at the back of the kitchen.

Helen smiled. "Thanks, Mum. You're a star." She finished making her drink, sat down opposite her and swallowed a huge gulp of milky coffee.

To move back in with her mother after John had died had seemed the obvious solution. John's army pension barely paid the rent and Helen had battled with the demands of looking after her children, finding a job to pay the bills, running a home. It had been a compromise, but one heavily outweighed by her mother's devotion to the boys and her flexibility when it came to childcare: helping with homework, driving them to clubs, collecting them from school when necessary. It would have been very difficult to find a nanny so committed and flexible enough to withstand the anti-social shifts imposed by the police force.

They were so close that Helen could not imagine life without her. But sometimes that closeness inevitably meant arguments, disagreements, as they got under each other's feet. Two women from different generations, wrestling with contrasting lifestyles. And, as the years passed, they found themselves clashing more and more.

Compromise had become habit, but Helen became aware that they couldn't continue like that forever. Finally, twelve months ago, they bought this new house together, building a granny flat on the side with adjoining doors for access. Jane Lavery now had her own living room, bedroom and bathroom; a gesture intended to give both women their independence. But, in spite of this, she still spent the majority of her time in their shared kitchen.

She looked across at her daughter. "What time is Robert's football this morning?"

"Eleven o'clock," Helen replied. "Perhaps you'd better take Matthew with you? He's in no state to be left on his own."

"No problem. What time do you think you'll be back?"

"No idea I'm afraid."

"The golden hours." Jane Lavery sighed. Having lived with a senior police officer for most of her life, she was well versed in police terminology.

"You've got it. Anything could happen. Are you sure you can manage?"

"Two teenage boys and a footy pitch," her mother's lips curled into a smile, "I think we'll manage."

Helen rose and moved around the table to place her empty mug in the sink. She placed a hand on her mother's shoulder. "I'll keep in touch."

Jane Lavery lifted her own hand and placed it over her daughter's. "Don't worry about us. We'll be fine."

HAMPTON MORTUARY WAS a grey, pebble-dash building located in the west of the city, the opposite side to Cross Keys station. In normal circumstances the journey would take around half an hour, but the traffic was busy this Saturday morning, due to early onset of Christmas shoppers, and it was well after 10am by the time Helen and Townsend battled through the congestion.

The monitor on the wall buzzed as Helen pressed it. A voice answered and she announced their arrival, watching as the door clicked open. Inside, the mortuary was surprisingly modern, having benefited from an injection of cash the council needed to spend at budget year-end, the previous year. The work had only just been completed. The newly tiled floor shone in the reception area, the desks looked as if they were straight out of IKEA and the walls were gleaming in freshly painted magnolia.

They made their way up to the lab. As they donned gowns, overshoes and gloves, they could see Charles through the lab windows. The naked corpse was laid out flat on its back on a waist height table. Charles hovered around it, examining and measuring external wounds, recording his findings into a tape recorder which was cast aside as he photographed the body from various angles.

"Good morning," Helen said, as they walked through the doors.

"Morning!" he replied, without looking up.

Helen looked at the corpse and thought how different the victim looked unclothed. Older somehow. It was surprising how clothes masked a multitude of sins. The skin on his stomach was sagging into wrinkles, the cheeks of his face sunken deeply and his hair seemed thinner than the previous night. The lacerated wounds across his torso sat like leeches on the blue tinged skin.

Charles continued to photograph the victim from

different angles. "I've already started, I'm afraid," he said, his eyes focusing on his work. "Came in early and stole a march. I've only got until midday. Sarah has this Christmas Fayre thing organised and I'm supposed to be selling the mulled wine." He turned sideways and smiled up at Helen sheepishly. "Simply forgot all about it, so I'm in the dog house." He noticed Townsend and stood up to face him, holding the camera away at an angle, as if it smelt badly.

"Charles this is Inspector Simon Townsend, my deputy on the investigation," Helen said. Charles nodded at Townsend who lifted his head slightly in acknowledgement.

"You'll forgive me if I don't," Charles looked down at his gloved hands which were already smeared with stodgy blood. As Townsend nodded, Helen allowed herself a gentle smile. Charles had always been the archetypal gentleman. He reminded her of her father in so many ways.

"How's it going?" Helen asked as he placed the camera down on a table behind him.

"Fine, thank you." He turned back to his work, leaving them standing there silently.

She glanced around at the pathology lab and felt a rippling shiver run down her spine. The labs always felt chilly, although it wasn't particularly cold in there. No matter how many corpses she had seen during her service, there was something unnerving about the smell of dead people which chilled her to the bone. A strange, clinical, musty smell. Years ago, a friend, Clare, had married into a family of butchers. When her new husband came home at the end of the day Clare would insist that he shower immediately because he always smelled of mince. It was as if it were deeply embedded in the pores of his skin. She wondered what Charles smelled of when he finished a busy day. Was it possible for the living to smell of the dead?

"It is as I thought," Charles said eventually. "There are six wounds in all and I think it very unlikely they were made by a regular kitchen carving knife. Look here and here." He moved his fingers over the lacerations. "You see on one side the wound is a smooth cut, but on the other the edge is torn. I would say you are looking for a knife with a smooth side and an opposing serrated side—possibly a hunting knife."

"Any signs of a struggle?" Helen asked, watching Charles avidly.

"No. No defensive wounds to speak of and not much under the fingernails either. It seems that he knew his attacker."

"Is it possible he was drugged and lured into the house?"

"No reason to suggest that from his external condition. It looks as though he was standing facing his attacker for the blows, but I will, of course, run toxicology tests."

Helen became aware of Townsend's silence and glanced sideways at him. He stood wide-eyed, although his eyes were completely averted from the examination, focusing instead on the grey, speckled flooring. Surely this couldn't be his first post mortem? She looked away and allowed herself a wry smile. She had thought she was doing him a favour by inviting him to attend, building some bridges, whereas really she was putting him through hell.

When she looked back at him she noticed that the

colour had now drained from his face. He looked decidedly green around the gills but, no doubt, his pride was not going to allow him to say anything. In many ways it was strange, but post mortems never affected her like that. The only time that she had experienced nausea was during her first pregnancy when the smell of cheese, any variety of cheese in fact, made her retch. She hadn't been able to go near a delicatessen counter for three months.

"Inspector, would you pop outside and give the station a ring to see how they're getting on with things?" she asked, fully aware that use of mobile phones inside the building was forbidden.

He nodded and left the room with haste.

Charles ignored his exit, immersed in his work. Several minutes passed before he finally spoke. "You will see that all six wounds are concentrated in the torso area. I would say that the blow to the heart was definitely the first—it was a good hard incision, the others were more like firm, quick jabs." He pointed to the bottom right hand rib cage. "This one here appears to have splintered the rib, but I doubt completely broken it."

She watched him in silence for a moment before asking, "What about time of death?"

"Again, as I thought. Death occurred before five o'clock, probably in the two hours preceding." She nodded as Townsend opened the door and leant in. He obviously had no intention of returning, having completely removed his gowns.

"Ma'am. Can I have a word?"

She turned to Charles. "Excuse me for a moment, would you?" Charles nodded without looking up and she went out of the lab to join Townsend in the room next door.

"Yes?"

"I've just spoken with DS Carter at the station. They've checked with Anna's work colleagues who confirmed that she left at four-thirty yesterday. They have also retrieved CCTV footage from Tesco which shows her entering the store at four-fifty and, more importantly, leaving at five-thirty-five."

"What about the old school friend?"

"Still working on that one."

Helen sighed. "Dr Burlington's just confirmed that the murder weapon had a serrated edge, so it couldn't possibly have been a kitchen carving knife. She looked at her watch. It was twelve o'clock. "I don't think we have any choice but to release Miss Cottrell on bail. As it stands at the moment we don't have any evidence to keep her." She looked up at Townsend. "Would you make the arrangements for me while I finish up in here?" He nodded, visibly relieved.

As Helen walked back into the pathology lab moments later, Charles was concentrating on making a 'y' shaped incision with a scalpel from shoulder to shoulder and down to the pubic bone.

"Charles?" she asked, "Is there anything else you can tell me?"

"Are you off?" He looked up at her as she nodded. "I'm just about to do the internals, but I can send you all that information in my report. There is one more thing I would like you to see though." He walked around to the other side of the body, pointing to the top of the right arm. "Look here," he said. She moved her eyes across a large area where the skin seemed to have been removed.

"This is most interesting," added Charles, gazing at the bare tissue which glared back at him.

"Has the skin been cut away?" Helen asked, puzzled.

"Yes, it would appear a rough area of around four inches square has been purposely removed." Charles re-examined the area in question, a sharp 'v' appearing in the middle of his forehead. "Most strange. Looking at the damage to the tissue below, I wonder if it may have housed a tattoo? I didn't notice it last night as it was covered by clothing. Presumably our attacker removed it and then re-covered the area. If so, it seems they were at pains to keep it under wraps."

Helen stepped back and looked at him, perplexed. "You're saying the assailant removed his tattoo?"

"You'll need to check of course, but that would be my guess."

WORTHINGTON, ONCE a village in its own right before extended housing had swallowed it up into Hampton, was situated on the very edge of the city boundaries and surrounded by open, rolling countryside. Anna looked out of the window of the patrol car as they drove towards her parents' suburban home, transfixed by the world carrying on around her as if nothing had happened.

The female police constable had given up making conversation and they sat in silence as she turned into Broom Hill Lane, a winding, country lane that stretched through the heart of Worthington. They passed the group of horse chestnut trees that Anna and her friends had called "conker heaven" as children, and drove over the bridge above the river where she had waded through in her Wellingtons, searching for treasure. It was an idyllic place for a child to grow up. Everybody had known everyone.

Before they reached the heart of the old village, they turned off into Worley Close and the patrol car pulled up outside number 12, a white seventies-built semi-detached. "Shall I come in with you?" the police officer asked, noticing the look of anguish on Anna's face.

"No... Thank you. They are in. The car is there." It wasn't facing her parents that bothered Anna, it was all the twitching curtains, eyes peering through slatted blinds—or was she being paranoid? She jumped out of the car and headed around the back of the house, past her father's Volvo on the drive and into the back garden. She stood underneath the old oak tree for a moment, looking at the long garden where she used to play. Water droplets bounced off her shoulders as the bare branches swayed in the light wind.

Anna spotted her father, halfway down the garden in the greenhouse and walked towards him. He had his back to her. "Hi Dad," she said, leaving the door open behind her. His body jolted, as if she had startled him, and he turned around to face her, instantly opening his arms and encasing her as if she had been a child of six or seven. They stood clasped in silence, before he stepped back and looked at her.

"Are you OK, my dear?" he asked.

"Yes, I think so," she replied wearily. "Tired and hungry, that's all."

"Sounds like you've had quite an ordeal." Edward Cottrell scratched the remaining wispy hairs on his balding head awkwardly.

"I'll survive. Think I'll just go in and try to catch some sleep." He nodded. This is what she loved about her father—he asked few questions. Most girls confided in their mothers, woman to woman, but for Anna it had always been her father she had turned to. And he instinctively knew that she would tell him all about her living nightmare when she was ready, in her own time. It had always been this way and she loved him dearly for it. "Where's Mum?" she asked apprehensively.

"She was in the kitchen when I came out, about two hours ago." She could see a sympathetic smile playing on his lips. The garden was her father's solace and he spent many an hour out here, nurturing, weeding, watering.

"Guess I'll see you later then." Edward nodded as his daughter shut the door of the greenhouse behind her and headed back up the garden, through the conservatory at the back of the house and into the kitchen. Anna breathed a sigh of relief when it was empty. As she indulged the exhalation, her stomach kicked out, reminding her she needed food. She reached for the breakfast cupboard and pulled out a box of cereal, standing beside the counter absent-mindedly as she tipped and poured until her mouth was full.

She felt a warm feeling around her feet and looked down to see Cookie, wrapping himself around her ankles. He was a handsome cat, his fluffy fur an array of different shades of tabby greys. "Hi Cooks," she said as she bent down, stroked his head and rubbed underneath his chin. He looked up into her eyes and she offered him a piece of breakfast cereal between her thumb and forefinger which he licked clean.

Cats had always interested Anna. They were completely consumed in their own world, their own needs. Not like a dog that, once trained, did as they were told and aimed to please. Instead a cat's behaviour was almost like that of a psychopath. They didn't live by any morals, didn't show empathy or remorse. Her mind wandered. *A psychopath—like a murderer?* She shivered.

"There are plenty of bowls in the cupboard." The crisp disapproval in Kathleen Cottrell's voice disturbed her thought process and she jumped, cereal tumbling out of the box as she turned to face her.

"Hi Mum." She looked over at her mother's expressionless face. "Um… Sorry. Couldn't wait."

"Do you want some coffee?" Without waiting for a reply, Kathleen Cottrell turned her back on her daughter and flicked the switch on the kettle.

"Tea, thank you." They stood in silence for a moment as Kathleen busied herself with cups, spoons, tea, sugar. As the vapour rose from the kettle, she made the drinks, stirring them excessively and turned back to face her daughter.

"Are you OK?" she asked, sipping her hot drink gingerly.

"Just tired," Anna answered, averting her glaze.

"Do you want to tell me what happened?"

"Not right now. I just want to sleep." She looked up in time to see her mother's brow furrow.

"All this commotion and you don't feel the need to explain yourself?" Her tone was getting louder.

"I'm sorry about the party."

"So am I," Kathleen said tightly.

Anna looked out of the window, through the conservatory, into the garden, willing her father to come in and lighten the atmosphere.

"Well. Aren't you going to explain yourself?"

"What is there to say?" Anna clenched her teeth, feeling her face flush.

"Well it seems to me plenty, if the last twenty-four hours are anything to go by?"

"I'm sure Will's already filled you in," she replied, feeling far too old for a lecture.

Her mother stared at her, forcing her into defeat. "OK. I came home from work yesterday to find a man murdered in my flat, was arrested, questioned by police and spent last night in a cell. They released me this lunchtime, when they finally realised that I'm not a mad, knife-wielding murderer. OK?" Anna felt the tone of her own voice rising, her head aching. At this moment her father walked in.

"No, it's not OK. This isn't the kind of thing that happens to normal people like us." Her mother's voice was splitting in panic, bits of words crackling haphazardly out of her mouth.

"Kath, dear, please. Leave her alone," Edward Cottrell interjected gently.

She completely ignored his comments, failing even to acknowledge his presence in the room. "There must be an explanation. I mean... Do you even know who this dead person is?" Her pitch was getting higher now, her breathing excessively rapid, as she approached hyperventilation.

"No idea," Anna replied, raising her hand and pressing it to her forehead to soothe the ache that felt like a volcano preparing to erupt. "The police said he was called Jim McCafferty." Kathleen Cottrell's face instantly froze, as if she had been plunged into icy cold water, her eyes almost popping out of her head. She was struggling for breath. Anna had witnessed many of her mother's tantrums over the years, but this was the first time she had ever seen her visibly petrified.

"Mum, what is it?" She looked over at her father whose face was as white as stone. "Dad? Do you know this man?"

Her father coughed, a gesture that appeared to help him regain composure. "Your mother's having a bad day, darling. You go up and sleep and we'll talk later."

"You do know him, don't you?" she asked suspiciously.

"I think he might be an acquaintance from many years ago. That's all," her father said.

"What do you mean 'an acquaintance'?"

"Look, why don't you go and get some sleep?"

"I want to know," she insisted. "I think I have a right to know since he was killed in my flat."

Her father inhaled slowly through his nose and sighed loudly. "It's been a difficult weekend. We're all tired. Your mother has made up the bed in your old room for you. We can talk later." He enunciated every syllable of the last line. Anna looked from her father to her mother who had put her head down now, lost in thought. It was clear she was not going to get any further explanation right now.

Weariness blocked the frustration seeping through her pores. Defeated and exhausted, she headed upstairs.

Her old bedroom was at the end of the corridor at the back of the house and her parents hadn't changed the decor since she had lived at home. The lilac walls and white lacy curtains had been her mum's choice but, despite holding years of embarrassment when she had taken friends up there to entertain as a teenager, it now looked very welcoming. She allowed her body to fall into the soft, comfortable bed and wrapped the duvet around her as sleep enveloped her weary limbs.

FIVE

THE FIRST THING that struck Anna when she awoke was the smell. Her nose had grown accustomed to the scent of thick bleach in the cell, so much so that she could almost taste it. Her old bedroom was full of the fake, floral aroma of an air freshener.

She pulled herself out of bed, still dressed in the clothes she had worn the previous night, and stretched. They felt itchy and uncomfortable. The jogging top had turned sideways and, as she lifted it, she could see there was a mark on her side where the zip had rubbed. She reached over, grabbed the robe off the back of the door and peeled off the top and trousers, feeling wonderfully liberated as she threw the robe around her shoulders. Her hair had fallen loose and was hanging in a messy heap around her face and she pushed it back, tying it in a knot at the nape of her neck. The digits on the alarm beside her bed read ten o'clock. She had completely slept through from the previous afternoon.

Anna's stomach growled, reminding her that it had been a couple of days since she had eaten a proper meal, and at the same time she was hit by an overwhelming thirst. Making her way out of the room and across the landing, she almost ran down the curved staircase towards the kitchen. It felt a bit like her old student days when a group of them would come home after a big night out with the "munchies", picking spots of mould out of old bread and jostling for the toaster. The memory made her smile.

She busied herself with preparing her breakfast with the haste of someone late for work, drinking fresh orange juice from the carton to quench her thirst. There was no mould on this bread. By the time she started on the first slice of toast, water bubbled and steam rose into the air from the kettle. Piling more buttered toast on to her plate and making a huge mug of tea she crossed the carpeted flooring and planted herself on the majestic, oversized sofa in the lounge.

Anna saw that her father's car was missing from the drive. The silence in the house was heavenly. When her stomach was full she stretched out on the sofa and glanced absently around her parents' lounge.

It looked as though it had been prepared for a magazine shoot. Copies of *Homes & Gardens, Country Living* and *Woman* were fanned out in the middle of a polished coffee table; anniversary cards stood neatly, side by side, along the window-sill; two china cats sat demurely on the mantel over the ornate fireplace; beige cushions were strategically placed in diamond shapes on the backs of both of the large, dark brown sofas. She looked at the bookcase where books were arranged in height order, containing the kind of bound book sets that were advertised in Sunday supplements, and frowned. It looked perfect. Too perfect.

Anna thought of her own little flat, her bookcase where the books were scattered, some stood vertical, others lay on their sides, depending on what she was reading at that particular time. She also kept a pile of her favourite books beside her bed, so that she could dip in and out of them, to cheer herself up at the end of a bad day. There were ethnic throws over her sofa and a couple of squidgy cushions for extra comfort. It was lived in, homely. She felt a longing in her chest, closely followed by a sudden rush of resentment at the situation imposed upon her. Staying here was going to be a nightmare…

The sound of the phone ringing broke her thoughts, making her jump. She leant over and grabbed it quickly, "Hello?"

"Hi Anna. Is that you?"

"Ross!" Anna felt her insides fill with warmth. Anna and Ross had met when she had joined Carrington Grange Community College, two years previous.

"I've been worried. I keep ringing your mobile, but it's permanently switched off."

The sound of his voice felt like a baby's comfort blanket. "The police have kept it. You heard what happened?"

"Yeah. Your dad phoned me on Friday night when the party was cancelled. Then I got a visit from some detectives on Saturday morning. Is it true what they're saying?"

"Depends what *they're* saying," she replied cagily.

"That you found a body in your flat, a man who had been stabbed to death?"

"Yes, that bit's right." Her body recoiled.

"Christ, Anna. You must have gone through hell?"

"Kind of."

"Why didn't you ring me?"

"I was indisposed."

"Not you, in a cell? I mean…" He paused for a moment. The line crackled as he continued, his voice full of astonishment. "How did you cope?" Ross had often teased Anna about her habit of leaving doors open, humorously accepting it as a personal quirk. But that was Ross. He found the fun in everything.

"Not very well. Anyway, they released me yesterday once they'd established that I'm not some cold-blooded killer. But they kept all my stuff. I'm staying with my folks for a few days until I can go back to the flat."

"Do you want to go back?" There was a note of concern in his voice.

"At the moment, I have no idea. All I know is that I don't want to stay here for long." She looked around the room at the pristine decor and cringed.

"Why don't you move in with me? You already have a key." Anna smiled. Ross' place was organised chaos. He usually had two or three bicycles in the lounge, one of which was in pieces whilst he was learning how to mend the brakes or change a tyre. There was always a mound of old washing up in the sink and his bedroom closet was empty, his clothes piled in the laundry basket; he either ironed them when he needed them (which was normally the case for work) or wore them until the creases fell out.

"Thanks, I'll be OK. I'm sure it's only for a few days."

"How are the parents?" he asked cautiously.

"Bearable, at the moment. Well actually..." She broke off and strained her ears. Was that a car engine she could hear?

"What?"

"It's all a bit strange really," she continued, her voice almost a whisper, "I don't think they quite know how to cope."

"Kathleen all over. She's probably still smarting over

having to cancel the party. All those wasted vol-au-vents…"

"No, I'm serious Ross. This is different. I've never seen them like this. It's as if they are not telling me something."

"Like what?" The silence was heavy. "You're just being paranoid. You are right though, things will be different. They're bound to be. You've all been through a terrible ordeal. I think they call it shock. What you need is a massage…"

She interrupted him urgently, "But they *knew* him." She could hear a key being inserted into the lock.

"What?"

"The dead man," she lowered her voice, "they knew his name, said he was an old acquaintance." There was a creak as the front door opened and she could hear footsteps brushing against the soft, carpeted hallway.

"What?" he said incredulous. "What do you mean knew him?"

"Morning!" she shouted, as her father entered the room. He looked over, momentarily startled at the loudness in her voice then, seeing she was on the phone, nodded and walked straight through into the kitchen.

"I guess you can't talk now?" Ross said.

"Not really."

"OK… Look, can I get you anything?" The concern had crept back into his voice.

"No. Errr… Yes, actually there is a favour you could do for me?"

"What?"

"Get me a cheap mobile phone would you? At least we can keep in touch until I get my own one back?"

"Sure. I'll see what I can do… Are you still coming today?" His voice was awkward. Anna felt a twinge in her heart. She had completely forgotten that it was Ross' mother's birthday. They had been invited to his parents' house for a family tea.

"Oh, Ross, I really don't think that is a good idea," she replied gingerly. "I mean everyone's bound to ask questions and I don't want to take the limelight off your mum's birthday." *And I don't want to have to face all those questions*, she thought to herself. "It is your mum's day, after all."

"OK. I understand." If he was disappointed, it didn't show in his voice.

"Give her my love won't you? I'll send her some flowers next week."

"Sure." This was one of the things Anna loved about Ross. He was so undemanding.

"Anything else?"

"Oh, yeah. A lift to work would be great tomorrow. The police kept my bike."

"You are going to work tomorrow then?" He seemed surprised.

"Yeah. I think I just need to get everything back to normal as soon as possible. You know, put this weekend behind me." She sounded as though she was trying to convince herself.

"No worries. I'll pick you up around eight-fifteen. Are you sure you're OK?"

"I'm fine, really."

"All right. And I'll try and drop you a phone over later today, after I've seen my mum."

"That'd be great. It'll be really good to see you."

"You too."

By the time she replaced the receiver and walked into

the kitchen her father had disappeared into the garden to tend his beloved green friends, no doubt.

She thought about Ross' offer: *Move in with me*. It wasn't the first time he'd mentioned it. In many ways it was tempting. She'd never have cold feet at night, he'd be able to massage the knots out of her shoulders whenever she needed him to, she could slouch on the sofa without worrying about creasing the cushions.

But, as a couple, were they ready for more commitment? There was no doubt in her mind that she loved him. Not the kind of love you feel for a short-term boyfriend, a deeper, more special feeling. They had been together two years and did already practically live in each other's houses. Maybe they were? *No...* It wouldn't be right. Even if they were ready to take the next step, she didn't want to be forced into it. And she loved her flat. Why shouldn't he move in with her, when the time was right?

Anna lifted her arms above her head, indulging in the feeling of her muscles stretching. She ran her hands over her hair. It felt greasy and limp. Realising that she hadn't showered since Friday morning she grimaced and made her way back upstairs to run a hot bath, thanking her lucky stars for her parents' combi-boiler. Back at the flat she had to wait an hour for the immersion to heat a tank of water before she could even contemplate a soak.

After washing her hair and cleansing her body she closed her eyes and lay back, allowing the deliciously hot water to soothe her weary limbs. She lay there for a long time. For the first time in days she was slowly starting to relax and feel like her old self, her mind momentarily discarding the events of the weekend like a bad dream. She was alone, with only the steamy bath water and her thoughts for company.

She thought about her parents. Anna knew that Kathleen's own parents had died when she was five years old, leaving her to be raised by her Aunt Kate. She often wondered how it must feel to lose your parents at such a young age. Her mother had always been very attentive, bordering on controlling. But, in spite of Kathleen's bouts of domineering, sometimes irascible, behaviour, Anna always firmly believed that she genuinely wanted the best for her. Like her choice of career: Anna had wanted to be an artist and do a degree in ceramics, but she yielded to her parents' wish for her to read economics and pursue a career as a secondary schoolteacher. Hadn't a stable career given *them* a good lifestyle?

But going away to university had been a turning point, the new-found freedom making her more independent. Although she returned to a teaching job in Hampton (which her mother had seen advertised in *The Telegraph*) she had refused to move back in with them, instead renting the flat in Flax Street. She visited her parents regularly, but could never imagine what it would be like to live with them again. Until now...

Something was nagging away at her. The look on both her parents' faces yesterday when she mentioned Jim McCafferty was as clear as the light of day. They knew something about him, something that had chilled her mother to the bone, something that they had been unwilling to discuss. What were they keeping from her? She wasn't a little girl anymore, to be protected from the harsh realities of the world. "We'll talk about it later." That was a laugh. The Cottrells never *talked* about anything. And where were they this morning? Was she being paranoid or were they avoiding her? What she needed now were answers.

The water had cooled and she reached over and ran the hot tap until the heat burnt her toes. As she lay back, she reflected on the episode on Friday evening. She hadn't really allowed herself to wonder much about what had happened in her flat on Friday afternoon. In fact, she'd almost concluded that it was a burglary gone wrong. It made sense really. A few other houses in Flax Street had been broken into only a month or two before. But now she wasn't so sure. Who was Jim McCafferty? Why her flat? These questions were starting to feel like an irritating itch she couldn't scratch.

With these thoughts still in her mind she reached forward, pulled out the plug, even though the water was still burning her bare skin, and jumped out of the bath. As she padded through to her bedroom, the thick, wool carpet cushioning her damp feet, she could hear a strange, whimpering noise. She stood still for a moment and listened. All she could hear was the sound of her own breathing. Then it came again.

It must be Cookie, she thought. He had an annoying habit of pushing the door closed whilst inside her parents' room, so that he could sleep on the warm patch where the central heating pipes ran beneath the doorway. Her father replaced the carpet, a few months earlier, when the cat had found himself trapped there and tried to claw his way out. Since then the door had been propped open by an old, heavy paperweight. But there was no sign of the paperweight today, and the door was firmly closed. She reached for the handle, pushed it open. Cookie emerged, wrapped himself around her ankles purring loudly and slunk away down the stairs.

She had just turned to go into her room next door when she heard the whimper again.

Confounded, she stepped back and pushed the door open wider so that she could see into the room. The curtains were still closed although it was around midday, a peculiarity most uncharacteristic for Kathleen Cottrell. Anna squinted to see in the limited light that seeped through the doorway, following the gentle moans. Eventually she found the source. Curled up in a ball on the bed, just like a cat, her head tucked into her hands, was her mother.

Kathleen Cottrell looked up at her. Smudges of mascara littered her wrinkled face. Anna's mouth fell open, momentarily bewildered, before instinct kicked in and she moved to her mother's side, sat on the bed and wrapped her arms around her.

"Oh, Anna. My little girl. What have I done?" Kathleen choked on her words as her body slumped on to her daughter's chest, her whines developing into sobs. Anna was not sure how long they sat there, she cradling her mother's limp body, stroking her hair. Even as her mother's breathing steadied and the tears dried, they didn't speak. It was as if neither of them knew what to say.

Finally, Anna became aware of a distant car on the road outside. The routine noise seemed to prompt Kathleen to sit up on the edge of the bed, reach over and grab a square, black purse from her bedside table. Anna stared at her mother as she fumbled with the metal clasp, finally clicking it open to withdraw a Marlboro and a silver box which bore the illegible, worn markings of an old engraving. Expertly, she placed the cigarette to her lips, lit it and took a long, deep drag.

This was her mother's one vice and Anna, not a

smoker herself, loved it. As a child, she had thought it a glamorous habit, relishing the calming effect it seemed to have on her mother's mood. And, in spite of how much it had irritated her husband, Kathleen had never been able to kick the habit, yielding to reduce her usage to ten a day, to "calm her nerves". These days she restricted her indoors smoking to the conservatory. The very presence of the black purse in the bedroom was completely out of character.

Anna watched her in silence for a moment. Her mother had aged considerably over the past forty-eight hours. Dark shadows appeared under her eyes, her usually manicured hair sat limply on her head. A flicker of stray ash landed on Kathleen's trousers and she brushed it off instantly.

"Mum, are you all right?" Anna asked gently.

"Fine dear, thank you," she replied, taking another deep drag.

"What upset you so much?"

"Oh, nothing dear. It's just me being silly." She had heard this cold dismissive tone in her mother's voice before. This was the moment when she would clam up, wouldn't offer explanation. Anna wasn't going to let her get away with it. Not this time.

"What did you mean—'What have I done'?" she said, looking her straight in the eye.

Her mother deliberately averted her gaze. "What?" she asked, shaking her head, as if to remove any bad thoughts.

"You said, 'What have I done?'" Anna repeated, stressing every syllable, her eyes glued to Kathleen's face.

"No I didn't. You must be mistaken." She rose

quickly and stared at the red, digital numbers on the clock on her bedside table. "Goodness, is that the time?"

"Mum, I need to know." Anna heard the desperation in her own voice.

Ignoring her daughter's pleading she added, "I must get your father's lunch. Coming down?" And, without waiting for a reply, she headed out of the room and down the stairs.

"I need to know!" Anna shouted after her in pure exasperation, as she sat there staring despairingly at the carpet.

Anna gripped her head. Her mother had always been self-obsessed, a total hypochondriac. Every little stomach pain had the propensity to be bowel cancer. Every headache could be the basis of a tumour. In Kathleen Cottrell's world the glass was always half-empty. Was she over-reacting to the extraordinary events that had befallen her family over the last few days? Or, was there something more to this? Anna felt there was. Something strange was going on and she felt completely and utterly cut out of the loop.

A STRONG, musty odour filled the air as Helen walked into Jim McCafferty's home. It smelt like a mixture of stale cigarette smoke and an old, mildewed cellar in desperate need of ventilation. She resisted the temptation to throw open the windows, instead glancing around at the one reception room which the front door led into. It was a relatively modern house, less than ten years old. The stairs led out of the lounge and there was a doorway on the far wall leading into the kitchen.

Helen scratched the back of her neck. The pattern on the brown carpet was no longer distinct, masked by bits of clothing, flakes of mud fallen from boots, pieces of food and dust, that had littered it for so many years they had now become part of it. The itch moved down her back and into her legs. Apart from the two green, cigarette stained chairs, a pine TV stand in the corner and a pair of old, sun-bleached curtains at the window, there was little else in the room. Helen wasn't surprised to see the empty spirit bottles and beer cans that were lined up beside the chairs. The autopsy report she'd received that morning highlighted a fatty, oversized liver, consistent with heavy drinking.

Something was bothering Helen and, as she could hear her team moving around, searching the floor above her head, she realised what it was—the mantel was empty apart from an old fashioned clock that ticked loudly. There were no photos on the walls. The room was devoid of those everyday objects we collect and treasure, those photos that record our memories.

She walked through to the kitchen. The sink was full of several days' washing up and an overfull ashtray sat on the work surface in between a jug kettle and a pile of opened post. She flicked through the post, a mixture of junk and bills, which felt strange through her rubber gloves. A letter touting for house insurance, a bank statement, telephone bill, a letter from the Department of Work and Pensions about income support. Right at the bottom of the pile she found a card in a grey envelope.

She pulled the card out. It had a drawing of a bottle of wine on the front underneath the words "Happy Birthday". She opened it and read the inscription inside: *"Happy Birthday, Dad. I've found her, and when I come out we'll all meet up."* It was signed *"Rab".* That was it. Not *"Love, Rab"* or, *"Thinking of You, Rab"*. Just *"Rab"*. She turned over the envelope to examine the postmark. It read October 2010. She screwed up her eyes to try and make out the obscured franking mark. There was no doubt it was HM Prison—but the envelope was smeared and she was unable to make out which prison.

IT WAS AFTER three o'clock when they finished searching the property and returned to the station. DS Pemberton looked up as she walked back into the incident room. "Anything of any use?"

"Rubbish." Before she was able to speak, she heard DI Townsend's dismissive voice behind and turned around to glower at him. He noticed her expression, shrugged his shoulders and strolled past her silently.

"The guys have bagged up a few bits and pieces." She walked into her office and he followed her as she opened her briefcase. "It was all very impersonal really," she added, "no photographs, no ornaments."

"Lived on his own," Pemberton said thoughtfully.

"Without a doubt," she replied, then, changing the subject, "Anything from house-to-house?"

"Not yet. Seems he pretty much kept himself to himself. Might get a bit more tomorrow, when the local shops open."

"What about in Flax Street?"

"Nothing. Nobody saw anything. In fact, they all seem to have been out last Friday afternoon."

She sighed. "I found this amongst his post." She pulled out a sealed plastic wallet containing the birthday card and envelope, and handed it over. The detective turned it over in his hands.

"Rab, Scottish for Robert," he said. He looked at the

postmark on the envelope. "This is quite recent. We'll check back through the prison records."

"Do you think we can trace which prison?"

"Quite possibly," he replied.

"Good. Anything back on forensics?"

He looked up at her. "Nothing yet."

Helen frowned. "Keep chasing, will you?" She looked past him, through the open blinds, into the incident room. There was no doubt that they were working, moving around, but in a malaise of weariness. It was like watching a film in slow motion.

Pemberton followed her gaze. "They're all knackered."

"Come on." She walked out into the main room and rested her right hand on one hip, lifting her jacket slightly.

"Can I have your attention please?" The muffled chatter hushed. "Thank you for all your hard work this weekend. We have made some real progress," she tried to sound upbeat, positive, although she knew they would be fully aware that the leads were quickly drying up. She pulled back her cuff, made a play of checking her watch. It was three-thirty. "Let's call it a day. Go home to your families. We'll start back again tomorrow morning, eight o'clock sharp." A roar went up around the room and she smiled to herself as she turned and walked back into her office to collect her things. Nothing more could be done today.

THE FIRST PERSON Helen saw when she arrived home just after four o'clock was Robert. He was sitting in the lounge, playing on his Xbox. His face lit up with a smile when she walked in.

"Hi, Mum!" She bent down to hug him and kissed

his forehead, affectionately pushing his unruly, brown curls out of his eyes.

"What are you playing?"

He looked back at the screen. "Lord of the Rings. Are you finished for the day or do you have to go back to work?"

"Done for today, darling. I'm going to cook us a roast dinner."

"Wicked." Robert had always been small for his years and the sofa juddered only slightly as he jumped with excitement. "Can you help me with my homework? It's algebra and I don't get it." He looked up at her, his dark eyes shining.

"Of course. We'll do it together after tea." He focused back on the screen now. She'd lost him to his game. She stood, placed her hand on his head briefly and moved out of the lounge, bumping into Matthew in the hallway.

"Oh. Hi, Matt," she said, resisting the temptation to hug him. He wasn't always in the mood for hugs these days.

"All right," he nodded slightly. She looked up at him, her eyes resting on his shaved head. He used to have thick, dark brown hair, which he liked to push up into soft, trendy spikes at the front of his head. Until a week ago. *Was it really only a week?* Last Saturday he left to go into town, a perfectly normal trip with his friends, only to return looking like a nightclub bouncer. Helen recalled the moment she'd first glimpsed it. She had walked into the kitchen as he pulled his head out of the fridge and gasped, "Wow! What have you done?"

"It's *my* hair," he replied indignantly.

"Was," she said, but her attempt at a joke was lost. He had stomped out of the room. He was right, of course, it was his hair. But she had always taken him to the hair-dressers in the past. This time he made his own decision, with no discussion. Her mother had been calmer (although she'd openly admitted to Helen that she didn't like it later, when they were on their own). "Are you pleased with it?" was all she had asked him as he passed her in the hallway. "It's OK," he'd shrugged, before disappearing to his room.

Helen was aware that he was growing up, not just physically, but also mentally, hormonally. She never seemed to say the right thing these days.

"How are things?" she asked, hoping to sound cool, relaxed.

"Umph. All right," he grunted this time, reaching into his pocket for his mobile phone.

"I'm making dinner," she added brightly.

"OK," he said without looking up. She'd lost him. He was already texting, his fingers busily moving over the buttons.

She walked into the kitchen to find her mother sitting at the table, head stuck in a book.

"Hi." She flashed her a weary smile and crossed to the fridge.

Jane Lavery put the book down. "Hi, darling. How's the case?"

"Hectic, drying up, desperately in need of a good lead…" She turned to face her, rubbing her forehead. "How was your day?"

"Not bad actually," she mused, "beat Matt at Wii bowls." A look of triumph appeared on her face. "What about *you*?"

Helen couldn't resist a grin. Jane Lavery was a very "hands on" grandmother. Thoughts of her own day darkened her face. "You know, the usual. Frustrating—hindered by the fact that I have an incompetent inspector who is negative in front of the staff and conspicuous by his absence most of the time."

"Oh. Not good. Anyone I know?" Married to James for the majority of his service, Jane Lavery had become the quintessential "police wife". Together their social circle was dominated by faces or partners of faces from within the force. A circle which reduced slightly after James' retirement and more so after his death, but there were still a few names that she maintained contact with, from time to time.

"Townsend. Simon Townsend. Just come back from the Met. He used to work here eight years ago."

"Doesn't ring any bells."

"Anyway," Helen said, keen to change the subject, "we are not going to discuss work tonight. I'm making dinner."

"I was thinking we should have a take-away. What about Chinese?"

Helen looked at her mother in surprise. "You, eat Chinese on a Sunday? Are you feeling all right?"

She shrugged a shoulder, tilting her head to the side. "Forgot to take the meat out of the freezer."

Helen stared at her a moment. It wasn't like Jane Lavery to be so disorganised. Her mother was still talking about the meat, the freezer, her day, when Robert walked into the room, breaking her train of thought. "Ahhh, Robert, fancy a Chinese?" Jane asked quickly.

"Yeah, great!" he said. Helen wondered at how easily her children could be persuaded by the lure of a take-away.

"But I was going to cook…" She watched them share

a glance, a smile. She felt the conspiracy, could see it in their eyes.

"Aww come on, Mum," pleaded Robert.

"OK, OK," she replied, lifting her hands in the air. "Chinese take-away it is."

As Robert dashed out of the room to look for menus, Helen's mother looked back at her, her eyes holding the kind of intimacy you only experience with the closest people in your life. "How are you?"

"Oh, you know," she said. "How's Matty been?"

"Back to normal. We haven't let him out of our sight all weekend."

"He just grunted at me in the hallway."

Her mother rolled her shoulders. "Hormones. A teenager's prerogative."

Just then Matthew and Robert crashed into the kitchen, already arguing over the menu that Robert clutched fervently. It would appear the take-away was a very popular idea.

An hour later, they sat down to a wide selection of Chinese food, helping themselves to portions of their favourite dishes, all talking at once. Even Matthew seemed to have relaxed. Helen opened a bottle of red wine and everybody laughed when Matthew balked at the smell. She sat back and surveyed her family. They each looked happy, healthy. She thought of Jim McCafferty and his sad life, his bare home. Right now, she felt truly blessed.

When dinner was over she helped Robert with his homework while her mother stacked the dishwasher. Bodies started to disappear. Robert went up to bed and Matthew retreated to his room.

Her mother finished her wine and placed her glass

on the table. "Well, that's me," she said, her voice slur-ring slightly.

"Sure you don't want to share the last few drops?" Helen said, holding up the bottle, tilting her head to one side cheekily.

"I think I've had enough." Jane Lavery rose from her seat, wobbling slightly. "That was a lovely evening. Thank you," she said.

Helen chuckled to herself. Her mother had never been able to take her drink. "See you in the morning," she said as she watched her shuffle out of the room.

After pouring the remainder of the wine into her glass she relaxed back into her chair. It had been a pleas-ant evening. Her family were fed and content. *Family, it's a funny thing. You can't choose your blood relatives. In fact, it's a bonus if you get along with them at all.*

She took another sip of wine and let her mind wan-der. What was missing? A partner. Someone to cud-dle up with on cold nights, share the last few drops of wine with, someone to have dinner with her fam-ily, watch a DVD, go to the theatre, make love—she couldn't remember the last time that had happened. *How sad is that?* Over the years she had indulged in a few affairs, but they were restricted to quick flings on training courses and petered out soon after. Where would she meet anyone like that? Somebody she could truly share her life with?

Not in the job, that's for sure. The police force was well known for its incestuous relationships. It was also renowned for the fact that it had the highest divorce rate of any profession in the UK. No, it would need to be somebody outside of the job, she was convinced of that. And who would want to have a relationship with a thirty-six-year-old widow with two teenage kids who still lived with her mother? Not exactly an exciting prospect. Her sad relationship prospects still on her mind, she reached for her laptop, pulled it out of the bag and switched it on.

The investigation. They had no real leads, were in pursuit of no recognised suspects. She had seen the concern in her mother's eyes earlier, recognised that same look before as Jane Lavery watched her own husband, in the midst of a murder enquiry, work painstakingly around the clock in pursuit of that hidden clue, that small scrap of evidence, that would lead him to the killer. *What would James do?*

Helen chewed the side of her lip. This was the reason Helen joined the police. For *this* job. She wasn't ambitious in the material sense. She had never wanted to attend meaningless meetings, making meaningless decisions, chase meaningless statistics to impress her superiors or the politicians that ultimately called the shots. To lead a murder investigation, to catch the bad guy, to be like her dad. But what if she wasn't good enough? What if she had just been kidding herself all these years?

Whilst the screen was coming to life she looked up at the kitchen clock. It was ten o'clock.

SIX

CROSS KEYS POLICE station was located just off the main ring road roundabout, a brick-built 1980s construction, originally intended to be the new Hampton HQ. But by the time the building was complete the trend for out of town headquarters had begun. Instead it became a new sub-station to address the needs of a rapidly expanding city. Over the years it had been extended in the form of two portable units, erected on the tennis courts at the back of the building, next to the car park. It was one of these units that housed the incident room.

By the time Helen had reached the car park a drizzle had started, the result of soft rainclouds moving in overnight. It was that kind of fine, constant rain that deceived you into not using an umbrella, but soaked you in minutes. She crossed the car park quickly and entered at the back door.

The incident room was dark. She switched on the main lights and made her way into her office, hung her damp jacket over the back of the chair, tucked her wet hair behind her ears and leant down to fish her notes from her briefcase. Resting her elbow on the table, head on hand, she went through her logbook from beginning to end, making endless lists and notes that would form the basis of her morning briefing. If she was going to miss anything, it wasn't for the want of trying.

Some time later a phone rang in the distance and she

looked up to see that, oblivious to her, the office had come to life. So consumed in her work, she had ignored the gentle hum of computer fans, the murmur of voices, the sound of keyboards clicking.

A few moments later there was a knock on her office door. She looked up as DS Pemberton peered around the door before she had time to respond.

"Morning."

"Morning, Sean. What can I do for you?"

He lifted a pad and read notes from it. "Miss Cottrell called to ask when she can have her bike back, Andrew Steiner phoned from *The Hampton Herald* and the Super's on his way over. He flashed his eyes up at her as a warning at the last remark.

"Thanks." She nodded as Pemberton retreated, quickly moving papers around her desk to represent some kind of tidiness. Although having worked for Superintendent Jenkins for three months, Helen could not claim any more acquaintance with him than on the day they first met. An acutely private man, he never discussed his personal life. She often wondered if he even had one. His dark eyes penetrated the surface, as if to read your thoughts, but gave nothing away in return. His intensity, only rarely broken by the odd smirk or joke (usually of his own making), and lack of personal contact made for an awkward working relationship.

When she looked up again Superintendent Jenkins was strolling across the incident room to her office. In his mid-fifties, his head boasted a full head of grey hair which was remarkable in contrast to his thick black eyebrows and lashes.

"Morning, Helen. How's it going?"

She stood and nodded at him. "Morning, sir. Good, thank you."

"You've charged your suspect then." He looked across at her in mock surprise.

She forced a polite smile and asked, "Did you read the report I emailed you?" as they both seated themselves, either side of the desk.

"Yes." He wiped a fleck of dust from the sleeve of his jacket and raised his head to look at her. "Any developments? Some new evidence, a sudden breakthrough?" A crooked smile tickled his lips. He continued to tease her, although she picked up the serious undertone. It was certainly in everyone's interests for this case to be cleared from the statistics as quickly as possible—and Superintendent Jenkins was well known for his dislike of protracted investigations.

"No, sir, no change. We are waiting on forensics and DNA which I have fast-tracked so they should be back this morning."

"Fast-tracked," he replied, nodding to himself. "Good. From what I understood, this looked like an open and shut case," he said, his brow creasing as he adjusted his position and crossed one leg over the other, a gesture which made his body appear at an angle.

"As you can see there appears to be much more to it," she replied.

"Your report was certainly very detailed."

"Thank you." She wasn't sure whether or not this was a compliment.

"Why don't you brief me on what I need to know?" His eyes, now serious, fixed upon her.

He hasn't read it, she thought. She considered mentioning that she had stayed up until midnight preparing it, but decided against it.

Helen sighed inwardly, then relayed an overview of the case. As she finished she added, "We are now looking at the possibility that our victim may have been killed by a third party, since Anna Cottrell appears to have a substantiated alibi. We are building up a profile of the victim and looking into Miss Cottrell's background..."

"The removal of the tattoo bothers me," he interrupted, rubbing his chin.

Helen considered this point. Further examination of Jim McCafferty's police record confirmed that he had a "love heart" tattoo at the top of his left arm. Officers at the time had reported that there was some illegible writing inside the heart (the letters were all smudged together) and McCafferty had refused to clarify. Helen pondered the significance of its removal herself. Why did the killer remove it? Did it have anything to do with the words contained within the heart?

"We've run it through the police national computer and carried out checks with national agencies," Helen said. "So far, we cannot find any cases which share the same characteristics, either an obsession with tattoos or skinning in general."

"I still don't like it," he continued. More chin rubbing. He stared into space. "Helen, I think you might benefit from some assistance on this case, perhaps from an experienced Senior Investigator?"

She stared at him warily. "What do you mean?"

"Well, if it is more complex than we originally thought, as it certainly appears..." He rubbed his chin again. "I wonder if George Sawford would be free for a few days?"

A feeling of dread hit Helen. She had rubbed shoulders with DCI Sawford in the past and, whilst she had to agree he boasted a wealth of experience at managing murder investigations, he was certainly not known as a team player. If George was brought into the investigation, with her lack of knowledge and experience she would almost certainly be marginalised. "I don't think that's necessary. We still have plenty of leads to follow and I'm confident that the victimology profile will lead us to the killer."

He sat back and surveyed her for a moment. "This is not a criticism, Helen. George would work alongside you, as a mentor more than anything. We need to be sure that we don't miss anything that a possible review team might pick up."

"It's a bit early for a review team." Independent Review Teams carried out an audit of investigations that reached a dead end, usually between two and six weeks after the crime.

"I'm quite aware of that, Helen. But we need to show, at every stage, we have taken the correct course of action. Imagine if there is a complaint to the Police Complaints Authority? They'll home in on this being your first major inquiry and scrutinise your every move."

Helen took a deep breath to keep herself calm and chose her words carefully. "I appreciate the offer. And yes, perhaps it would help to have somebody to bounce ideas off, should I need it. But I don't need another SIO on the case yet. Give me a chance. Please?"

He sat back and stared at her. "Fair enough, I'll give you a few more days. Keep me updated on any developments. I'll have June email you George's number, just in case."

That's you covering your back in case I mess up, thought Helen.

"Anything else?"

"I wanted to have a word with you about Acting Inspector Townsend." She emphasised the word "acting", hoping it would add some weight to her argument.

"Simon Townsend. Good man by all accounts, just joined us from the Met."

"Yes, but rather lacking in motivation." She was tempted to include his lack of experience, but, in view of the Super's reservations in her own abilities, decided against it.

"Oh, I'm sure you'll pull him round."

"That's the problem. He's supposed to be my deputy, but he spent half the briefing smoking a fag in the car park the other night." Superintendent Jenkins' eyes widened at this remark. She'd finally got his attention. "Look, sir, in view of what you've just said, I think assigning a dedicated DI, with major incident experience, *within* the team would be a better idea…"

"Helen, I don't need to tell you that we have a real shortage of substantive Detective Inspectors at the moment," he interrupted, dismissively. "Hell, your own DI is on extended leave in Australia. And I've still got officers investigating the train crash near Worthington at the weekend. That's without all the officers we've lost, or are about to lose—those leaving the provinces, lured by the inflated pay packages of the Met. We need to encourage more people like Townsend back."

"But, I…"

"I'm sure it's just teething problems. Show him who's boss and he'll soon pull into line." He stood, making it clear the conversation was at an end.

"Let me know as soon as you have anything. We need something to feed to the press, and fast. As soon as they find out our principal suspect has been released they'll be all over this like a rash. This is sensational heaven for the pen boys."

She slumped back into her chair, defeated, as he left, shouting "Morning" across the office to Townsend, no doubt to rub further salt into the wound. Whatever happened, she needed a result fast.

Helen grabbed her bag and headed out of her office, through the incident room, and out of the building into the fresh air. She reached into her handbag and pulled out a packet of Dunhill's and an old blue, plastic lighter she kept for emergencies. She stood under the doorway, sheltered from the damp drizzle as she lit the cigarette and took a long, deep drag. It felt good. She hadn't been a regular smoker in years, but, every now and then, she needed to indulge.

There was a flurry of activity in the incident room when she returned a few minutes later. When she reached her office, Pemberton and Townsend were waiting for her. She looked around at them, anger still clouding her vision. "Is there a problem?"

"Ma'am, the DNA results are back," Townsend said, handing her a buff, A4 file. There was a change to his attitude. An injection of enthusiasm.

"No forensics?" she asked.

"No, not yet, but these are just in and you really need to read them," Pemberton interjected, failing to disguise the excitement in his voice. She stared at them. They were both glowing, like delighted little boys on Christmas morning.

"What do you mean?" she asked as she opened the file.

"You are not gonna believe it," Pemberton said.

She looked up at the detective, frustrated. "Well, spit it out, whatever it is. It's going to take me a good ten minutes to read this and you've obviously already…"

"There's a family link."

"What?" She screwed up her forehead, perplexed, not sure whether to listen to the detective or start reading the report first.

"There's a link in DNA between the suspect and the victim." Pemberton looked triumphant.

Helen stared at him in astonishment. "How do you mean?"

"Jim McCafferty is a member of Anna Cottrell's family. A very close member."

IT SEEMED TO Anna that a dark cloud of mist had descended over the Cottrell household when she got up the next morning. Breakfast in the kitchen with her father was a sober affair. Few words were spoken and those only out of necessity. After lunch, the day before, her mother had retired to her bedroom with a migraine, not to be seen again. Her father had disappeared into the garden until dark, then gone to bed under the pretence of an "early night". He appeared cagey, as if he were walking a tightrope of despair, as if at any moment she would ask an awkward question and he would tumble off into doom. But she didn't feel like asking questions today. In fact, she was probably the only person in the country who was really looking forward to going to work on this Monday morning, restoring some kind of normality to her life. Questions could wait until later.

She had just finished her coffee when she heard the

phone ring. Her father answered and passed it over mouthing, "It's your boss."

Anna reached for the handset and wandered into the lounge. "Hi, Jason. I'll be there in a half an hour," she said, reaching down to stroke Cookie's head.

"How are you, Anna?" His tone sounded uncomfortable. Cookie purred and nestled up closer to her ankles.

"I'm OK." She hesitated, not too sure how much he knew. No doubt the grapevine would be well at work already, and that was if the police hadn't spoken to him. "I just want to get everything back to normal really."

"No problem. I can see that. But I'm sure that you'll need some time to sort out your home and things. We can arrange some special leave, Anna, in view of the circumstances."

"That's all right. I'm staying with my folks at the moment. I don't need…"

"I insist, Anna." The interruption startled her. Her hand froze. "You've had a huge shock. We, that is… I would rather you took some time to get yourself together and return to work when all of this is behind you." That explained the awkwardness.

Cookie nudged her hand, but she kept it still. "Oh."

"Do you have any lesson plans for today?"

"In the top drawer of my desk. It's unlocked."

"Take the week to sort yourself out." Anna blinked. This was a command, not a request. "Just keep me informed, will you? And let Erica know if you have any lesson plans for the rest of the week?" Erica was the school secretary.

"Of course." She watched as the cat wandered away into the kitchen. "Errr. Thanks, Jason."

"No problem. Take care."

She switched the button to end the call and stared at the handset, perplexed. She was beginning to feel alienated. Suddenly she remembered her arrangement with Ross, grabbed her new mobile from her pocket and selected his number, hoping to catch him before he left.

"Hi, Anna." He sounded as if he was still half-asleep. "I'll be there in twenty minutes."

"That's why I'm ringing, Ross. I'm not going in today. There's no need to pick me up."

"Oh... Everything all right?"

"I'm not sure really. I was just getting ready when Randle phoned and told me to take the week off..." She stuttered in her rush to deliver the words. "Special leave. To sort out my life, I think."

"Wow. That's generous for Randle."

"That's what I thought." She fidgeted, suspicion creeping into her head.

"They're probably waiting for it all to die down a bit. The kids are bound to have heard about it in the news. If they put two and two together..." He hesitated.

"They wouldn't know my address," Anna said defensively.

"It's probably just a precaution. Don't worry. I'd better go. I'll pop in tonight after work." As he rang off she heard something on the radio and headed back into the kitchen, straining to hear the news report.

Her dad had left the room and she stared at the radio as it bellowed the words out. "The dead body of a middle-aged man was found on Friday evening in a flat in Little Hampstead. A young woman, known to be a local schoolteacher, is currently helping police with their enquiries..."

She leant forward and switched off the radio as realisation hit home. It was only a matter of time before the press tracked her down and connected her with Carrington Grange. Perhaps Randle was right. The school certainly wouldn't welcome any disruption caused by press attention.

Anna walked back into the lounge, looking out of the front window absent-mindedly. She was starting to feel very alone. It reminded her of when she was back at junior school, in Year 6. Some fellow pupils were penning graffiti on the back of the bike sheds. She hadn't been keen to join them at first, but they cajoled and persuaded, flattering her artistic talent. Although she knew it was wrong, she believed them when they said they were in it together and they would stand together when caught. But on the day it was discovered she was there alone, silently putting the finishing touches to a drawing of a rock guitar. As she was brought out into the middle of the playground and confronted by her form teacher, she watched her classmates stepping away as if they had nothing to do with it, leaving her to face punishment alone. In the same way today she could feel more and more people gradually retreating, although this time she had done nothing wrong.

And then she saw it, through the front window. The police car indicated and turned into her driveway in all its glorious bright colours. Maybe they were bringing her bike back? She hoped so. She really needed some good news today. She made her way to the front door and opened it before the policeman in uniform had time to ring the bell.

"Morning officer," she said brightly.

"Anna Cottrell?" The seriousness in his inflection was disconcerting.

"Yes." She felt her face fall.

"I need you to come down to the station with me. We have some more questions for you."

ANNA WATCHED TWO detectives enter the room and close the door behind them. She was baffled. The only contact she'd had with the police since her release on Saturday was a telephone call requesting her bike back. What on earth could they possibly need to ask her now?

She continued to stare at them as they arranged their paperwork on the table and fiddled with tapes and recorders. Anna recognised the oversized detective from her first interview, but the female detective who sat opposite her was new. She was dressed in a charcoal suit, the white shirt underneath open at the collar, and had an air of practicality about her. She wore no jewellery and her dark, bobbed hair was tucked neatly behind her ears, her face showing only a trace of mascara, perhaps a little blusher.

"Good morning, Anna," she said finally. "You've met Detective Sergeant Pemberton already," she said nodding to her colleague, "and I am Detective Chief Inspector Lavery." There was a squeak as Will adjusted himself in his chair next to her. She glanced sideways at him. His face suddenly looked very alert. She shot him a puzzled look, which he failed to notice, and turned back to the detective.

"Anna, I would like to ask you some more questions about Friday evening," DCI Lavery continued.

"I've already told you everything I know."

"I realise this is difficult for you, but it would be most helpful if you would just help us with a few more issues."

Anna shrugged. "OK." *What else could there be?*

The detective placed three sheets of paper face down on the table. One by one she turned them over, her fingers squeaking on the glossy paper. They were photos of the dead man, taken from various angles. Anna cringed. Her stomach churned and she averted her gaze, just as acid bile rose into her mouth, forcing her to swallow.

"Have you ever met this man before Friday evening?" the detective asked, once all the photos were face up.

"No, I've already told you…"

"Are you sure? Take a closer look."

Anna forced herself to look at the pictures again, then looked up at the detective alarmed. "What is all this?"

"Do you know his name?"

"Jim McCafferty. Your colleague here told me on Friday evening." Anna looked from one detective to another. *What now?*

"Have you heard that name before?"

"No. Not before Friday. Never." She started to shake her head.

"I'm afraid I'm struggling to believe you."

Anna looked back at her defiantly. "I don't care what you think. I'm telling the truth." She could feel the tone of her voice sharpen as she struggled to keep her composure.

"His name has never been spoken in your house before Friday?"

"No." *Not before Friday.* She wondered at the significance of this.

"Then you may be surprised to discover that the DNA results are back and they are very puzzling." Anna continued to return the detective's stare. It was as if they were the only two people in the room. "They reveal a familial link with the victim."

"What?"

"He is a member of your family."

"What?" Her body jolted as if it had been struck by a pulse of electricity. She sat forward. "Do you mean? Is that why my mother and father have been acting strangely?"

"Excuse me. May I have a word with you, Detective?" Everyone's eyes focused on Will at the sudden interruption. "In private?" he continued. "It's important." DCI Lavery's face creased into a frown. "It's important," he repeated, pressing every syllable.

DCI Lavery sat back in her chair and sighed. "OK."

"Will," Anna cried, "what's going on?" He put up his hand to silence her.

Her face clouded over as the DCI announced a break in the interview. The tape was switched off and both detectives rose and left the room followed by Will, closing the door behind them. She felt outraged and, not for the first time, as if she were being treated like a child in an adult's world. Wasn't Will supposed to represent her? What was so secret that he couldn't discuss it in front of her?

The door opened and a female officer in uniform stepped in. She glanced at Anna and then looked away, standing just inside the door. Her brown hair had been highlighted with a russet tone and she wore it scraped off her face into a bun at the back, lifting her eyebrows slightly. She stood so still that she reminded Anna of a shop mannequin.

Restlessly, Anna fidgeted in her chair and looked at her watch. It was eleven o'clock. She wondered if the

police would be speaking to her parents about Jim Mc-
Cafferty. Perhaps they were here now?

She shuddered as she remembered the chilling look
on her mother's face when she mentioned his name.
What could have terrified her so much? And her behaviour afterwards? Usually, when Kathleen Cottrell
got upset, she got angry and shouted—she shouted a
lot—but to sob like a baby? No, that was definitely not
her style. And those words, "What have I done?" Was
she referring to Jim McCafferty when she uttered those
words? Anna swallowed hard.

The sound of the door clicking open broke her train
of thought. Will walked back into the room. He looked
straight at the uniformed officer. "Would you give us a
moment please?" She nodded and left the room, closing the door behind her.

Anna gripped the sides of the chair tightly. Anger
turned to frustration as she glared at him. "Will, what
is it?"

When his eyes finally met her gaze they were sor-
rowful, like a puppy pleading forgiveness for chewing
the back of a sofa.

Anna could feel the bottom drop out of her stomach.
"Will, please?" She stared up at him desperately. "You
have to tell me what's going on?"

He was silent for a moment, as if he were trying to
find the right words. Finally, he looked directly at her.
"Anna, I need to tell you something and I need you to
be calm."

She stared back at him with fear in her eyes, a rab-
bit startled in headlights. "OK."

"This isn't easy for me, so please bear with me until

I've finished." She continued to stare up at him expectantly, nodding her head slightly.

"When you were three years old, you were adopted by Edward and Kathleen Cottrell. Jim McCafferty was your biological father."

"No," Anna shook her head in disbelief. "This isn't happening." She could hear the sound of her heart pounding in her chest.

"I'm sorry, Anna. I'm very sorry to have to be the one to tell you." He looked around the room in despair. "In here… Like this."

Anna opened her mouth to say something, but her voice caught in her throat. She closed it again. She shook her head as if it were wrong, as if he were mistaken. She focused on the linoleum flooring which was speckled in black and grey, put together in a mock tile effect, wondering who would create such a design. *Were there companies who focused on designing flooring for police stations, cells, interview rooms?*

She became aware of Will's face in very close proximity to hers and turned her head to face him, her hands still gripping the sides of the moulded chair. He was crouched beside her.

"Can I get you anything?" he asked tenderly.

"I need to go to the ladies' room."

"Of course." He stood up. "I'll take you there. It's just at the end of the corridor."

One by one, Anna peeled her fingers off the plastic and stood. Her legs felt shaky and her eyes were set in a wide, trance-like state.

Anna couldn't remember the walk down the corridor. It was like a whirlwind. She walked into the empty toilets and immediately headed over to the basins, turning on the tap and splashing water on her crimson face. The cold water soothed her burning skin momentarily. She lifted her head to look at her reflection, staring at herself for several minutes. The face looked familiar, but she didn't know who the hell she was looking at.

SEVEN

THEY RETURNED TO the interview room to see two Styrofoam cups of coffee on the table, steam rising out of them, diffusing into the cool air around. Anna hadn't spoken to Will since they had left the room. She had no desire to speak to anyone. At this moment she felt as if she were piloting a plane which had descended into a tailspin, unsure of her surroundings or how to correct her position.

She sat down as the door opened and the detectives entered, seating themselves opposite. Placing her hands around the white cup, the warmth providing some bleak comfort, she lifted it to her lips, not noticing the lack of sugar usually craved by her sweet tooth. She gazed at the grey wall behind them, staring at nothingness, hoping her gesture might provide a few more precious minutes of respite.

It was as if both detectives were telepathic. They sat and waited patiently until she replaced the cup on the table before they restarted the interview. She was aware of tapes being switched on again, voices in the background.

Finally, Detective Chief Inspector Lavery spoke up. "Anna." She waited until Anna looked her in the eye. "We understand that you've had quite a shock." Anna looked away instantly, feeling her face flush in anger. "But we need you to stay focused," she continued gently, tilting her head in an attempt to regain eye contact. "We just have a few more questions to ask you."

Anna bent her head, rubbed the fingers of her right hand hard up and down her forehead and looked up at the detective, allowing her hand to drop loosely on to her lap. More than ever, she really wanted to get out of here.

"Can you tell me whether you recall hearing the name Jim McCafferty before today?"

Anna stared at the tape for a moment, watching the spools wind around slowly. She lifted her eyes and spoke directly at the DCI. "I'd never heard his name until your colleague here," she nodded at Pemberton, "mentioned it in the interview on Friday night."

"Have your parents *ever* mentioned the name McCafferty to you?"

"Never... Well, not until Saturday."

"Oh?" The detective leant in towards Anna.

"When I mentioned his name they seemed to sort of know him—said he was an old acquaintance." She felt herself cringe. "It kind of makes sense now. I wondered why they were being so cagey."

"How do you mean *cagey*?"

"As soon as I said his name, they both looked as if they had seen a ghost."

"Did you have any idea that you were adopted?"

"What?" Her face screwed up in horror. "No. I thought I was just... Well, you know, I thought they were my real parents."

"You never suspected anything?"

"Why should I?" She shook her head incredulously. "They brought me up as their own. I don't remember anything different." Silence hovered in the room for several minutes. Anna could literally feel the cogs turning in her own brain. "That explains it," she concluded finally, as the penny finally dropped into place.

"What?" Detective Pemberton asked.

"They've never said things to me like—'You've got your father's smile' or, 'you take after your mother, she was good at swimming.' My friends' parents would say things like that to them and I always wondered why my parents never did. When I was young, I asked them several times, like when I won an award for my reading in Year 3—'Do I take after you Daddy?' And my father would just say, 'You've always been a clever girl, Anna'."

Anna stared at the walls, her brain searching through its depths, examining memories from her youth. "And they never had any early photos of me. When I was in Year 4 we had to take in baby photos of ourselves. You know, a game so we could guess which one belonged to whom?" Anna was gazing into space now, talking to nobody in particular. "Mum didn't have any of me. She said a whole box of photos was lost when they moved to Worthington, so I had to take in one of her instead. I was really embarrassed at the time because it looked so old-fashioned." Anna dropped her head realising, with chagrin, that these were going to be the first of many memory recollections over the next few days. Many occasions when the clues were there, screaming out at her, but she had always failed to notice who she really was.

As THEY DROVE into Worley Close the rain was coming down in a steady stream, blurring the windows. So much so that she almost missed the police car heading out. *Almost*. Will pulled up outside number 12 and cut the engine. Anna undid her seat belt and swung round to face Will who, it seemed, was deliberately avoiding eye contact, instead staring up at the road ahead.

"You knew, didn't you?" she asked finally.

He turned to face her, resting his right hand on the steering wheel. He didn't need to speak. It was written all over his face.

"How could you have kept it from me?" she pleaded. Will had been a family friend for as long as she could remember. His son, Julian, was the same age as Anna and, at gatherings, Will would always play footy in the garden with the two children, or roll around on the grass, pretend fighting. He was like a fun uncle. Since adulthood, she had always seen him as a friend, an equal, not simply one of her parents' friends. This made the disappointment and betrayal all the heavier to bear.

"It wasn't for me to say," he answered finally, looking back at the road.

"Who else knew?" she asked, but as soon as the words left her mouth she regretted them. Once again, his face displayed all the answers. Everyone: family, of course, and their entire circle of friends, she guessed. All of them, closely guarding their precious little secret. She imagined them talking, huddled in bundles at parties and gatherings over the years. "Poor little Anna. She has no idea where she comes from." She could taste sick in her throat.

He looked back at her. "I'm sorry, Anna, truly I am. But your parents do love you. You must know that?"

"Don't lecture me about happy families. You know mine well enough to know what we have been through over the years, walking around on hot coals trying not to upset my neurotic mother. In fact, you know more about my family than I do." She noticed his mouth move as if he were about to speak, respond in some way, but didn't hang around to listen. Pushing the door open, she leapt out of the car, muttering, "Thanks for the lift," before slamming it shut and marching up the pathway and around to the rear of the house.

Anna never heard the sound of Will's engine, his car turning and pulling away down the road. She walked doggedly in through the conservatory and into the kitchen. Relieved to find it empty, she headed straight up the stairs to her bedroom and her white bedside table, opening the top drawer. Here were the remnants of her old stuff, things that she hadn't used in years, belongings that she hadn't seen the need to take with her but always intended to sort out, sooner or later.

The top drawer contained a couple of old magazines. She carefully lifted them out. Underneath was an instruction manual for an old mobile phone and some cookery recipes. Her fingers searched urgently and, frustrated by the bare wooden bottom, she pushed everything back into the drawer haphazardly, closed it and moved on to the next one down.

She lifted out her old exam certificates, beneath which was a favourite essay from university, the diary that she started keeping in her first year at uni, but only managed to write daily entries until the end of the second week in October. There were some old receipts which were curled up at the edges. Eventually, in amongst the fluff and bits of glitter at the back of the drawer, she found what she was looking for—a pile of photographs.

Anna pulled the photos out of the drawer, brushed the dust off the edges, and sat on the bed flicking through them, one at a time. These were old photos, taken in the pre-digital age, when people actually developed and kept all the copies. She'd retrieved them from one of her mother's clear outs, memories that told the story of her life which she meant to put in an album some day. There was one of her playing the violin, very poorly she recalled, in her final concert at primary school; another of her and her parents on a sun scorched beach in Corfu, one of them all on her graduation day, another of her and her father holding a huge pumpkin they had grown in the vegetable patch, when she was ten.

As she flicked through the photos her eyes searched desperately for similarities, small signs of a resemblance between her parents and herself, frantically holding on to her own thread of reality. She wanted more than anything to find something. Some kind of connection to dispel the science, prove the experts wrong. But the more she searched, the more the stark differences jumped out and slapped her across the face. In his younger years her father had shared a similar hair colour, not chestnut like hers, more a light sandy brown. Her mother had fair features and blue eyes, unlike her own which were dark brown. Her father was average height and build, her mother a pear-shaped size fourteen, both in stark contrast to her petite frame. As she scanned each photograph her frustration grew and tears pricked her eyes.

She stopped when, halfway through the pile, she reached the photo of her mother that she had taken in for the game at primary school. Her nostrils flared. Defeated, she tossed the pictures to one side and reached into her pocket for her mobile phone, her fingers working the keys with a sense of urgency.

"Hi, Anna, what's up?" Ross' soothing voice felt therapeutic, relaxing the tense muscles in her neck.

"Ross, sorry to bother you at work. Can you do me a favour?"

"Sure. You only just caught me. I've a class in a few minutes."

"Can I come and stay with you for a few days?"

"Yes, sure you can. But what's happened? I mean... are your parents all right?" He sounded concerned.

"They're fine, just doing my head in. I'll explain everything later."

"OK." She could feel him nodding at the other end of the line. "Do you want me to pick you up?"

She glanced at the hands of the bedside alarm clock. It read twenty-five minutes past two. So much had happened since she had spoken to him that morning. It seemed like days had passed, rather than hours. "No thanks. I'll make my own way over. I'll see you back at yours."

"No problem." He didn't sound particularly surprised. "I'll be back around five-thirty."

"See you then. And thanks." She pressed the button to end the call, straightened her body and went downstairs.

It took Anna a while to locate her parents. They weren't in the kitchen, which was their normal haunt, and she couldn't see her father in the garden through the conservatory window. Rain had been falling all day and the windows were masked with scattered patterns of water droplets. She was still straining her eyes to search through the wet windows when she heard murmurs coming from the lounge.

She stood in puzzled silence for a moment, as if

any movement would block her hearing. Her parents rarely ever sat in the lounge during the day. She heard another voice, quiet, almost a whisper. Yes, somebody was definitely in there. She headed for the lounge door and opened it.

Kathleen and Edward Cottrell sat together on one of the large sofas, her left hand enveloped in his. The shadows under Kathleen's eyes had grown darker in contrast to her pallid complexion. Her cheeks were sunken and she looked as if she had lost half a stone in the last few days. Edward, usually so calm and in control, looked tired and worn, older somehow.

They startled Anna and it was several seconds before she realised why. This was the first time she had ever seen them hold hands. Her parents looked up at her sheepishly, like a pair of toddlers interrupted whilst drawing on the walls.

Kathleen was the first to speak. "Why don't you sit down, Anna?" It was more of a command than a question and it felt like a red rag to a bull. Anna balked, a lifetime of domestic repression fuelling a rage within her.

She creased up her whole face and leant forward. "What?" she said, incredulous, nostrils flared, eyes boring into her mother. Kathleen jolted her head back, affronted.

"Sit down, darling." Edward's soft, silky voice spoke now. But Anna was not in the mood to be disarmed.

"How dare you tell me what to do!" she snarled.

"Anna, you need to calm down," Edward said, arching his forehead, a look of deep concern in his eyes.

"I'll make a cup of tea," Kathleen said, rising from her seat.

"Oh yes, you do that, Mum. Make a cup of tea. A cup of tea," Anna repeated, "that'll sort everything out."

"Anna." Edward stood now and stared at her.

She glared back at him as her mother left the room. "Just tell me why?"

He looked at her and blinked, as if he didn't know what to say.

"Go on, I'm dying to hear it. Tell me why you decided to keep the grand secret from me all these years. Poor little Anna, the desperate, adopted girl. How come everyone knew but me?"

"Anna. Sit down. Please?" She could see his eyes were watering. A lump rose in her throat and she moved across to the other sofa, tripping over the rug and finally falling into the seat. Her ears burned in clumsy embarrassment which only served to exacerbate her anger.

Over the years it seemed that her parents had mastered the art of sticking a plaster over problems and moving on, always treating the symptom instead of the cause. The problem, whatever it was, would then never be mentioned again, swept under the carpet as if it never happened. She was determined it was not going to happen this time.

Her mother re-appeared with three mugs of tea, carefully balanced on a tray which she set down on the coffee table in front of them. Anna watched as she retrieved coasters from a drawer in the dresser and set them out on the table. She couldn't stop herself from rolling her eyes. *That's it, carry on as normal. Let's pretend that nothing's going on here.*

She waited until her mother sat down before she spoke again. "How could you *not* have told me that I was adopted?" she asked.

Edward lifted his hand and scratched his ear uncomfortably. "We did what we thought was best, Anna."

"For who, you or me?" she asked, blinking as a sharp pain seared into her head.

"For all of us," he replied.

Anna looked at her mother, who had lifted her tea to her lips. She looked as though she wasn't part of the conversation.

"Were you ever going to tell me?"

"What good would it do?" His face slackened and his voice grew quieter, as if someone had turned the volume down.

"How can you say that," she said drily, "especially when everyone else seems to know? Surely I was bound to find out sooner or later?"

"First, everyone didn't know. Only family and our oldest friends, those who have known us since you joined our family. Second, we always felt that we were a strong, loving family and you would never need anything else."

Anna stared at him, her eyes wide. He had no idea how she was feeling.

"I remember the first time I set eyes on you." Kathleen finally spoke, staring into space. "You were three years old." She smiled to herself, as the memory warmed her heart.

"This isn't about you," Anna cried, the tone in her voice rising. "What about me?"

Kathleen's face fell as she looked at her daughter. "We gave you a good home, opportunity. You'd never have had any of that where you came from!" she shouted back at her daughter, turning her nose up disapprovingly.

"How would I know?" Anna retorted, competing with the decibels in her voice.

"I'm not sitting here listening to this." Her mother stood, glared at her daughter and marched out of the room.

"I don't believe it," Anna said, shaking her head. "Typical. No answers to any questions and now *she* feels aggrieved. Why does it always have to be about her?"

"Don't be too hard on your mother."

This was too much for Anna. She stood and raised her hands to her head which now felt as if it was splitting in half. "I'm going to stay with Ross."

"Anna, please."

She couldn't miss the desperation in his voice. "I need some time to think," she replied, turning to face the door as she closed her eyes in an effort to control her erratic breaths. "I need a few days." As soon as she reached the hallway she flew up the stairs hastily, keen to reach her bedroom before the tears came tumbling down.

EIGHT

HELEN PUT OUT the cigarette, walked back in from the car park and stopped beside the water cooler, filling a plastic cup. As she drank she indulged the feel of the icy cold water flowing through her body. She watched the hive of activity around her in the incident room, detectives going about their business, trying their best to find a cold-blooded murderer. That was the thing with murderers—some were racked with remorse, afraid of incarceration, but almost relieved when they were caught, as if justice would wash some of the guilt away. Others played a game of cat and mouse, relishing the notoriety the chase provided in the media. But calculating, cold-blooded murderers were the worst type. They were engaged in a completely different game: one in which they went to great lengths to prevent you discovering their identity at all costs.

She made her way across to her office and reached into her bag, rummaging around for the Paracetamol. By the time she had placed two in her mouth and swallowed them back there was a knock at the door. She looked up in time to see DS Pemberton's face appear.

"How did the meeting go?" he asked.

She sighed. Having spent the last hour with the press office, discussing their media strategy, they concluded that, after the short statement released to the press on Saturday, they should release another appealing for witnesses. There wasn't enough fresh information to warrant a press conference at this stage. But they couldn't hold them off forever. "Poor. We've released another statement, appealing for witnesses, but we need something to feed the beast and fast, before they start printing what they want to. The train crash just outside Worthington put us on the back burner for the weekend, but now they're looking for something new."

He nodded. Many a previous investigation had been thwarted by the press carrying out their own partisan enquiry. "You have several messages." He walked into the office and closed the door behind him, his face grave.

"What's up?" she asked, suspicious.

"Sergeant Samson called from custody. He has your mother and your son, Matthew, downstairs. You need to give him a call."

"What's happened?" Her eyes widened. "Sean?"

"I didn't ask all the details. I believe it has something to do with smoking cannabis." She didn't miss the smile that danced on his lips. "Give Dave Samson a call, he'll fill you in."

"Right." Helen drew a deep breath in through her nose and let it out slowly.

"A Mr Devereaux from St Edmund's School also called. He wants to speak to you urgently."

She nodded, speechless, hard eyes staring into space. She hadn't imagined her day getting any worse. "Anything else?"

"Forensics results are back."

She looked at him eagerly. "And?" He untucked a pink cardboard file from underneath his arm and passed it over but his face was flat.

"Nothing."

"What do you mean?"

"Nothing." He shook his head as he spoke. "No prints, no DNA that doesn't appear to match Anna or her boyfriend. It looks pretty clean."

"Do you have any good news for me, Sergeant?" He shook his head.

"What about the son?"

"We're working on it."

"See if you can speed things up there, please. I have a strong feeling that he might hold some answers."

She waited for him to leave the room before she dialled the custody suite.

"Cross Keys Custody, Sergeant Samson speaking." The line crackled as he spoke.

"Dave, it's Helen Lavery."

"Oh. Hi, Helen. You got my message?"

"Yeah. What happened?"

"Matthew was caught smoking cannabis behind the gym at school with a couple of other lads. The school called us so we brought them in. Since we couldn't locate you, your mother came down to be his appropriate adult for the interview."

She raised her free hand and massaged her forehead. *That's all I need.* "Where is he now?"

"He's been given a caution. I believe he's still in the interview room with his grandmother. Want me to send him up?"

She thought for a moment. "No. Put him in a cell for a bit, will you? Maybe it'll knock some sense into him. I'll be down in a bit."

"Sure thing." She heard him muffle a chuckle.

"And Dave?"

"Yes?"

"Give my mum a cup of tea, would you?"

"No worries."

"Thanks."

She replaced the receiver and put her head in her hands. How could she have two sons that were so completely different? Robert struggled academically, particularly in maths and science, but he was a sociable lad with a pleasant disposition, plenty of friends, always being invited to go bowling, swimming, on sleepovers. His school reports always read the same: "He tries hard", "Very obliging", "Always willing to have a go".

Matthew was a whole different ball game. He was blessed with the brains. Like his father, he had a practical as well as an academic mind, excelling at maths, science, design technology. He wanted to build aircraft, but despite having a clear career path since primary school, he constantly needed pushing. And now more than ever. Over the last couple of months she'd needed to nag him to do his homework, caught him feigning illness to miss school. And now drugs.

Helen raked her hair away from her face as she telephoned the school and spoke to the headmaster's secretary who made an appointment for three-forty-five.

By the time she joined her mother and retrieved Matt from the cell he looked diffident, and the party of three drove back to St Edmund's in silence. She glanced at him in the rear view mirror a couple of times but decided words would be futile at this stage, afraid that her own anger may provoke her to say something she would later regret. No, it was better to let him sweat it out for the moment. At this stage she needed to concentrate her efforts on limiting the damage.

St Edmund's High School was situated only a couple of miles from the station. Luckily, Hampton's rush hour traffic hadn't yet kicked in and they arrived in less than ten minutes. The school was a modern build, less than fifteen years old and completely lacking in character.

They made their way directly to the headmaster's office and knocked on the door. Mr Devereaux had managed St Edmund's comprehensive for the last seven years, during which time he had turned the school's results around, so much so that it was now one of the leading comprehensives in the county, a fact which had increased his popularity with the governors. However, parents in general were sceptical about his success. He was known to be a deep disciplinarian and had the highest expulsion rate in Hamptonshire; fuelling parents' arguments that he simply got rid of underperforming kids in order to improve the school's ratings.

Devereaux answered the door almost immediately. "Good afternoon, Mrs Lavery." He shook her hand, his fingers feeling like sweaty sausages against her own, and nodded to Jane Lavery before turning to Matthew. "You can wait outside," he said firmly.

The two women followed the headmaster into a small office, dominated by a large desk, upon which papers, books, photographs were all arranged in an orderly manner. Helen glanced across at her mother who raised her eyebrows. Helen couldn't help but think what a contrast this desk was to hers at work. She winced at the musty smell which filled the air.

As they seated themselves opposite him, the desk between them, Helen stared at the man who poured his body into the seat beneath him. They'd met on a couple of occasions in the past at open evenings and both times she witnessed his boldness, his tendency to boast about the school's achievements. She was also acutely aware of his reputation for bullying parents into submission, as if they were an extension of his pupils.

"I assume you know why I have called you here?" She caught a slight lisp in his voice as he spoke.

"I have heard the police officer's account." Helen nodded. "Perhaps you would like to give me yours."

Devereaux looked at her suspiciously. This clearly wasn't what he was expecting. He looked across at her mother, but Jane Lavery's face gave nothing away. He shuffled in his seat, folded his hands together on the desk in front of him.

"Well," he cleared his throat. "Matthew was caught smoking marijuana behind the gym during break this afternoon."

She smiled inside at his use of the term "marijuana". He sounded as though he had just stepped off the set of *The Wire*. "I understand there were other children involved?"

"Yes, three in total."

"And how many joints did they have between them?"

He tilted his head back, surprised by her bluntness. "Just the one, as far as I am aware." She nodded, a gesture intended to encourage him to continue. "However," he continued hastily, "that doesn't make the offence any less serious." She stared at the headmaster, expressionless. "School policy is to call the police which, as you are aware, we did." She nodded and they sat quietly again. It always interested Helen how uncomfortable people were with silence. Eventually he added, "The lockers were searched but no other drugs were found."

"So this was a group of teenagers, curiously meddling with drugs?" she asked finally.

"I'm sure that I do not have to remind you, Mrs Lavery, of all people, that marijuana is a class B drug." His lisp dragged out the "s" in class. She wondered how much fun the school kids had with that lisp. Kids could be so cruel when they wanted to be.

"Not at all, Mr Devereaux," she replied. "But let's not get carried away here. Matt's results are good, as I'm sure you are aware, and this is the first time the school has ever found the need to formally discipline him." Helen knew she was walking a fine line. Matt's last test results had still been reasonably high but, in view of his rebellious behaviour over the last few months, his lax attitude towards homework, it would only be a matter of time before they started to deteriorate. Intelligence alone could only bolster him in the short term.

"It's still an offence and against school rules," Devereaux declared, clearly exasperated by her calmness. "And I have no choice but to suspend him for a week."

Helen frowned. "That seems rather harsh under the circumstances. He has already been cautioned by the police and you can be assured he will be punished at home. It's not as if he was supplying the drug to others, or had his own personal supply in his locker." She was tempted to ask about the other boys, about where the drugs had come from, but thought better of it. That line of questioning could rebound and hit her in the face, especially if Matt had obtained the joint himself.

"Rules are rules. I can assure you that if we had found any further evidence, then your son would have been expelled immediately, irrespective of his grades. The school governors are resolute on the issue of drugs."

Helen decided to quit whilst she was ahead. In her experience, one week's suspension was not unreasonable for possession of an illegal substance on school premises. "What about work in the meantime?"

Her acceptance threw him off balance momentarily. He stared at her. "Ah, yes well… I can get his tutors to email him work so that he doesn't fall behind with the curriculum. If that is what you wish?"

"Of course. I'm sure the school wouldn't want his grades to be affected." She stood indicating the end of the conversation. "Thank you for seeing us."

He nodded, flabbergasted, as she walked out of the office followed by her mother.

The car was quiet again on the drive home, the silence only broken briefly when they stopped to collect Robert from his friend's house, his mood instantly subdued by the sombre atmosphere in the car.

Helen considered the effects of the punishment on Matt's life. *What would John have made of all of this? Would he have handled it differently? Been harder on the boys?* At times like this she longed for him, for his support.

When they reached home Matthew bolted for his room. *You're not getting away with it that easily*, thought Helen.

"Mum, do you know where my rugby shirt is?" piped up Robert as they removed their coats and hung them up in the hallway. "I need it for tomorrow."

"Ask your gran to find it for you," Helen said. "I have a special purpose to attend to," she muttered under her breath, reaching the top of the stairs before she had even finished the sentence.

Matt was lying on his back on the bed when she

walked into his room without knocking. He quickly sat up, lifting his head backwards, a look of horror on his face.

"Is this where I get the lecture?" he asked, warily.

She stared at him for a moment. He looked more like his father every day. "Was this the first time?" she asked, ignoring his question.

"Yes."

"And the last?"

"Aren't you going to ask me where I got it from?"

"The school and the police have already done that," she said curtly. She looked him up and down. He was so young, so unspoilt. Or was he? *The haircut, the drinking, the drugs*. When she spoke again her tone was softer. "I would like to know *why*, though?"

He shrugged. "Seemed like a laugh at the time."

"Is there anything wrong at school, anything you would like to talk about?"

"No." He snorted through his nose.

The snort touched a nerve with Helen, hardening her reserve. "Listen, I understand that you are growing up Matthew. I understand that you want to experiment, try things. But make it the last time you experiment with cannabis. OK?"

"Why? Because you're worried about how it will affect you. Worried about your job, your reputation?" He stared at the blank wall opposite. It seemed that his boldness would fizzle out if he made eye contact.

His outburst surprised her and when she finally spoke her tone was steely, her eyes hard. "This isn't about me, Matt, it's about you. About how a police caution and a school suspension will look on your record when you apply to Engineering College."

He shifted his posture uncomfortably. "I'm not going to Engineering College," he muttered.

"What?"

"I said I'm not going…"

"I heard what you said," she interrupted. "What do you mean you're not going to Engineering College? I thought you wanted to build aircraft?"

"No. You want me to build aircraft." He virtually spat the words out of his mouth. "I want to fly them."

Helen was flabbergasted. "Since when?"

"Forever." He stared at the wall, avoiding her eyes.

"Why haven't you said anything?"

He looked at her now and she could almost feel the hackles on his back rising. "Because you'd never listen. Not after what happened to Dad." His voice was quiet, as if he were revealing a secret.

Helen was aghast. *After what happened to Dad.* The words transported her back ten years. John had just returned from two months in Sierra Leone. She remembered the relief she felt having him back on British soil, the exhilaration at seeing him again. Two weeks later he died.

He was on an army training exercise, being routinely transported from Nuneaton to Leicester. The helicopter crashed into a field just a few miles from the runway, the pilot and all four passengers killed instantly. A few minutes later they would have landed at the base.

There was an investigation—of course. The inquest heard that there were no reports of mechanical breakdown. Could it be weather conditions? It had been very foggy that evening. Or pilot error? Nobody would ever know. Three months after his death the coroner recorded an "open verdict". Helen was beside herself. What did that mean?

She plagued the army for answers. It became an obsession. Grief turned to anger as she desperately looked for somebody to be held responsible for taking John's life. And inevitably, eventually it made her ill. Her life began to fall apart at the seams. Until she had no fight left in her.

One day, she had been sitting at the table helping Matthew draw a picture. It was almost Christmas. The boys had decorated the house with streamers, tinsel, baubles. She felt the tears come out of nowhere, streaming down her face, but couldn't seem to stop them. Matthew looked up at her and said, "Mummy, don't cry again. You can have my picture if you like. That'll make you happy." It was an epiphany moment. The words of a small child lighting up the darkness that flooded her brain. Suddenly, she realised John was gone. There was nothing that she or anyone else could do to bring him back and, for the sake of the boys, she needed to move forward and put the accident behind her. Shortly afterwards she applied to join the police.

But Helen had been anti-military ever since. Any mention of them made her seethe. She would switch the TV over if there was an army documentary on, tut at the radio if the presenters were reporting war news. Over the years she tried to curb her behaviour for the sake of her children. But, maybe she had not tried hard enough? Had it really been that obvious? Had she tainted her children with her own opinions? It took her a moment to gather her thoughts.

"Matt, it's your life," she said gently. "If you want to become a pilot."

"I want to join the Air Force." It was his turn to interrupt now and she couldn't fail to miss the tears that were gathering in his eyes.

But the words still winded her, as soon as they left his mouth. *Air Force. Military.* Her throat constricted.

She forced her mouth to move, desperately trying to hide her own feelings. "Oh."

He glanced across at her. "I still want to go to university," he continued, as if he were selling the idea to her. "They do a course at Staffordshire where you went. Aeronaut or something Technology. It's a degree course. You can join the RAF after that."

She nodded and stared into space, not quite trusting her voice. Thoughts filled her brain. *Military, war, battles, flying, accident, death…* She shuddered inwardly. Maybe he would change his mind? Do the degree and join an airline? The thought of him piloting an aircraft wounded her enough, but the Air Force… The thought of history repeating itself…

She looked askance at her eldest son. His eyes were filled with a mixture of relief and anxiety. Swallowing her own pride, she tried to push the tarnished thoughts out of her mind. "I'll do a deal with you."

He narrowed his eyes. "What do you mean a deal?" he asked tentatively.

"Well I imagine piloting is very competitive." She fought to keep her voice even. "Your grades would have to be perfect…"

He groaned.

"Listen, this is important. If you really want to become a pilot then you need to work hard at school and stop pulling stunts like today."

He scowled.

"It's up to you Matt, but if you're prepared to show me that you can work hard, that you are committed, then I will support you all the way."

He looked up, eyes shining in amazement, "Really?"

"Really," she said, her mouth still tight. She couldn't seem to manage a smile to accompany it. "That should keep you busy while you are grounded for the next month."

Matt laid back down on his bed and groaned again, swinging his arms up over his head.

As Helen closed the door to his room behind her, she could feel her heart racing, a rush of blood to the head. She sat on the top stair, placing her head in her hands. She thought about John, how they had both met at Staffordshire University all those years ago. She was studying law, he mechanical engineering. Matthew was a lot like his father: annoyingly clever, never having to graft for his grades. It was just after graduation that she discovered she was pregnant, scuppering her plans to join the police service.

As she cast her mind back to those early years, tears filled her eyes. They were so young. And it was a struggle. She had been so proud of John when he left Sandhurst, eventually becoming a platoon commander in the Royal Electrical and Mechanical Engineers.

She remembered those long periods on her own with a young baby. John was often away for weeks, sometimes a couple of months at a time. But when he was home—life was wonderful. He was a great father, very hands on, couldn't do enough with his family...

The gentle hum of her mobile phone distracted her. She pulled it out of her pocket and answered abruptly, "DCI Lavery," blinking to fight back the tears that appeared to be breeding in her eyes.

"Ma'am, sorry to bother you at home." She immediately recognised Pemberton's accent, although he didn't formally introduce himself. "We've had a bit of a breakthrough." The excitement in his voice grabbed her attention.

"What?"

"We've managed to trace the victim's son. His name is Robert McCafferty, known to his friends as Rab."

"Good work."

"There's more. He's only just been released from prison."

Helen clutched the phone hard. "When?"

"On the day of the murder."

Excitement turned to adrenalin. "What was he in for?"

"Armed robbery."

"Go get him."

"We're on it. Spencer and Dark are on their way."

"Great. I'll be at the station in twenty minutes."

"Right."

"And, Sean?"

"Yes?"

"Don't start anything until I get there!"

NINE

ANNA WASN'T SURE how long she had sat on her bed, frustrated at her inability to cry properly, the lump in her throat growing bigger. She couldn't remember when she had felt this bad.

There was a knock at the door and she looked up as her dad entered.

"I'll give you a lift over to Ross' house." He spoke firmly, clearly having recovered his composure.

"No, don't worry…"

"I insist, really. I know it's a difficult time for you and I want to help. If I've wronged you, it was only with the best intentions. You have to understand that?" He sat on the edge of her bed, his eyes soft. "I'm here to make it right."

For the first time in days Anna couldn't resist a small, choked smile. This had been his favourite phrase when she was a child. If she'd had a bad day or somebody had been mean to her in the playground, she would climb up on to his knee at bedtime and pour it all out. He would listen intently, offering a little advice at times, but the conversation always ended the same way, "I'm here to make it right." Sitting here on her bed with him again folded back the years. Years ago those familiar words made everything right with the world. Her smile faded. She wasn't a little girl anymore and she hadn't been for a very long time.

"OK. Just give me a few minutes. I haven't got much. It won't take long to pack." As he nodded and left the room she tried to block the feeling of guilt worming its way into her heart.

They drove across town in silence. Anna watched the road in front of her, her eyes focused on nothing as her head mulled over the recent events in her increasingly tumultuous daily life. Her thoughts reached her mother.

"Has Mum always been difficult?"

The question, out of the blue as it was, seemed to startle her father momentarily. Several seconds passed before he said, "You shouldn't be too hard on your mother. She's had a difficult life."

"But why can't she talk about things, be reasonable without going off on one?"

"She has a lot of good qualities."

Anna raised her eyes to the roof. "That's not what I asked."

"She just finds emotions difficult to deal with."

"Hasn't that been hard for you over the years?" *How have you stayed with her?* She thought.

"To truly know a person is to understand them," replied her father. His eyes didn't leave the road. "Everybody has their little foibles, things that mean a great deal to them, but little to others. Everyone has a story."

Anna folded her arms and stared across at him. "What's her story?"

Her father turned into Castrell Street and pulled up at the curb halfway down, outside Ross' Victorian, mid-terrace house. "She's had a difficult life," he repeated.

"Why, because her parents died when she was young?" She raised her eyes upwards again. Frustration itched away at her.

He looked at Anna and sighed. "Anna, your mother's parents didn't *die* when she was young." The emphasis on the word die got her attention.

"What? Great, more lies." She sunk into the seat.

He ignored her and continued, "They abandoned your mother when she was five years old. Old enough to have a memory, but too young to care for herself."

Anna's mouth dropped.

"They didn't want her. She went to live with her aunt and they never saw her again." He stared blindly out of the window. The two street lights nearest to them weren't working. This, coupled with the absence of any house lights, the residents not returned home from work yet, made this part of the long road seem chillingly gloomy.

"I don't believe it," she said, dubiously shaking her head.

"It's true."

"Are they still alive?"

"No. Her father died a few of years ago, her mother just last year."

"Where did they live?"

"In Birmingham. Less than an hour's drive from here."

She blinked. "So nearby?"

"Yes. Your mother always secretly thought that they had gone abroad. She told the rest of the world they died. It seemed to make the rejection easier for her to bear."

"Why has she never told me?"

He exhaled slowly. "The family kept it quiet, did everything they could to keep the authorities out of it. Your grandmother's sister took her in."

"And Aunt Kate brought her up."

"In a manner of speaking," he said wistfully. "I think she did love your mother in her own way, but she'd had no children of her own and didn't really know how to look after a child. Plus she had rather an eye for the men."

"What do you mean?"

"When Kate met a new man, she would shower your mother with gifts, new toys to keep her busy so that she could concentrate her time on him. They would invariably move into his house, from what I can make out, and your aunt kept the home spotless—your mother was only allowed to play in her bedroom on her own. To be seen and not heard in the true old-fashioned sense." He paused again, his face momentarily frozen in sadness, before he continued, "But as the relationship turned sour, they would leave, usually in a rush, and most of the toys and belongings would be left behind. They moved around a lot, so your mother had little opportunity to make friends. This continued until she was sixteen years old." He swept the palm of his hand across his forehead.

"What happened then?"

He looked across at Anna. "She left school at sixteen and got a job in the local supermarket. There, for the first time she earned a wage, made friends and started to feel settled. When her aunt was ready to move on again she refused to go, shared a house with a group of students instead. I was one of those students in my final year at college. We were married a year later."

"Why has she never told me? Why all the lies?"

"We are all crafted by our experiences, Anna. Your mother wanted you to have a childhood which was as near to perfect as possible. She wanted you to grow up into a happy, balanced adult—not haunted by her past.

This is why we didn't tell you about the adoption." He shook his head. "It could have had a profound effect on you during your formative years."

"There's no such thing as perfect," Anna said dismally. With the engine extinguished, the car was beginning to feel cold. Anna shivered. "Why was I adopted?"

"After we got married she was desperate to have our own children. But it wasn't meant to be. So we applied for adoption and you came along. And that made our family complete in her eyes. She had her home, her daughter and her husband and, over the years, has managed to forge some friendships. She is not a bad person, Anna. She just needs to be understood."

"Why didn't she get some counselling?"

He glanced sideways at her. "Your mother has seen many therapists over the years. This is how I know so much. I went to many of the sessions with her."

Anna baulked at this remark. "When? How could I have not known?"

"She wanted to protect you, I guess. In some ways she wanted our family to be almost too perfect." *Almost too perfect, her life, her home, her family; almost.*

"Is that everything?"

"Everything. No more secrets." The relief in his voice was palpable.

Anna stared out into the darkness. It must have been difficult for her father to keep all this under wraps over the years, allowing the secrets to fester within, knowing that one day they may surface and he would have to deal with the consequences.

"What will Mum say when you tell her you've told me?"

"I won't say anything for a while," he said slowly, "I

need to find the right time." Over the years he'd learned how to manage the mood swings of his unpredictable wife. "I'd be grateful if you don't say anything either." Anna nodded. "This is difficult enough for her. But you are grown up now and you have a right to know, to understand why we made the decisions we did."

He opened his door and climbed out of the car to retrieve her bag from the boot. Anna sat still for a while, frozen to the spot as if all of the blood had drained from her body. She wondered how many shocks a girl could take in a day. Right now she felt full to the brim.

She forced herself to get out of the car and walk towards the house, leaving the car unlocked behind her. When she finally joined him and walked into Ross' hallway her dad bent down to remove his shoes.

"Don't worry about that, Dad," Anna said quickly, waving her arm behind her. "Ross isn't bothered about things like that." He followed her into the lounge.

"Wow!" She watched him look around the room, taking in the bicycle parked under the front window, the folded bike in the far corner; various bike pieces set against the wall. "You sure he's in the right job?" Edward continued. "It looks like he should have been a mechanic."

"His parents thought teaching would give him more security." She glanced sideways at him as he set down her bag.

"Shall I wait with you until he comes home?"

She shook her head. "No need."

"Oh. OK then." He seemed awkward, not quite sure how to leave things. He reached into his pocket and pulled out a piece of paper holding it out to Anna.

"This is my mobile number. For your new phone."

"Thanks. I'll text you my new number."

"What about clothes, your other things?" he said finally.

"I haven't much. I've been wearing the old stuff I'd left at home, but that needs washing now. I've got a few bits here that'll keep me going and I'm sure Ross'll lend me a few of his tops."

"Right, well…" He turned to leave.

"Dad." The urgency of her voice pulled him back. "Thanks for everything." She leant forward and wrapped her arms around him. She didn't see him close his eyes, relishing the comfort of the moment. When she pulled back his eyes were watery.

She stepped away and looked at him sheepishly. "Can I ask one other question?"

"Go ahead."

"Do I have any brothers or sisters?" She bit her lip as his face folded. The question pained him, like an arrow through the heart.

His eyes grew sad. "There was a brother," he stared at the floor, his voice quiet.

"Really?"

"Yes, but don't be too disappointed Anna. The last we heard of him, he was doing a long stretch at Her Majesty's pleasure."

WHEN ROSS WALKED through the door she was curled up on his one sofa in front of the fire, watching *Pride and Prejudice*. It was her favourite adaptation, one of her own films she left here months back and, although she had seen it numerous times, it was a welcome respite for her tired brain.

"Hi!" He leant down and kissed her on the cheek.

"Guess what?" He stood back and raised his arms. A paper bag hung off the end of each hand. "I've got take-away—Indian, your favourite."

She smiled up at him. "Better find some plates then."

They moved into his galley kitchen and she placed two plates on the breakfast bar at the far end. They laid out lamb samosas, onion bhajis, poppadoms, chicken balti, king prawn rogan josh, basmati rice, and tucked in. Ross opened a couple of beers and handed her one.

"How was school?" she asked.

"Same as ever," he said, a bored look covering his face. "I had the charming 10A for DT this morning and that sleazeball Fenton chucked a stapler at Gary Roberts when my back was turned. Gary's sporting a wonderful bruise on his head, missed his eye by a fraction." He shook his head. "I'm hoping this is going to be enough to suspend him this time. To tell you the truth, I can do without both of them. They're a liability."

"No change there then. How was Randle?"

"Didn't speak to me really, apart from the usual. A few of the others asked about you."

"What did they say?"

"Not a lot. Just that they were concerned about you. Wanted to help. Some said they had been trying to ring you on your mobile and couldn't get you. I didn't tell them you had a new number."

"Thanks." She didn't relish the prospect of all those sympathy calls.

He reached his hand across the table and took hers. "Are you all right? I've been worried about you." His eyes were gentle, concerned.

"I think so." Anna pressed her lips together in a faint smile. "Thank you."

"Tell me about *your* day?" he said, as he leaned forward to grab a large prawn, coating it with rice before placing it into his mouth.

"You wouldn't believe it."

He looked up. She had got his attention. "Try me," he mumbled through a mouthful of food. "I can't imagine anything worse than finding a dead body in your flat."

"Oh, you just wait." She stared at him for a while, then sighed and described her day, finishing up with the revelation of her having a brother, thought to be in prison. Anna picked at the food as she spoke whilst Ross seemed to shovel it down as if he hadn't eaten for a week.

He blinked at intervals, jolted back at times, wide-eyed in surprise, but waited until she had completely finished before he spoke. "Sounds like you've had quite a day."

"You could say that. I feel bruised and battered, as though I've been used as an emotional punch bag."

"What are you going to do now?"

"I don't know. I need some time to think. It's too much to digest in one go." He nodded and they continued to eat in silence.

"If I can do anything to help…"

"Sure, thanks."

As they were finishing up a thought nudged Anna. "Ross?"

"Yes?" he said, helping himself to another poppadom and dipping it into a generous portion of mango chutney.

"Do you think I should tell the Detective Chief Inspector about my brother? She gave me her card and asked me to call her if I heard anything."

He thought about this for a moment as he crunched

away. "It's up to you. They're bound to have spoken to your parents." He picked a stray crumb off his sweater, put it into his mouth. "I guess they'll work it out sooner or later. That's why they're called detectives." He smiled, but the joke was wasted on Anna who had started clearing away the empty boxes and bags. Her stomach felt fuller than it had in days.

Ross took out the rubbish while she washed the dishes. The waft of cold air that raced into the kitchen as he walked back through the door made her jump. She turned suddenly, too suddenly, catching the edge of a wine glass on the drainer. The crash of the glass hitting the floor reverberated throughout her whole body.

"Miss Cottrell, that's a record," Ross said jollily. "We should re-name you Clumsy Cottrell." He was giggling now. "That's three glasses in a month." She could hear him chuckling in the background, but froze amongst the splinters of glass that littered the floor as her eyes blurred, her shoulders began shaking, letting the tears overflow and race down her cheeks.

Ross rushed to her side, ignoring the crunch of glass under his shoes, turned her around and pulled her into his arms. He held her tight as the grief exploded into uncontrollable sobs.

Time stood still. Eventually, as her breathing slowly regulated itself, he kissed her gently on the head, moved her over to the breakfast bar and sat her down, whilst he cleared up the shards of broken glass. Anger having abated, the release felt good, and when the tears finally dried up she sat in silence, her body numb, watching the slow movement of the brush sweep across the floor.

"Are you all right?" Ross looked over at her tentatively.

"I think so," she nodded, raising her eyes to look at him. "Why is this all happening to me?"

"Bad luck I guess." He leant the brush against the wall and made his way over to her, wrapping his arms around her from behind.

She turned to face him. "Sorry about all this."

He snorted, caressed the back of her neck tenderly and locked his soft, brown eyes straight on to hers. "Don't be silly, it's not your fault. Just wish I could do something to help."

"There's nothing anyone can do at the moment."

"Would it help to talk some more?"

She scrunched up her nose, trying to pick through the mist swirling about her brain, "No, I don't think so."

"What would you like to do?" he asked.

She shook her head. "No idea. Something to take my mind off things."

"How about bowling?"

"I'd rather do table tennis."

"Come on, I'll thrash you at table tennis." She followed him into the lounge as he set up the TV and games console. Despite the fact that Ross nearly always won, it felt good to play ball games for a change. The Wii was much kinder to the uncoordinated than a real court.

When they exhausted the sports, they switched to some dancing game where you had to copy the moves, which Anna couldn't remember the name of. As the third tune finished, Ross collapsed on to the sofa with laughter. "You really are the most rubbish dancer I've ever been out with."

She sat down next to him, panting slightly, and smiled. "Beat you at cycling though, didn't I?" He grinned back at her, stretching out his arm, pulling her towards him. Anna breathed in deeply. She loved the smell of Ross. His hair was vanilla and his body a mixture of sporty shower gel and Armani Pour Homme aftershave. An addictive scent that seeped into his clothes.

He kissed her on the side of her neck, tenderly. "You smell lovely," he whispered into her ear. *Just thinking the same*, she thought. Her stomach flipped as his nose brushed across her cheek. He kissed her gently at first, slipping his tongue in softly. His left hand hugged her neck, the right moving slowly down her back as he gradually became hungrier. Anna trembled as she surrendered herself to him. Ross was the perfect antidote to stress.

It was almost eight o'clock when she untangled herself from his arms. She pulled the throw off the back of the sofa and stroked his tattoo. For some reason Anna loved the neatness of the small blue sign of infinity on his upper arm. She bent down, kissed him gently on the cheek, covered him over and pulled his long, fleece sweater over her head. It reached her thighs and she relished Ross' scent on her as she walked back into the kitchen. Ross was sleeping soundly, lost in that satisfied, relaxed sleep that only sex can induce.

As she leant over and flicked the switch on the kettle, she saw the creased business card she had left on the side, the card the Detective Chief Inspector handed her earlier. A pang of conscience hit her and she dialled the number impulsively.

It rang five times and she was just about to hang up when the ring tone changed, as if it had been diverted, then a male voice answered. "DS Carter?"

"Oh. I'm sorry to bother you. My name is Anna

Cottrell. I wondered if I could have a word with DCI Lavery?"

"She's interviewing at the moment. Can I help you with anything? I'm working on the same investigation."

"Well errr…" Anna hesitated for a moment. She didn't know DS Carter and didn't feel comfortable telling him about her brother, which suddenly seemed very silly. "I just wanted to know if I could go back to the flat and get some clothes," she said weakly. "I'm running out of things to wear."

"Right," he said. "I don't think that'll be too much of a problem. Let me make some enquiries and I'll come back to you."

"OK."

"What number can I get you on?"

She gave him her new mobile number and hung up, a barrage of thoughts entering her mind. Anna blinked and tried to make some sense of the fuzz in her head. There were two questions that kept screaming out at her. Who was the DCI interviewing *and* did they have a new suspect?

TEN

Helen breezed into the interview room later that evening and was instantly startled at the sight before her. Robert McCafferty was striking in appearance, the kind of man that would send a group of women into a flutter when he walked into a room; multiple hands checking hair, smoothing clothes, hoping to impress him into noticing them. But it was the resemblance to Anna which really caught her. Their facial features—the dark eyes, set against olive skin and chestnut hair. They could have been twins.

She sat opposite him, resting her hands on the table between them. "Hello, Robert. I'm DCI Lavery and this is DS Pemberton." He nodded in acknowledgment, a dark lock of hair flopping over his forehead.

"I'm aware that you've had quite a shock." She needed to tread carefully. He had only just formally identified his father's body a short time beforehand. "First, I'd like to say that I'm very sorry for your loss." She watched as he pushed the corners of his mouth down and nodded again in solemn acknowledgement. "Are you sure you are up to talking to us today?"

"Anything to help." He pronounced his words strongly and definitively, but they had a soft, musical edge. She imagined he didn't spend many nights on the town without charming some young lady into his clutches.

"Thank you. DS Pemberton here will take some

notes while we go along. Would you like a cup of tea, coffee perhaps?"

"I've just had a coffee, thanks."

"Right. Why don't you start by telling us about your father?"

"What do you want to know?"

"Anything you can tell us about your father will help us build up a picture of his life and may, eventually, lead us to his killer. Why don't we start with your relationship? Were you close?"

Robert scratched his head and thought for a moment. "Not particularly."

"What makes you say that?"

"My mother died when I was eight years old. I was fostered out after that."

"Did you still see your father?"

"I used to go back to see my dad sometimes, on visits, but they wouldn't let me live with him. He was an alcoholic."

"That must have been hard."

He shifted in his seat. "We coped."

"Did you love him?"

"What kind of question is that?" He sat back, clearly affronted. "He was my father. He didn't abuse me or neglect me, he just drank himself into a stupor to take away the pain of losing my mother, so he couldn't take care of me. But when he was dry he was great. Of course I loved him." Helen watched his reaction carefully, focusing on his body language, looking for signs of animosity, latent resentment. So far there were none.

She pulled back. "How did you find out your father had been killed?" she asked, softly.

"I'm sure if you don't already know it, you'll soon discover that I was released from prison on Friday…"

"What were you convicted for?"

"Armed robbery. It'll all be on my file." He gave her a hard stare before continuing, "As I said, I was released on Friday. I'm staying with friends at the moment. I tried to call Dad a couple of times on Saturday and then Sunday, but couldn't reach him so I went down to his house today." She nodded, encouraging him to go on. "The house was covered in blue and white police tape so I spoke to his neighbour who told me about the murder. I couldn't believe it. I only saw him a month ago."

"Which neighbour did you speak to?"

He paused, switched his gaze to the other detective who was scribbling notes on a large pad.

"It's OK," Helen said reassuringly. "We'll draw it up into a statement and you'll be able to read it all through before you sign it."

He shrugged his right shoulder. "If it helps."

"So, which neighbour did you speak to?"

"Number 27." He hesitated, thinking hard. "I think her name is Mrs Hart."

"What did she say to you?"

"Sorry?"

"How did she tell you about your father?"

"She was surprised that I didn't know. Grabbed the paper and showed me the news report. I haven't much bothered with the papers this weekend, what with just coming out of prison and all that."

"It must have been quite a shock."

"One hell of a shock."

"And what time was this?"

"I suppose I got there around ten-thirty. There's no

point in going over any earlier. He doesn't get up early
in the mornings." He fidgeted uncomfortably. "Didn't."

"And what did you do then?"

"To tell you the truth, I didn't know what to do. I read
the news report and then I saw the address and couldn't
believe it. I had to go down there to Little Hampstead
to check for myself."

"Why?"

"What do you mean, why?"

"Why did the address shock you so much?"

He looked at her for a while, appearing to be considering his options before he continued. "It's a long story."

"No problem. We're not in any hurry."

"I don't think it will be relevant."

"Why don't you let us be the judge of that? Anything
to do with your father's life is of interest at the moment."

"OK," he continued, but his reluctance was obvious. "I have a sister. Her name is Anna. We were separated when our mother died of cancer and our dad hit
the bottle. She was three and I was eight at the time. I
haven't seen her since. 22a Flax Street is her address."

Helen tilted her head to one side. "How did you
know?"

"What?"

"If you haven't seen her since she was three, how did
you know that this was her address?"

He sighed. "I have tried many times over the years
to make contact with her, you know, through social
services. I wrote letters and took them to my father to
send off. When I was old enough I wrote on my own.
But Anna was adopted and her new parents refused all
contact. She is now an adult, so I found her myself. I

had planned to arrange to meet up with her—all of us meet up—when I came out of prison."

"Did your father know her address?"

"Yes, I gave it to him when I saw him last month. But we agreed that I would make the first contact." He snorted. "I doubt she will be interested now."

"What makes you say that?"

"Well, would you?"

Helen ignored the question. "Were you and Anna close?"

"When we were younger? Very. When Mum died and Dad crashed out, I practically looked after her on my own. Until they took her away from me."

"That must have made you very angry." He shrugged in response. "What happened to you?" Helen said.

"As I said, I was fostered out. I had a couple of false starts, I guess I was a bit of a handful at first, but stayed with the same family from thirteen, until I got my own place when I was seventeen."

"How did it make you feel, being separated like that?"

"What do you mean?"

"Did you feel anger or resentment towards your father?"

"What?" He screwed his face up indignantly. "I didn't kill him if that's what you're asking me." He rolled his eyes.

"Nice theory," he continued, "but wrong. I've never hated my father. I hate what he puts through his body. I hate the way it makes him behave. I don't want to be like him, I couldn't be more determined to build a different life for myself, but I don't hate him. He's still my dad. And it wasn't him that took Anna away from me.

It was social services. And I hate *them* for it." His nostrils widened as he emphasised the word *them*.

"We have to follow every line of enquiry." Helen dropped her tone a level to mollify him. "I'm sure you appreciate that. No one is suggesting that you killed your father, but we do need to eliminate you from our enquiries. Where were you between two and six o'clock last Friday afternoon?"

"I didn't get out of Ashwell until late afternoon. There was some kind of…" he hesitated, searching for the right word, "disorder—that's what they call it, happens when a few prisoners kick off. We were on lock down for most of the day. You can check with them yourselves—the prison'll confirm it. My friends I'm staying with collected me around five. It took us well over an hour to get back here, so I wasn't back before six."

"Thank you. Did you see your father much while you were in prison?"

"No, I was placed too far away. Started off in Nottingham, then they moved me to Leicester. For the last three months I've been at Ashwell in Rutland, an open prison, so I could come home a few weekends. I was supposed to go there sooner, but they didn't have any space."

"You've moved around a bit then?"

"Yeah, they do that to you. Don't like you to get too settled, make too many criminal associations. Might affect your rehabilitation, if you get my drift? No problem for me, I just wanted to do my time and get out. I kept my head down and did as I was told."

"Did you write to each other, phone maybe?"

"I rang him on his birthday a couple of times, sent

him the odd card." He lowered his eyes. "He wasn't really one for letters."

"But you visited him a month ago?"

"Yeah. I was on weekend leave."

"How did he seem?"

"All right. Not exactly dry but at least he was off the wacky baccy."

"He used drugs?"

"Only weed." He allowed himself a wry grin. "Couldn't be doing with anything you inject. Far too squeamish. But he seemed to have laid off it recently. Probably ran out of cash."

"Did he seem edgy? Worried about anything?"

"No more edgy than usual. He's always on the edge when he needs another drink."

"How long did you stay?"

"About half an hour."

"What did you talk about?"

"Anna mostly. He was really looking forward to meeting her." He grew sad.

"How well do you know his friends?"

He shook his head. "Not too well. There's a couple he's known since we were kids that I know, but since he moved ten years ago, I think he lost contact with quite a few."

"What about his supplier?"

Robert raised his hands. "No idea. I don't touch the stuff. I've watched what has gone through him over the years. It's enough to put anyone off."

"Are you aware of anyone who he may have upset, somebody who may have a grudge against him perhaps, or may wish to hurt him?"

"No."

The room became quiet. Robert was staring at the floor, churning over his thoughts. Helen sat very still and cast her eyes over Jim McCafferty's only son. She could see nothing in his demeanour, his manner, or his words that indicated guilt on his part. But she wasn't going to be fooled by the charming façade. This man had been part of a ruthless gang of armed robbers who, eight years ago, charged into a bookmaker's in the early evening wearing ski masks. A male cashier was shot in the tussle that followed. Luckily, the bullet clipped his arm and he lived, otherwise Rab would still be sitting in a cell right now.

"What about you, Robert?" she asked finally.

"What do you mean?"

"Is there anyone who may have had a grudge against you, anyone you have upset, in prison maybe?"

He narrowed his eyes, sat back in his chair, "You think this is to do with me?"

"We have to investigate every area."

"No, I told you, I kept my head down and did my time."

She looked him in the eye. "Did you grass anyone up at the trial?"

"Absolutely not." He jerked his head back, gave her an antagonistic stare. "Go through everything. You won't find anything on me."

"What about the guys you did the job with?"

"We're still on good terms. It was a job that went wrong." He cleared his throat. "I was only given two years less than them because I wasn't armed. Just the driver. The judge made that perfectly clear at the trial."

"Thank you. That will be all for now. You've been most helpful. Can you please give your present address and contact details to the detective, along with a list of all associates and friends of your father, and yourself."

"Why do you need my friends' details?"

"We need to follow up all lines of enquiry. We can't rule anything out at this stage."

He nodded and sighed, chewing the inside of his lip.

Helen rose to leave the room. Just before she reached the door, she turned around. "Your dad, does he drink locally?"

"No, he usually walks up to *The Black Bull* during the week, *The Wagon and Horses* on a weekend."

Helen raised her eyebrows. "That's quite a walk."

"You're not wrong. Both must be between two and three miles away from home, but that was the way he liked it. He was bred a Weston boy—did his food shopping there, too—what bit he bought. Might be worth a try for you guys? He's pretty well known around there."

"Thank you. We'll do that. Just one more thing?"

"Yes?"

"The tattoo on the top of your father's arm. I couldn't make out what it said inside the heart?" The mortuary had assured her that this area of the body would be well covered when he formerly identified it.

Rab didn't flinch. "Just our names—Robert and Anna. I'm not surprised you couldn't read it. It wasn't a very professional job when it was done and that was well over twenty years ago."

ELEVEN

"RIGHT EVERYONE, you've all no doubt heard the news that we have traced the victim's son." Helen's eyes darted around the room as she spoke. "For those of you who weren't here, he came down to the station to talk to us yesterday evening." She went on to summarise the main points of the interview, listing them individually on the whiteboard. Some sat and scribbled notes, others leant against desks, or stood at the back, digesting the new information, all in rapt silence.

As she finished a voice spoke up from the back of the room, "At least we now know why house-to-house in the vicinity is like bleeding a stone," DI Townsend said, dejectedly. Echoes of agreement followed, the mutterings growing louder.

Helen glared at Townsend. She couldn't read him. His attitude seemed to change direction like the wind. She addressed the room again. "Listen, if Robert McCafferty's statement is correct then we need to set our net wider. Weston is now our focus of attention. This could be our chance." She waited until the cacophony of voices abated and all eyes were fixed on her once again. "I want people down to both pubs to talk to the landlords this morning. Let's go back to the beginning. I want to know who Jim McCafferty's friends are, what he does in his spare time, where he shops—anything you can find."

"Let's dig into Robert's background too," she went on. "Speak to the liaison officers at each of the prisons he attended. Who did he share a cell with? What was his discipline record like? Did he forge any particular friendships or make any enemies? Who visited him in prison? Look at the medical records—any history of drugs? Although Robert himself has an alibi we cannot rule out the possibility of his involvement, however small, at this stage. Did somebody kill his father to get back at him for something he'd done to upset them?"

Silence fell in the room. She glanced around. Twelve pairs of ardent eyes looked back at her. "Right, that's it. Any questions?" Heads shook. She pulled back her sleeve and checked her watch. "Let's get to it then. We'll try to meet back here at four o'clock."

A phone rang in the incident room and she was aware of footsteps behind her as she walked back into her office.

"Ma'am?"

She turned to face Pemberton.

"Andrew Steiner from *The Hampton Herald* has just phoned for the second time this morning and Chris Watts from *The Evening Chronicle* wants an urgent interview." He looked down at his list. "Oh, and Anna Cottrell is going back to her flat this morning to collect some clothes. Plus, the Super's just called. Apparently, he's already tried your mobile. He wants to speak to you urgently. Says if we don't get you to ring within the next five minutes he's coming down."

It was like being at the receiving end of a barrage of machine gun fire.

Helen thought for a moment. "Get me Jack Coulson in the press office on the phone, will you?"

Confusion filled his face. "What about the Super?"

"Belt and braces, Pemberton. Belt and braces." He stared at her as if she had just been admitted to a secure mental unit, and turned on his heels.

THE CHAIR THAT was usually occupied by Superintendent Jenkins' secretary was empty outside his office, so Helen approached the door and rapped it vigorously with her fist.

"Come in!"

"Morning, sir." He looked taken aback as she walked into his office, his expression clearly indicating that he was expecting someone else. "I understand you wanted a word."

Jenkins' office was on the top floor of the original building. A large room, there was a round oak table at one end, surrounded neatly with eight chairs, and a cabinet stacked with books at the other. His desk was placed in the middle at an angle, to allow a clear view of the top of the building opposite out of the large window. The whole room was immaculately tidy. The papers on his desk were stacked precisely, even the books on the shelf appeared to be arranged in height order. There were no photographs on his desk and none on the walls, apart from an abstract painting which looked like odd splodges of yellow and orange paint. She pointed at the empty chair opposite his desk, "May I?"

"This needs to be quick Helen," he said urgently. "I've a meeting with the Chief Con. in five minutes."

Helen held her head high, well aware that meeting face to face would prove somewhat disarming. "Sorry, sir." She sat down decisively. "I won't take up much of your time. Did you get the email I sent you?"

"Yes I did, but I need to speak to you about the press, Helen," he said, quickly. "I've had Andrew Steiner, Editor-in-Chief of *The Hampton Herald*, on this morning. Somehow, he's got hold of my direct line. He seems to think we have apprehended a suspect and wants to know if we plan to charge them." He scratched his head irritably.

Helen narrowed her eyes. The press loved to employ tactics to force their hand into releasing information. "Where'd he get that from?"

"It doesn't matter where he got it from," Jenkins retorted, the tone in his voice rising. "I take it from your reaction that you are not in a position to charge on Operation Marlon?"

Helen sighed inwardly at the choice of names allocated to police cases to distinguish investigations. More red tape. *Marlon*. This wasn't car crime, an organised drugs group. It was a murder enquiry. "No we are not. But…"

"Helen, in a murder investigation the rule of thumb is to get the press on your side from the beginning. If you don't, they'll go for the sensationalised angle and whip the public up into a frenzy."

"Yes, I am well aware…"

"Being aware is not enough," he snapped. He sat back in his chair and sighed. The dark eyebrows swung back. When he spoke again his voice was calm. "Perhaps we've given you too much for your first murder case?"

Helen could see where this was leading and rushed in quickly, "Certainly not. Now that we have traced Robert McCafferty, the victim's son, we have plenty of fresh leads to follow up."

"Have you spoken to DCI Sawford at all? Ran your ideas past him?"

"With respect, sir, as my superior, I'm running them by you. I have asked our press office to arrange a press conference later today and Robert will be present to appeal for witnesses. I'm confident that this new information will give us the break we need. We won't be releasing the removal of the tattoo at this stage. The last thing we want to do is to give the public the impression that it was a trophy and there are the makings of a serial killer on the loose. We need to convince them this is an isolated incident. But I didn't want to arrange a press conference until we had something substantial to give. Now that we have the son…" She went on to give him a laconic update of the investigation thus far. When she finished he was still glaring at her, but she could see that his reserve was wavering.

"Why wasn't I informed about the press conference?"

"I was just about to let you know. I'm sure you appreciate that the sensitive elements of this case require us to tread carefully."

"Sensitive?" His face contorted.

"I wanted to discuss it with you first, to make sure you approved of our strategy. I don't wish to reveal the adoption angle or Anna's biological link with the victim. I'd like to keep that information to ourselves for the moment. I want to see where the new leads take us first. I feel sure that the killer is close to the family in some way and keeping that under wraps at present may draw him in." He stared at her. "Plus Anna Cottrell is returning to her flat to collect some things today. I've got constables on scene and some undercover guys there watching…"

"That will only add fuel to their fire."

"Not if we handle it correctly." She stared at him in the short silence that followed. "Would you like to join us at the press conference? It's at one o'clock."

He thought for a moment. "No, I have a meeting scheduled, but don't forget that we are here to serve the public in general, and we are judged by what they print in the press—true or not. Are you sure you are up to this?"

"Absolutely. We are really starting to make some progress now."

He surveyed her a moment. "I can give you until Friday to come up with something. After that, I feel we need to bring in an experienced SIO to work alongside you."

He didn't miss the flash of anger in her eyes. "This bears no reflection on your abilities, Helen. Look upon it as a learning curve. Right." He stood, indicating their meeting was at an end. "I want to be appraised of every aspect of the investigation as it progresses. Call me when anything significant crops up. I don't want to be put in a vulnerable position again."

Helen dropped her head back in relief as she closed the door to the Super's office behind her. She wasn't under any illusions as to why he wanted this case solved swiftly. An Assistant Chief Constable position had just arisen in a neighbouring force and a quick result here would not only raise a positive public profile but, more importantly, look favourable on his application. Jack Coulson in the press office had been very informative on that point. Having a wife who worked in the human resources department meant he was very well versed on the political motivations of senior officers, as well as handling the media.

She made her way down the stairs feeling mildly relieved. During his short time in situ she had seen many officers leave his office licking their wounds after incurring his ambitious wrath. She couldn't help feeling she'd got off lightly this time. But she also knew her victory would be short-lived. If a result wasn't forthcoming by Friday she would become another pawn in his game, pushed aside for her alleged ineptitude, his latest scapegoat. And she couldn't afford to let that happen.

When she reached the car park, her phone buzzed. "DCI Lavery."

"Hi, darling."

"Hi, Mum," she said. It was good to hear a friendly voice. "How are things?"

"Fine. And you?"

She tilted her head on to one side and leant against the wall. "We traced the victim's son. He's given us loads more information to follow up on. Could be just the breakthrough we need."

"Great. Err… You need to speak to Matthew."

The sudden change in subject caused Helen to jerk forward slightly. Her heart sunk deep into her chest. "Why what's happened?"

"He came down last night after you'd gone, looking for you, muttering something about a party on Saturday."

"He's grounded."

"I told him that, too, but he said he needed to talk to you. When I said you weren't here he started muttering under his breath and slamming doors."

Helen furrowed her brow. It wasn't like Matthew to be rude to his grandmother. "What did he say?"

"I couldn't make out most of it. But he's definitely not a happy bunny."

Helen looked up at the sky. It was grey, angry. "He wants to become a pilot," she said.

"So I understand," her mother replied.

"You knew?"

"He has mentioned it a few times." Helen leant back against the wall. "The RAF could be the making of him," her mother continued gently.

The RAF. So he had spoken about that too. "Why didn't you say anything?"

"It's something that you two need to sort out together. I know how you feel about the military."

Helen rubbed her forehead with her free hand. The line buzzed slightly.

"He told me this morning he had spoken to you about it yesterday."

"Oh?" This sounded like a conspiracy. How many other people knew? "Did he also tell you I said I would support him?"

"Yes, but…" Jane Lavery hesitated.

"What?"

"He thinks you will support him to become a pilot. He said you didn't look very happy when he mentioned the Air Force."

What does he expect? Helen didn't want to have this conversation, not here, not now, not ever in fact. "I need to go. Thanks for letting me know about Matthew. I'll deal with him later."

As the line went dead a wave of nausea hit Helen. She had worked full time since Matthew had been five, studied for her sergeant, then inspector exams to improve her prospects, salary. She wanted to set her boys an example, as well as giving them every opportunity. Was she really doing the right thing? Would he be behaving any different if she'd stayed home all those years? She sighed to herself deeply and reached into her pocket. What she needed now more than anything else was a cigarette.

"THAT'S STRANGE," JESSICA KEEN said, moving to examine the fax she was holding from a distance. Jessica was one of three support officers, civilian staff who provided administration support to the investigation.

"What?" Townsend said.

She jumped, unaware that he had been standing directly behind her. He gave her the creeps.

"Oh, sorry, sir. It's just the routine checks on Kathleen Cottrell show that she was known by another name until the age of seven years."

"Really. That's interesting. May I?" He held out his hand and scanned the sheet, before adding, "I'll need to borrow this Jessica, to make some more enquiries."

"Shall I take a copy for DS Carter?"

"No need to bother him at the moment. He's up to his eyes in it. I'll brief him if it comes to anything. OK?"

Jessica swallowed. "OK," she said. Despite policy requiring all enquiries to be cross-referenced through the HOLMES system managed by DS Carter, she passed the piece of paper over. *Must be all right*, she resolved to herself. After all, he was the boss's deputy, wasn't he?

ROSS FINISHED HIS breakfast, looked up at Anna and smiled. Flakes of Weetabix poked out between the gaps in his teeth. "What are you up to today?"

She gazed out of the window at the bare tree branches dancing in the wind. "I don't know. I'd love to go for a ride but my bike's still at the police station."

"Borrow one of mine."

She smiled back at him. "What about the Brompton?" The Brompton was Ross' newest addition to his little collection of cycles, his current favourite.

His eyes widened teasingly. Instinctively, she reached out to punch him. "Yeah, sure," he said, as he dodged her fist. "Just make sure you fold it and take it wherever you go. It's a thief's market at the moment."

"No problem. I also need to get some clothes from the flat." She flinched inwardly. It felt strange to call it "the flat" and not home. But the truth of the matter was that it wasn't home at the moment. Recent events made sure of that.

"Are you going on your own?"

"It's my flat, isn't it?"

Ross blinked in surprise, his face tightening. "I just thought that you might want to go with someone at first, especially after what happened."

"I'm sure that the killer hasn't broken down police cordons and planted another body," she replied, hoping that he wouldn't see through her bravado.

"Ha ha," he said sarcastically, but concern was still etched on his face. "If you wait until tonight I'll take you over myself?"

"I can't. I couldn't possibly go another day without clean underwear." She gave him a cheeky stare and he laughed.

"Not a bad thought," he said, his eyes glancing into space.

"Be serious!"

"Well, borrow my car if you want, or go commando and I'll take you tonight, it's your choice. I'm going in on my mountain bike."

She could feel a hum in her pocket and pulled out her phone. "Hello!"

"Anna, how are you?"

"Hi, Dad. I'm fine, thank you." She nodded to Ross, pointed to the phone and moved out into the lounge.

"Just wanted to give you your messages."

"Messages?"

"Yes, you've got quite a few. I guess when your friends can't reach you on your old mobile, they're ringing here."

"Oh, sorry about that. Who called?"

She listened to her father reel off a list of her friends, work colleagues, even an ex-boyfriend who had asked after her welfare. It seemed that the news of the weekend's events had spread like wildfire in the bush. She made a mental note to call some of them when the murderer had been apprehended and some kind of normality returned to her life. Not for one moment did she entertain the thought that the offender may not be caught. To Anna, it was just a matter of time.

"Thanks, Dad. If anyone else rings, just tell them I'll be in touch soon."

"There's another one."

"Oh?"

"Robert McCafferty phoned." His voice was tainted with anxiety.

Anna's heartbeat accelerated. "Oh…" She tried to keep her voice calm. "Did he leave a number?"

"Yes."

"Will you text it over to me?" She cringed as she spoke the words.

"Sure. If that's what you want." He sounded dejected.

She cringed again. *This is uncomfortable.* "Thanks, Dad."

"Anna?"

"Yes?"

"Don't do anything rash, will you?"

"What do you mean?"

"If you decide to meet him, promise me something?"

"What?"

"He's a stranger to you. Make sure you take somebody with you?"

"Of course. I'm not a complete idiot." Keen to change the subject, she quickly asked, "How's Mum?"

"She'll cope." *No change there then.* She heard Ross coming down the stairs. "Listen, I have to go. Thanks again, Dad."

She clicked to end the call just as Ross walked through into the lounge in his cycling kit, rucksack on back.

"Everything all right?"

"Fine, thanks. That was Dad on the phone."

"So I heard. How are things?"

"Mum's still stressing, you know what she's like."

"Sure." He smiled sympathetically. "I'll see you later then. Have a good day." He put his arm around her shoulder, pulling her close to him briefly as he pecked her cheek and headed out. She listened as he manoeuvred his bike through the hallway, slamming the front door behind him.

Anna glanced at her mobile phone, still in hand. In a few moments she would receive her brother's number. Should she call him straight away? Perhaps not, perhaps she should wait until Ross was back and call him that evening? No, if she had meant to wait for Ross she would have mentioned it to him before he left for work... *This is something I have to do on my own.*

Anna stood under the shower for far longer than the usual perfunctory five minutes it took to shampoo and condition her hair, lather and rinse her body. Today she had time and she indulged, enjoying the spattering of water on her face, turning so that it ran down her back and through her legs until they were red raw. It seemed to be cleansing more than her skin this morning, the water penetrating beneath the surface.

By the time she wandered out of the bathroom in Ross' robe, hair bound in a towel which resembled a makeshift turban, she felt more relaxed than she had in days. She picked up her phone and examined it. The text message had arrived. She straightened, retrieved the number and pressed dial.

Counting the rings, a habit which oddly seemed to calm her acute rush of nerves—one, two, three; she stopped suddenly when a voice answered.

"Hello?" The male voice sounded smooth, friendly.

"May I speak to Robert McCafferty please?"

"Speaking." She drew a short, sharp breath, unable to speak. "Is that Anna?" His tone was gentle.

"Yes." *He doesn't sound like a criminal.* Anna flinched as soon as those words sprung into her mind. What was someone with a criminal record supposed to sound like?

"I thought so. Thank you so much for calling."

"OK," she answered, cringing at her unobtrusive inflection. She couldn't think of anything else to say.

"How are you?"

"Good thanks."

"Great. Listen, would you like to meet up?"

"Umm…" She hesitated momentarily, remembering her father's warning. Then, scolding herself inwardly for allowing the only information she had heard about her brother's life—whether right or wrong—to colour her first impression of him, she spoke quickly. "All right. When?" She had to give him the benefit of doubt. If he had, indeed, served a prison sentence, he could be a reformed character now.

"Are you doing anything this afternoon?"

"No." She reached up to support the towel which was starting to unravel on her head.

"Do you know Café Cliché on Feveral Street in Weston?"

"Yes."

"Good. Would you like to meet there at, say, three o'clock?"

"That would be good."

"Great, see you there."

She clicked the button to end the call just as the towel finally gave up and slipped down her back. It had taken less than two minutes.

ANNA WAS FLABBERGASTED at the scene she faced when she turned into Flax Street later that morning. She pulled in just past the corner, engine still running and surveyed the spectacle: a group of people, some with notebooks, others with cameras, stood directly outside the gap which led to her flat. The crowd of Hampton-shire press looked completely out of place in the usu-ally desolate Flax Street, like an army of Wood Ants in the middle of a desert. She looked around her. A police car was parked in the same position on the other side of the road. Focusing on the gaps between the bodies, she could faintly see the uniform of a constable blocking the aperture between the houses which led to the entrance of her flat.

Thinking quickly, she carefully reversed the car around the corner so that it was well out of sight. Grateful for Ross' baseball cap that she had used to cover her wet hair, she pulled it down over her face and got out of his old, red escort. She briefly hesitated, considering whether or not to try the back entrance but decided against it. In daylight that could draw even more unwelcome attention.

Anna sauntered, head down, up the street and hung at the back of the crowd. When she saw a small gap appearing she squeezed through it and gently pushed herself to the front of the group. Suddenly, just as she reached the police officer, somebody called out from behind, "Who's this?"

Immediately, she could feel all the eyes descend upon the back of her neck. Panic flooded her veins. "Hey, is that Anna Cottrell?" another voice from behind her shouted as the crowd pushed forward. She wasn't sure whether the police officer recognised her, or if it was the look of sheer desperation in her eyes, but suddenly things moved very quickly.

An arm rushed forward, grabbed her shoulder and forced her into the opening between the houses, shouting, "Go!" She ran for her life, through the gap and up the steps until she reached the entrance to 22a, her heart pounding her chest.

The door was wide open. A man in blue overalls was

working on the lock. He jerked his head back towards the opening as she reached him. "They're like vermin, aren't they?" Anna didn't answer. She pushed past him, not sure if he knew who she was or why she was here.

Without thinking she opened the door and plunged into the lounge, stopping dead in her tracks. The last time she had walked through here the dead, bloody body of a man, now known to be her biological father, sat up against the sofa staring at her. She closed her eyes and saw him, eyes wide open. Her head started to feel woozy, her feet stumbled and she clung to the wall to steady herself. Time stood still.

Moments later there were voices behind her. The police officer appeared in the doorway. "Anna? I'm PC Cartland. Are you all right?"

She opened her eyes and looked up at him, surprised to see that he was wearing glasses, a fact she hadn't noticed outside. "I think so." She looked around the room. Anna didn't know what state she expected to find her flat in. Would the walls still be covered in blood, would her curtains be splattered, the carpet covered in bodily fluids? She was almost surprised to see that there was no blood. But it didn't resemble her lounge room either. The walls had been washed down, the carpet cleaned. A strong smell of lemon detergent filled the air. The gold, gothic throw, usually strewn over the back of the sofa covered the whole of it, no doubt concealing bloodstains. The curtains had been removed from the window and her collection of ornaments, photos and pictures had been taken down from walls and shelves and were stacked neatly in the corner.

"Who cleaned up?" she asked finally.

"Your landlord. Organised new locks too," Cartland said, handing her a set of keys.

She blinked, just as if she had been disturbed from a trance, and said, "What about the press?"

"Oh, they won't come up here. It's more than their life's worth." His smile fell as he glanced towards the door. "Getting you out of here might be a bit more of a challenge though."

She ignored his last comment. "I need to get some stuff from the bedroom." She pointed towards a door. He nodded and followed her through a small passageway which contained two more doors, both of which were open. A gleaming white bath could be seen through the first doorway, a chair strewn with clothes the other. She stopped in her tracks and turned to look at the policeman at the entrance to her bedroom.

He put his hands up. "I'll leave you to it, Miss Cottrell. I'll be waiting outside."

She waited until he had walked back through to the lounge before she crossed the threshold into her bedroom. It looked pretty much as she had left it last Friday morning: the duvet pulled roughly over the bed, an old jacket placed over the clothes on the chair in the corner. The police would have been through it, checking everything, looking for clues, anything that may implicate her in, or connect her to, the crime. A feeling of violation pressed against her. If she had learned anything over the past few days it was that nothing in her life was private anymore.

Anna moved over to the wardrobe and reached up to pull down her trolley case. Then, changing her mind, she pushed it back and instead reached for her old rucksack, the one she had used when she had travelled through Asia with a friend during their final summer holiday from university. Fumbling through her wardrobe and into her drawers, she started packing her clothes, shoes, coat, underwear, in a haphazard manner.

Her rucksack was like a Tardis, swallowing her belongings. When she was satisfied she had enough clothes, she threw some of her favourite books in and started looking around for her address book and iPod. She checked the bedside drawer, the bookshelf, even looked under her bed. They were nowhere to be found. Had the police taken them? She was mulling this over when a noise came from outside.

Anna peered around the curtain edge. The group of journalists and cameramen had doubled in size, covering the width of the street, their desire for news fuelled by her presence. A car was trying to navigate through the middle of the assemblage and they were rapidly clearing a passage.

Anna stood and watched them for a moment, concealed behind the fabric, as the car finally disappeared down the street and they regained their original position, like vultures descending on their prey. She wondered what possessed people to become reporters. How could they go through school, university, in pursuit of good grades with the idealistic attitude that they would be performing a public duty, keeping people informed; only to be reduced to badgering and harassing the good people of this world into supplying that special picture, or that all-important trashy, gossipy news story?

And were people really interested in such trash? Realisation kicked her in the stomach. Even at the mere suggestion that she *might* have been a knife-wielding murderess, then sadly they were. What a coup, what a good story this would make. If they got one odd line of a quote to put in their miserable story, a picture of her peering guiltily around the edge of the curtain, it would make their day worthwhile. The thought made her jolt her body away, so suddenly that she lost her footing, slipped and fell back on to the bed, catching an empty vase on her bedside table with her hand.

She heard footsteps through the small passage and managed to sit up, just before the door opened. "Is everything all right?" PC Cartland asked.

"Fine thanks," she replied, stumbling as she stood, looking up with ashen cheeks. "Just an accident."

"Are you hurt?"

"No, I'm fine, thank you."

He looked at the broken glass. "Want some help to clear that up?"

"That would be great. There's a dustpan and brush under the sink." He disappeared and she stared at the floor, cursing her clumsiness.

As he returned, and started to sweep the shards of glass out of the thin pile carpet, she fastened her backpack and shot another look at the window. "They're getting restless," she said.

"Let them." He stood, looked across at her. "Is there a back way out of this place?"

"Yeah, but you have to garden hop a bit. I've done it a couple of times for a joke when I've been drunk. Never done it in daylight though."

"Is it visible from the road?"

"No, you eventually reach a gate in the last garden which leads to the pathway." She looked back at the window again. "They won't have worked it out."

"Think you can do it with a rucksack on your back?"

"I'll give it a try. Give me ten minutes." She hauled the pack over her shoulders and made for the door.

FIFTEEN MINUTES LATER, the men and women of the press rushed forward as PC Cartland re-emerged from the gap between the houses to join his colleague who was keeping the crowd at bay. He held his hands up. "You all might as well go home, there's nothing to see here."

Numerous necks craned, peering over his shoulder, perplexed when Anna didn't materialise behind him.

"What's going on?" shouted a gruff voice from the side. "Where's Miss Cottrell?" called out another. The policeman side-stepped the bodies and walked down to his car at the end of the street. He could still hear the distant cries of disbelief as he started his engine and drove slowly away.

IN ALL OF the commotion nobody seemed to notice the tall, blond man with the receding hairline, standing at the back of the crowd. His pale, blue eyes bore holes through the crowd as he stood perfectly still, a rapt smile on his face. When he saw her enter the flat earlier, adrenalin flooded his veins—just as it had the very first time he'd laid his eyes on her photograph. She was even more beautiful in the flesh. Beauty that would be preserved in death like an alluring painting.

He wasn't surprised she had crept out the back, through the gardens. He patted his pocket gently. No matter. He had all the information he needed, for the moment.

THE CALL CAME in just before twelve. DS Pemberton's voice bounced with excitement.

"Ma'am? A checkout assistant in the Weston One Stop Shop saw a stranger with Jim McCafferty on the day of the murder. He knew Jim, he came in weekly, but he'd never seen this man with him before."

"Excellent." Helen smiled and closed her eyes. "Did you get a good description?"

"Not great, but they also have CCTV. We're bringing the tape back to the station now."

"Well done, Sergeant." *Finally*...thought Helen.

TWELVE

HELEN WATCHED THE CCTV footage over again, trying to convince herself that she would see something different. Like when you watch a great film for the second time and you notice new backdrops, images, characters in the background. But the shop was using the same tired old tapes and re-recording over them, time and time again, so much so that the images were blurred, scratchy. She could barely make out Jim McCafferty, let alone his acquaintance. Frustrated, she switched it off.

DC Rosa Dark had researched Rab's prison record. He was right, he certainly kept himself clean, lived by the rules, a model prisoner by all accounts. Perhaps the press conference later would reveal something? Helen had principally arranged the press conference to give them a story. Rab could sit on their front page for the next couple of days, appealing for witnesses, reassuring the public that it was an isolated incident. Get them off her back, for the moment, at least. But it also served another purpose.

She would be sitting right next to Rab and his every move, word, mannerism would be recorded, not only by the media, but also by themselves. Afterwards, she would watch the recording, focusing on his body language, again looking for any signs that he was not being completely truthful. If unsure, an expert on non-verbal communication would be brought in to view the tape.

Convinced that the key to solving this murder lay close
to the family, she needed to utilise every opportunity to
watch them all very carefully. He may have an alibi but
that didn't mean that he wasn't involved in some way.

Helen also knew that some killers felt compelled to
return to the scene of the crime. Much has been written
about the reasons for this: sometimes through general
curiosity, sometimes it makes them feel more power-
ful and in control, sometimes they sensed a close bond
with the victim... For this reason, she'd planted undercover police officers, alongside those guarding the
crime scene, at the flat this morning to watch Anna's
return. She knew Anna had an alibi and was practically convinced that she had nothing to do with the
murder. But, it happened in her flat... What were the
words Charles had used? *"He intended on creating quite
a show."* Was the murderer directing the kill at her?
Maybe he wanted to get her attention? And he may return to be close to her.

Now that the CSIs had finished with the crime scene,
and the residence was secure, the press would be pulling back from Flax Street. But not before the morning's
events had offered her a chance to check out another
hunch. Detectives were currently checking the number
plates of all vehicles parked in Flax Street that morning, looking for individuals who weren't residents and
weren't linked to the press. Of course if the killer was
there, then he may have parked well away and walked.
But, it was worth a try...

Helen sucked her lips and grabbed her pad. She wrote
down all the family names that were swimming around
her head. Kathleen, Edward, Jim, Rab. Then in the middle she wrote Anna in capital letters. She was the link

between them all. *What am I missing here?* An idea crept into her mind. Anna. She looked at her watch and dialled her number.

"Anna?"

"Oh. Hi." She sounded surprised, as if she were expecting someone else.

"I heard that you called the incident room last night. Just wondered if everything was all right?"

A slight hesitation followed. "Umm… Yeah fine, thanks."

Helen frowned. *She didn't sound very sure.* "Did you get everything you needed from the flat this morning?"

"Yes, thank you… Um, Detective…" Another hesitation.

"Helen."

"Sorry?"

"Call me Helen."

"Oh. Right… Helen, did you know that I have a brother? I mean Jim McCafferty has a son?"

So that was it. Helen narrowed her eyes. "We have discovered that, yes," she answered slowly. "When did you find out?"

"My father told me yesterday."

"Ahhhh."

"Have you spoken to him?"

"Your brother? Yes, he came down to the station to make a statement." A picture of Rab McCafferty's face appeared in Helen's mind. Chestnut hair tumbling over deep, dark eyes. "What do you know about him?"

"Not much. Only what Dad has told me… I heard he's been in prison."

She's fishing. Helen cleared her throat, said nothing. She didn't want to give anything away.

"Is he a suspect?"

"No. Anna, what is all this about?"

"He's asked me to meet him."

That explained her hesitation. "I see."

"Do you think I should go?"

Helen was taken aback. A momentary silence followed as she gathered her thoughts. "Well, that is up to you, Anna, but it might be prudent to take somebody with you, or at least tell someone where you are going."

"You don't think he's safe?"

"I didn't say that. But, I'm sure you wouldn't usually go to meet a complete stranger on your own, without telling someone where you were going."

"Thanks. I'll bear that in mind." She sighed out loud, as if she was trying to decide what to do.

Helen decided to change tactic. "How are things going with your parents?"

"I've moved out."

More changes. "Oh?"

"I just needed a few days to think. Because of the whole adoption thing. I'm staying with Ross."

"Your boyfriend, Ross?"

"Yes. Sorry, I guess I should have told you. It all happened so quickly."

"Right. I'll update our records." An awkward silence followed. Helen jotted herself a note to update the system. She glanced at her pad. *All lines lead to Anna.* "Look, would you like to meet up for a coffee later? There are a couple of things I would like to go over with you."

"I'm a bit busy this afternoon."

"Meeting your brother?" She tucked a stray strand of hair behind her left ear.

"Yes." The line crackled.

"What about this evening then?"

"That should be OK."

"Good. Do you know Hayes on the High Street?" Helen loved Hayes, a privately owned coffee house she occasionally visited for a quiet coffee on her own, when she had a day off in the week. It gave her time to think.

"Yes."

"Shall we meet there? At, say seven o'clock?"

"OK."

"Fine, see you then. Anna?"

"Yes?"

"You have my card. You can call me whenever you like."

"Thanks. Bye."

Helen replaced the receiver and stared again at the notes on her pad. What was she missing?

ANNA SLIPPED HER phone back into her pocket. The Detective Chief Inspector wasn't giving much away. Was she deliberately refusing to divulge any information regarding his prison record, or was she bound by some confidential code? She sighed. It seemed that everyone was set on treating her like a child.

Perhaps he wasn't a suspect but he was connected to the murder in some way? Hadn't she read somewhere that most people are killed by a member of their family or a close friend?

The quiet in Ross' house was deafening. Since her return from the flat, she'd unpacked her rucksack, leaving her clothes and belongings in neat piles on the bedroom floor and fixed herself a cheese sandwich for lunch. With nothing else to do, she shifted around on the sofa, restlessly flicking through the endless house renovation programmes, chat and game shows that swamped daytime TV. Finally, she switched it off and glanced around the room. Her eyes rested on the dresser at the far end. The floor around it was littered with bicycle parts, but it wasn't these that caught her eye. On the edge of the dresser, wire and plug sitting on top, was Ross' laptop.

She leapt up and grabbed it, plugging in the leads beside the sofa and turning it on. As soon as it fired up she clicked on to the Internet and logged into Facebook. A search revealed several Robert McCaffertys, most of whom had no location listed, apart from a few in the States. She looked at the photographs. A heavily, bearded man with shaggy, brown hair stared back at her; another with long, blond hair and blue eyes. Could any of these be her brother? She sucked in a deep, frustrated breath as she remembered her father's words—"The last we heard he was detained at Her Majesty's pleasure." This was hopeless. How long had he been out of prison? Would he even know what Facebook was? The plain truth was that any one, or none, of these could be him.

She looked up Feveral Street and traced the route she would need to take later. It was half past two. Guessing it would take around thirty minutes to bike to Weston, she calculated that if she left now she could cycle. It might diffuse some of the pent up frustration and apprehension she was feeling and settle her nerves.

Anna crossed into the bathroom, washed her hands and raised her head to look at herself in Ross' circular shaving mirror. She let her hair loose from its band, shaking it down her back. It still felt damp underneath and there were kinks in it where the tie had been. She stared at her face in the mirror. Should she put on some make up? Make a bit of an effort? What does one usually do when they meet their brother for the first time? The first time in memory, at least.

She reached for the hairbrush and ran it through her hair before tying it back, resolving to go for minimal make up—just a touch of mascara and blusher to cover the pale patches, the toll the last few days had left on her usually clear complexion. For some reason she wanted to make a good impression on Robert McCafferty. Even if she decided she didn't like him, it was important that he liked her, although she had no idea why.

As she was leaving the house she grabbed her phone and turned it off. Maybe it was irresponsible but, in spite of all of the good natured advice bestowed upon her, she felt that for the first time in her life she had to face this alone. Whatever happened this afternoon, she would deal with it.

It was one of those misty November afternoons when it never really feels like it's going to get light. Droplets of dew clung to the bare branches of trees. People made their way mostly by car, those brave enough to travel by foot all wrapped up, their shoulders hunched in an effort to shut out the cold. Nobody, except the most hardened cyclists took to their bikes in this weather, but Anna loved the feeling of the fresh air flowing into her lungs. She didn't even mind the cold chill today, nipping her face. The sheer freedom of the great outdoors made her feel vital, alive.

She glanced down at the bike as she slowly braked on the approach to the junction marking the end of Ross' road. It was a treat to ride such a high spec bike, the Brooks saddle felt so comfortable.

"Hey!" The man's voice took her by surprise. She

looked up, braked hard. She had almost plunged straight into a pedestrian in the road, just a few metres in from the junction. Wolf-like eyes glared at her from beneath a pulled-up hood. He seemed to appear from nowhere.

"Sorry! Are you OK?" she called in a shaky voice, over her shoulder as he rushed past her. He put a hand up and continued to march up the road. "I'm so sorry," she called loudly after him, "I didn't see you." But it was too late. He had disappeared in the distance. *He can't be hurt*, she thought and shrugged it off, placing her feet back on the pedals. But the encounter niggled away at her, an unresolved puzzle, as she cycled across town. It seemed such odd behaviour to rush off so quickly like that. What was the hurry?

JUST BEFORE THREE o'clock, Anna passed the sign for Weston. Known for its less salubrious neighbourhoods, Anna was surprised when she rode through the main shopping area and spotted a designer boutique flanked by a launderette, and a French delicatessen.

As a child she recalled forging a friendship with a little girl at ballet class who lived in Weston. She remembered being invited to her house to play. Her mother flatly refused to go to "that side of town". It was as if something bad would happen to her if she crossed the boundaries. Anna was forced to wait until her father was free to drive her at the weekends. Despite noticing the odd run-down shop or boarded up house, her attention fuelled by her mother's dislike of the area, she had enjoyed these visits immensely. But the place had certainly changed now, the opposite of its former self.

She reached the coffee house on Feveral Street, sandwiched between a privately owned bookshop and a One

Stop Shop, pulled up outside and hopped off the Brompton cycle. After removing her helmet and gloves she
clicked four times: first the back wheel was folded, then
the front wheel twisted around, the handle bars folded
down, finally the saddle was dropped. She hauled it
up next to her body, keeping her promise to Ross, and
entered the café. The mixture of a log fire burning on
the far wall and the strong smell of coffee mixed with
spices made the Café Cliché feel invitingly warm.

There were only a few tables occupied and she quickly
disregarded the lady sitting on her own on the sofas next
to the fire. There was a middle-aged man, busy reading
a newspaper, who didn't even look up, and a younger
man sitting on one of the leather sofas in the window.
As her eyes met his he stood immediately, a gesture
obviously intended to invite her over to join him. *He
doesn't look like a criminal*, she thought.

"Anna?" He held out his hand which she shook
warily. "It's good to see you at last. I'm Robert, but
everyone calls me Rab." His eyes sparkled, his wide
grin was easy on the eye. She licked her lips, not quite
knowing what to say and removed her coat.

As they squashed down into the sofas opposite each
other, Anna stared at her brother for the first time. He
shared her dark features with the addition of a swarthy
face that looked as though he would have a permanent
five o'clock shadow, however regularly he shaved. His
navy sweat top hung loose over his jeans which fitted
snugly over thighs that wouldn't have looked out of
place on a rugby field.

"Why Rab?" she asked. *No wonder I couldn't find
him on Facebook.*

"It's what our mother used to call me. Scottish for Robert."

"Oh."

"Can I get you a coffee, perhaps something to eat?" He gestured towards the menu and she smiled awkwardly, leaning over to grab it.

"This is all a bit strange, isn't it?" he added. She looked up from the menu at his mischievous, crooked smile and wrinkled nose and couldn't help but chuckle.

"It is a bit," she agreed, wrinkling her own nose.

"Well, listen. How about we just sort of pretend that we're old friends who haven't seen each other for years? You order what you like off the menu, late lunch on me. If you're hungry that is?"

"Sure." She wasn't, but for some reason speech eluded her so she stuck her head in the menu.

"Can I help you?" Anna turned to see that the waitress had crept over to the table and was standing next to her. Her bleached, blonde hair was swept off her face, apart from a stray strand hanging down. One hand hung on to the tied cord of her long, black apron, the other held a pad and a pen. Her young eyes stared at Rab, agog.

"Yes, I'll have one of these focaccia breads with brie and grapes, and a plain, black coffee." Rab looked up and smiled.

"Certainly," she smiled back, raising her eyelids and tilting her head as she did so.

Rab looked across the table, "Anna?" The waitress followed his gaze and looked at Anna as if she had only just noticed her. Then she looked at the bike folded next to her and frowned.

"I'm sorry, but I'm going to have to ask you to move that," she said curtly.

"Why?" Anna asked, surprised.

"It's a health and safety hazard. Somebody might fall over it. You can park it outside." She pointed her pencil lazily at the pavement outside the window.

"I can't," Anna said. "It's borrowed and I promised my friend that I wouldn't let it out of my sight."

Rab looked across at Anna and then at the bike. He quickly flashed the waitress another smile. "It's really not doing any harm is it?" She looked back at him warily. "Aww, come on, it's not as if you're really busy." He looked around the café as he spoke and then back to her. Her taut face was clearly softening. "How about we keep an eye on it and if anyone comes near, then we'll move it straight away?"

"Well…" She hesitated. "OK then, but it is your responsibility. Make sure you keep a watch."

"Thanks." Anna caught him wink at her. Having forgotten what she wanted, she ordered the same as Rab. As the waitress retreated to the kitchen, she thanked him.

"You're welcome." He looked back at the bike. "I watched you fold it down outside. It's a mean feat of engineering. I've never seen anything like it. What make is it?"

"It's a Brompton, you know, a city bike." She pointed at the smaller wheels. "British made. They've become really popular over the last few years. This is the latest model."

He seemed genuinely surprised and got up to inspect it. "It's incredible."

"I guess."

Rab flicked the brake lever and fingered the gears. "This really is amazing."

"You like bikes?"

He looked back at her. "Any gadgets really. My nickname is 'Techy', that's what my mates call me." He moved back over to the sofas. "I've been fascinated by stuff like that ever since I was a kid. *The Gadget Show* is my favourite programme on TV."

Anna smiled inwardly. They didn't share that trait in common. "It doesn't belong to me. I borrowed it from a friend." Anna wondered why she hadn't said "boyfriend". Ross was, after all, her boyfriend. But somehow it didn't feel like the right time to make personal revelations. Rab was, as everyone had reminded her, a stranger. She could tell him these things later. If there was going to be a later...

"You said. But you like cycling?"

"I love it." She took a deep comfortable breath. "It's freedom."

"Do you drive?"

"Yes, but I don't have a car at the moment."

"Same here. I love to drive. Used to go-kart when I was a kid."

"Really, which track did you use?"

"Rightons. Just outside Worthington. Did you ever kart?"

"No." She shook her head. "But I grew up in Worthington. I wondered if it was that one. My friends and I used to go up to the track and watch."

He smiled. "Maybe you saw me?"

"You never know." Anna shrugged. "Where are you from?"

Rab held out his arms. "Weston. Born and bred."

Anna smiled politely and nodded. *That explains Mum's aversion to the place.*

"Don't you have a bike of your own?"

"Yes, well no…"

He raised his eyebrows and his eyes danced at her as the mischievous smile returned to his lips. "Yes or no?"

She cleared her throat. "The police have it at the moment." Anna watched his face fall, his eyes growing serious as comprehension hit home.

"Ahhh…" It was obvious from his expression that he hadn't wanted to reach this point. It was too early in the conversation to discuss recent family events. He looked absently out of the window. She followed his gaze. A man had stopped in the doorway of the shop on the other side of the road. He appeared to be looking over at them. She scrunched up her eyes, struggling to focus through the mist. He looked strangely familiar, although she couldn't think where she had seen him before. As he met her gaze, he seemed to turn abruptly to face the doorway. When he turned back he had lit a cigarette.

"Anna?" The sound of Rab's voice wrenched her attention back to the moment. "Are you all right?"

"Yes, just thought I recognised somebody."

He followed her eyes. "Where?"

"Across the road." But when she looked back the man had gone. Rab sat back and looked at her.

"Sorry," she said hastily, shaking her head.

"That's all right."

"I'm sorry for *your* loss too," she said, directing the conversation back to Rab.

He lifted his head, did a backwards nod, then turned to watch a white van pass by the window. When he finally spoke his voice was barely audible, "It's a tragedy."

Her heart swelled with compassion. "I'm so sorry, really."

He rubbed his hand vigorously over his forehead and faced her. "So am I. He was your father too, and he died before you could meet him again."

That thought hadn't occurred to Anna. She pondered it for a moment, before she said, "Why do you think he was killed in my flat?"

"No idea. I would like to find out though." His eyes glazed over for a moment. "He would have been so proud of you."

Anna fidgeted, changing position on the squashy sofa, and looked out of the window again. She could see from the reflection in the glass that he was now staring at her, a look of total bewilderment on his face.

"You didn't know, did you?" He spoke slowly, the perception in his voice startling her.

"What?"

"About us?"

She looked back at him. "I didn't know I was adopted, if that's what you mean."

"They never told you?"

"Never."

"I can't believe it." He was shaking his head now, astonished. "All those times I was told by the services we would be reunited, be together again. They would arrange visits... Soon, always soon... But as the years passed and I was moved from one foster home to another, I realised these were all lies. We were lost in the system, off their statistics and I would have to bide my time until I was an adult and could find you myself. I went through the normal channels but was blocked. Your people refused to give me access. So, I managed to trace you. But never for one moment did I think they wouldn't tell you." He looked as if he had seen a ghost. "When *did* you find out?"

"Two black coffees and two focaccias!" The crisp voice of the waitress startled Anna and she moved back, allowing her to lean over and place them on the table in front of them, before returning to the bar. Anna sat forward, grateful for the interruption, and reached for the sugar. She never drank black coffee. She busied herself with the spoon, shuffling the plates around on the table. When she finally looked up Rab was still staring at her, his eyes heavy.

"Tell me about our mother," she said finally, hoping to lighten the mood.

"Ummm…" He hesitated for a moment. "Well, she died when I was eight years old, and you were three. That's when, you know, you were taken away." Again silence.

"What was she like?" Anna reached for the mug and lifted it to her mouth, flinching as the hot coffee burnt her lip.

"She was lovely. You look very much like her. I have photos. I can show them to you sometime if you like?"

"I'd like that." She leant over and tore open another sachet of sugar.

"So, what do you do, for a living I mean?" he asked. "I guess you don't usually while away your afternoons drinking coffee."

She laughed. "I wish. No, I'm a schoolteacher."

"What age?"

"Secondary."

"Wow! Do you enjoy it?"

She watched him place a huge chunk of bread in his

mouth and thought about his question. It seemed that over the past few weeks prior to the murder, she'd spent a great deal of time moaning about the politics of ambitious colleagues at work, the cuts in the education budget, the Year 10 history class on Fridays that preceded PE being sheer hell—far too much testosterone flying around the room, reducing concentration in her male students. But during these few days away she'd really missed it. She craved the keen, enthusiastic faces of those with a thirst for knowledge that made her job feel worthwhile, coupled with the challenge of turning the odd new head and watching a flicker of interest grow. "Yeah, I guess I do. What about you?"

"Huh?"

"What do you do?"

"Oh… I've just qualified as a plumber. I'm looking for work at the moment."

"Do you like it?"

"Plumbing? Well I enjoyed the training, so I don't see why I shouldn't. Wait and see when I get out into the real world."

"Doesn't your training take you out and about, as well as in college?" An awkward silence followed. Anna looked out of the window again as a woman passed, pushing a pram. She stopped momentarily to retrieve a discarded toy, fallen from within. As she stood up she bent over the pram to caress the baby's head, her smile that of a doting mother, before heading off again.

"I trained 'inside'." He placed an emphasis on the final word. *So, he expected me to know.*

"In prison?" She shot him a surprised look.

"Yes."

"Oh." An awkward silence followed. "What did you do?"

"Sorry?"

"What did you go to prison for?" she asked boldly, inwardly recoiling. It seemed like the right question to ask, but she wasn't sure she really wanted to hear the answer.

"I made a mistake." He shook his head and averted his gaze, as if the gesture would wipe his past clean, like cloth on a whiteboard. "I made a mistake—once. I did the time and paid for it." He shifted uncomfortably, the leather sofa squeaking beneath him and ran his hand through his hair. When he finally spoke he looked directly at her, although his flat smile didn't reach his eyes. "Listen, can we talk about this another time?" His eyes were like deep pools and she guessed there was an awful lot going on beyond the surface.

Anna gave a concessionary shrug. "OK." *So he wants to hold back too.* She could be patient. "Sorry."

"It's fine, just that I'd rather not be judged by my past. Let's get to know each other first."

The word "past" sounded hauntingly familiar to Anna and, brimming like an over full tea cup, she certainly didn't wish to court any new revelations. Not today anyway. She noticed a book peeking out from the jacket slung over the back of the sofa.

"You like to read?" she asked, nodding to it.

Glancing back at the book, he smiled, looking visibly relieved at the sudden change in subject. "Yes, very much. You?"

"Yes."

"What's your favourite genre?"

"I like a bit of everything," she replied.

"Favourites?"

"Well—I do love Jane Austen. I know it's a bit girly but *Pride and Prejudice* is my favourite." When he nodded knowingly, she started. "You've read it?"

"Yeah, I had a lot of time on my hands *inside*." He laughed. "Took a lot of stick for it, mind you, but I wanted to see what all the fuss was about."

"And what did you think?"

"If we're talking classics, I prefer *Papillon*."

"Good book," she nodded.

"But I tend to prefer a bit of fantasy," he said. "Give me Terry Pratchett any day. Do you read fantasy?"

"Not so much, but I do love Pratchett. So. Favourites?"

He chuckled at her repeating his words. "Well," he narrowed his eyes cheekily. "I could say *Guards! Guards!* but you might consider that a bit of a guy book. So, I'll go with *The Fifth Elephant*."

"Angua the werewolf & Captain Carrot!" They both laughed out loud.

"*Interesting Times* too. I've always wanted to travel to the east."

Anna was in her comfort zone now. The conversation moved from books to travel, and she was surprised at how much she was enjoying herself. They ordered more coffee and this time she ordered a latte, allowing the afternoon to pass easily and comfortably with lots of laughter. When she next looked out of the window, it was dark.

She looked across at Rab. "What time is it?"

He checked his watch. "Nearly ten minutes to six."

"God! I have to go. I didn't realise it was that late."

She jumped up, grabbed her coat and motioned to sling it over her shoulders.

"It was fun, wasn't it?" he asked, his face widening into a grin.

"Great. We'll meet up again soon. If you like?"

"Sure."

"Give me a call."

He nodded. "Look forward to it."

"Errr. Can I ask one more question before I go?" She grimaced. "A serious one?"

"OK." He looked directly at her as she sat back down.

"How did we get separated all those years ago?"

"Dad crashed out after Mum died. He shrivelled up, turned to the bottle, so we were mostly left to look after each other. On the day they took you from me, Dad had disappeared again and I stayed off school to look after you. I guess it was probably the school that called them."

His eyes glazed over, staring into space as he recalled the memory. "They arrived in a police car, but I wouldn't let them take you. I locked us in the house until they assured me that we would go together, we wouldn't be parted.

"They drove us to this big, red-brick building. I'll never forget it. We were shut in a bare, white room together, with one of *them* sitting in a corner watching." His eyes were wide, but concentrated, as if he were reliving it on an invisible television. "You were sitting on my lap when a woman came in and said she wanted to talk to me alone, didn't want to frighten you. She prised you off my lap and you wailed. But she insisted, said it was only for a few minutes, it would be for the best. She took me away and closed the door firmly behind me. I never saw you again." His eyes were heavy. "I'll never forget your scream at that moment. It's haunted me for years."

Anna stared at him and swallowed hard. "I've always hated closed doors," she whispered.

THIRTEEN

ROSS WAS STANDING in the hallway by the time Anna had unlocked the door, arms crossed against his chest. "Where have you been?" he asked, with the resonance of a mature married man addressing a straying wife.

"You won't believe it," she replied, oblivious to his angst, a goofy smile stretching from ear to ear as she wheeled the bike in.

"This is no joke, Anna," he snapped. "It's gone half-past six. I've phoned everyone we know. I was giving you ten more minutes before I called the police."

"Why didn't you ring my mobile?" she said, taken aback, her face falling as she peeled off her outer clothing.

"Don't you think I've tried?"

She reached into her pocket, pulled out her bare phone. She'd completely forgotten that she turned it off earlier. "Damn. Sorry."

"I've been worried sick."

"Sorry, I didn't realise the time."

"Christ, Anna, how could you have missed it? It's pitch black outside, not to mention thick fog? And with those petty lights." He pointed at the Brompton and shook his head. "Are you trying to give me a heart attack?"

She could have cycled home with no lights at all for all she cared at this moment. "Sorry, really I am, but

I've had an amazing afternoon," she said as she hung up her coat and helmet. But Ross simply shook his head again and strode into the lounge.

He was sitting on the sofa by the time Anna joined him, wide eyes staring at a blank TV screen. "So where have you been?" he asked, not looking up.

"I went to meet my brother." She missed the muscle that flexed in his jaw. "Oh Ross, he's really nice—you must meet him. He's really interesting. I…" She stopped as he stood, nostrils flared. "What's wrong?"

"I don't believe this. You went to meet him? On your own? After everything that's happened over the past few days?"

She clenched her teeth. The last thing she needed now was a lecture, especially from Ross. "What do you mean?"

"He's a known criminal, Anna. Your father was murdered. You put two and two together."

"He's not a suspect. I checked with the DCI first." Her voice cracked in defence. She coughed slightly in an attempt to hide it.

"Oh, that makes it all right then, does it?" His face contorted sarcastically. "That doesn't mean he's not involved in some way. Don't you think it might have been wise to have let all this blow over before you arranged to meet up and do the happy family bit?"

"That's not fair."

"What's not fair? That you didn't tell anyone? Or that you went to meet a total stranger, known criminal even, days after finding the dead body of your biological father in your flat? Think about it for a moment, Anna. Doesn't that sound like playing with fire?"

I did think about it. And it was something I had to

do on my own, she thought. But she didn't want to risk hurting Ross' feelings, even if he was being so crabby. It wasn't his fault. "I met him in a public place," she said calmly. "What could happen?"

Ross shook his head. "If the events of the last few days have taught you anything, it should be caution."

"What do you mean?"

"Well *somebody* killed Jim McCafferty. Haven't you wondered why or who?"

"Of course. Hey…" she hesitated. "You think they're going to come after me?" Her face flushed.

"I didn't say that."

"But that's what you think."

"All I know is that there is a killer out there. And I would feel a lot happier if you would stay safe."

Anna was crying now, the tears flowing down her cheeks like a leak in a pipe gaining momentum. "I'm sorry."

The breakdown in her composure crushed his resolve. He reached out and pulled her to his chest, hugging her tightly. They stood there for a few moments before he spoke, "I'm sorry. I'm just worried about you, that's all."

She nodded, wiping the tears away with the back of her hand.

"Come on, let's go and get a take-away. You might as well tell me all about meeting your brother." He smiled. "I can see you'll self-combust if you don't!"

"I can't." She raised her head to look at the clock on the wall and gasped at the vertical hand pointing up. "I'm meeting Chief Inspector Lavery for coffee. I'm already late."

"Why?"

"I'm not sure really. Maybe she has some news."

He looked downcast. "Where?"

"Hayes."

"I'll give you a lift."

"I'll be fine really. I'm meeting a detective for goodness sake."

"OK. Take my car and be careful. Park right outside and call me when you get there."

"I'll be fine, honestly. I'm not a total imbecile, Ross, I can manage."

HELEN DRAINED HER coffee mug, rested back in her chair and glanced at the surrounding empty tables. Her day hadn't ended well. The landlords at Jim McCafferty's favourite pubs were not particularly helpful. Neither could recall seeing anybody out of the ordinary with him on the weeks leading up to the murder. Pemberton and Dark had gone back that evening to have another go at the regulars.

Left with a rather vague description from the checkout assistant at Weston's One Stop Shop of a tall, blond man with pale eyes (he couldn't even remember what he had been wearing), Helen had spent half an hour with the force technology experts before sending the CCTV footage out to an independent company in an attempt at enhancing and sharpening the images. *More money—that'll please the Super.* Then, to rub salt into the wound, just as she left work she received an email from Jenkins himself. It was a copy of an email he had sent to DCI Sawford, asking if he was available to assist with the investigation. He wasn't going to let this one go.

Home hadn't offered much solace. Matthew had been

quiet over dinner and retreated to his room thereafter. When she'd followed him, explained he couldn't go to the party on Saturday night because he was grounded, and told him to apologise to his grandmother for his behaviour, he had just shrugged and said "OK".

Helen exhaled a long, sad sigh. She missed John. *How different would things be if he was still around?* Matthew was five when he died. He still had memories of him. How had that affected him? She had always tried to be a mother and father to the boys, with the help of her own mother, but they did lack a strong male figure. Her own father died before the boys were born and John's parents were ensconced in Newcastle. They were lucky if they saw them once a year. Maybe he felt as though he had no one to talk to…

No one to talk to. Helen could relate to that. Often her head felt like a caged animal. She had no one, no one outside the family that is. Oh, she had friends, lots, but over the years contact had drifted off to weekly, monthly, then occasional phone calls. Demands of the job and commitments to her family didn't allow much time for anyone else.

Her eyes fell on the waitress who was leaning on the counter, reading a magazine, twisting her hair absent-mindedly around the index finger on her free hand. Helen pulled back her sleeve to look at her watch and sighed. It was seven-twenty. Anna was late. Perhaps she wasn't coming?

She thought hard. The key to solving this crime was associated with Anna—she was sure of it. *Does she hold it?* Helen didn't think so, but something in her past, present, her family life, her social circle, or wider family structure would lead them to the killer. Helen was so sure of this that she didn't want to let Anna out of her sight for long. Sooner or later, perhaps even inadvertently, something would slip.

The door burst open and Anna rushed in. "Sorry I'm late."

Helen stood. "It's OK. Thank you for coming." She gestured to the chair opposite and they both sat down. She couldn't fail to notice the red marks around Anna's eyes, but chose not to mention it. Not yet, anyway.

"Can I get you anything?"

Anna slipped her coat off her shoulders and sunk into the chair opposite. "I'll just have a latte, thank you."

The waitress sauntered over and Helen ordered a latte for Anna and a cappuccino for herself. As the waitress wandered back over to the coffee machine, Helen watched Anna blow into the palms of her hands, rub them together and then over her face.

"Hard day?"

"I don't know whether I'm coming or going," she replied. "One minute I'm right up there, the next I'm at rock bottom. I feel…" She hesitated for a moment, as if she was trying to find the right word. "Weary."

Helen nodded. "You've been through a terrible ordeal. It's understandable that you'll experience a whole gamut of emotions. There are people you can talk to you know."

"No, thank you."

She watched Anna chew the side of her lip. "How was it returning to the flat?"

"Strange." She managed half a smile. "They'd cleaned it up. It was a relief not to see blood stains splattered up the walls."

Helen tipped her head in silent acknowledgement.

"I wasn't expecting all the press attention though."

"Ahhh." She gave Anna a knowing look. The press were another ball game altogether, especially if you weren't used to their tactics. "Did you speak to any of them?"

"No, should I have done?"

"Not at all. I would prefer you to leave all that to us. An odd word or sentence misconstrued can mislead the press and whip people into panic. We like to keep them on a tight leash if we can." Anna nodded once in acknowledgement. "Don't worry. It'll die down sooner than you think."

The coffee mugs arrived and they sat in silence as the waitress placed them on the table and returned to her magazine at the counter.

Helen watched Anna wrap her hands around the large mug. "How did you get on with your brother this afternoon?" she asked.

"To tell you the truth, I haven't got a clue. There were so many things I wanted to say, but when I got there I couldn't remember any of them." She lifted her mug and sipped the hot coffee. "It didn't seem to matter though. We found plenty of things to talk about. He was very nice."

"I'm glad it went well. What did you talk about?"

"Books, travel. We appear to have a lot in common."

Helen nodded. "Did he talk to you about your father?"

"Jim McCafferty?" It still felt odd to Anna to think of him as her dad. "Not much. I asked him why he thought Jim was killed in my flat."

"Really? And what did he say?"

"He had no idea, but wanted to find out."

"Oh. Did he say how he planned to do that?"

"No." Anna was starting to get fed up with all of the questions about her meeting with Rab. "You'll have to ask him yourself."

Helen looked up. "I'll do that."

"He's very easy company," Anna said, absent-mindedly. Helen couldn't help but agree inwardly. Rab Mc-Cafferty had certainly charmed the pants off the press at the conference earlier that afternoon, praising the police for their efforts. She couldn't have asked for more. There were no outward signs, nothing in his body language or mannerisms to indicate guilt when they had watched the recording afterwards. But something was still niggling away at her. *The killer has to be somebody close to the family.*

"There are so many things I want to ask him," Anna continued, raising her mug to her lips.

"You'll have plenty of other opportunities."

"Sure. It's just all so confusing." Her eyebrows fused together.

"How so?"

"Well, it's like… Oh, I don't know how to say it."

"Try me," Helen said gently.

"It's like I don't know who I am anymore."

"Because of the adoption?"

"I guess so. It sounds a bit dramatic, but it almost feels like an identity crisis." She gazed out of the window into the dark street beyond.

"You are Anna Cottrell. The same person you were on Friday, before all this happened."

"But I'm not the same, am I? My parents aren't my real parents. I have a brother who I don't even know. A dad I don't recall ever meeting, who was murdered in my own flat. It's a mess."

"There's more to being a parent than blood alone. They raised you, nurtured you," Helen said. Anna looked away again unconvinced. "How are *they* taking this?"

"It's all right for them. They were in on the big secret."

"Must have been difficult though. To harbour that *'secret'* for so many years."

"Yes well, not as difficult as for me."

"Do you get along with them?"

"My mother is tricky, but it's not her fault. She's had a difficult life."

"How so?"

"Her parents..." she hesitated momentarily, "died when she was young."

Helen nodded. Anna's expression betrayed that she'd guessed the police already knew their background. "What about your father?"

"He's a wonderful man. Part of me genuinely feels sorry for him—trying so hard to please everybody over the years."

"He sounds very special."

"He is."

"Well then, you are very lucky to have him."

"I guess." Anna put down her mug and raised her arms, smoothing back loose strands of her hair away from her face before letting her hands fall idly to the table. She could feel her eyes warm as they started to fill up. "It feels like everything is broken and can't be mended, and in the meantime I'm suspended in limbo, not knowing who I am."

Helen's maternal instincts took over. She reached forward, took her hand. "Why not look on this as if you are turning a corner, a new opportunity in your life. Nothing has been taken away, just new people to meet and get to know. It's like a new chapter. It doesn't have to be one or the other, just an addition."

"I'm sorry. You don't want to hear this," Anna said, retrieving her hand, fighting the tears that pricked her eyes.

"It's fine, Anna. Really. You can talk to me anytime." She looked away and sipped at her coffee to give her time to compose. She needed to keep Anna calm. Calm enough to talk freely. Confide information. This way, something, somewhere, may drop into the conversation, a stray comment that could eventually lead them to the killer.

Helen loved this part of police work. She found people fascinating, watching their body language, their eye movement, their mannerisms, using silence to induce conversation. As she had moved through the ranks, the opportunities for face-to-face contact had reduced dramatically. Very few DCIs interviewed these days. That is what made this particular job so attractive—the people contact. She felt bad for Anna, it was a form of manipulation, but in a case this complex, she needed to keep probing...

"Do you have a new suspect?" Anna asked finally, dabbing the napkin beneath her eyes.

"We have lots of leads we are following up. Don't worry, Anna, we'll do everything we can to catch them."

"Them?"

"Him or her. The murderer."

Silence followed. "I've even argued with Ross," Anna said.

"He's probably just concerned for your safety. That's understandable. I'm sure you'll make up."

"I guess." Anna blew her nose noisily, placed the napkin in her pocket and looked up. "Why do you think this has happened to me?"

"We're looking into that. But you need to be completely honest with us. If there is anything you are not telling us, anything at all, however insignificant you might think it is, you must speak up quickly."

Helen sighed. She knew that meeting Anna like this was a very unorthodox approach, one that could easily be misconstrued by her colleagues. But, her father's experience had taught her two things: always keep your witnesses close, and sometimes you don't get results without bending the rules ever so slightly.

"I've already told you everything I know. There isn't any more." Anna sneezed suddenly, the noise eating up her words.

Helen pulled a tissue out of her pocket and handed it across the table. She watched as Anna took it gratefully, and blew her nose.

"What do you know of your biological father's background?" Helen asked.

Anna shook her head. "Nothing. I didn't even hear his name before this weekend. You could try my parents."

"We have spoken to them. They say they've never met him, only knew his name through court records." Helen lifted her coffee to her lips and sipped it. The cream stuck to her top lip and she licked it away quickly.

"What about your brother?"

"I thought he wasn't a suspect?"

"We're just trying to build up a background picture on the McCafferty family members. Did he talk to you about his relationship with Jim?"

"He mentioned they didn't live together much while

he was growing up." Her brow furrowed. "Told me that he was an alcoholic."

"But they kept in contact?"

"Yes, I believe so. And he saw him a month ago. He visited him when he was on home leave… You don't think he did it?" Anna leant back in disbelief.

"I have no reason to think that," Helen said reassuringly. "As I say, we are just trying to build up a picture of the family, friends, acquaintances—something that will lead us to the killer. It wouldn't hurt for you to be cautious though."

Anna shuddered. "Do you think they will come after me?" she asked, quietly.

"We have no reason to think you are in danger."

"But what if I am? I mean, his dead body was in my flat. There must be some reason for that?"

"It could mean something, or nothing. I don't want you to worry, Anna. We're doing everything we can to find whoever is responsible and in the meantime you have my mobile number, you can call me any time. However insignificant you think it is. I'm only at the end of the phone. If I'm in a meeting one of my team in the incident room will pick it up."

As if on cue, the buzz of Helen's phone startled her. She reached down and pulled it out of her bag, examining the illuminated dial. "I have to take this." Anna nodded, as she got up and walked out into the street beyond.

Helen pulled her suit jacket across her chest, cursing herself for not throwing her long coat over her shoulders before she'd descended into the cold evening earlier. The air was icy and she was relieved to finally end the call and return to the warmth of the café.

"Everything all right?" Anna said, as she approached the table.

"I think so," she replied gingerly. "I need to go I'm afraid." She sat down, picked up her bag, rummaging for her purse.

"Work again?"

"Home business this time."

Helen removed a ten pound note and placed it on the table between them. She looked across at Anna. "You're a teacher, aren't you?"

Anna met her gaze. "Afraid so. Do you have kids?"

"Yes, two boys, thirteen and fifteen."

"Challenging ages." She gave a knowing nod.

"You could say that. Robert, my thirteen-year-old is a saint, but Matthew is going through a…" she pressed her lips together and paused to find the right words, "difficult phase at the moment."

"Can I help with anything? I am the Year 10 counselling contact."

Helen inwardly shook herself tall. She liked Anna. *Maybe in different circumstances…* There was a fine line between keeping Anna close, keeping an eye on her, finding out who she has been with, why, when; and friendship. The conversation was becoming too personal. Right now, it just wouldn't be ethical. *Such a shame.* There was a side of Helen that genuinely liked Anna, and she would certainly appreciate some professional advice at this stage.

"Nothing I can't sort out." She smiled, keen to change the subject. "Can I give you a lift?"

"I've got Ross' car. It's just outside."

"I'll walk you to it."

"There's no need."

"I insist. It's on the way to mine."

When they reached Ross' car Helen held out her hand, a gesture so simple but so defined. Suddenly, their easiness became awkward as the professional relationship between them reinstated itself. Anna shook it. "Take care and keep in touch."

"Thank you. And good luck with Matthew." As Helen watched her drive away a thought nagged at her. Anna's comment about her mother—"She's had a difficult life." Helen wondered why she hadn't been alerted to any anomalies in Kathleen Cottrell's background? She made a mental note to check with the team first thing in the morning.

EVEN BEFORE ANNA had reached the Cross Keys roundabout, she could see the smoke rising up into the moonlit sky. She stared up at it. The closer she got, the bigger the smoke cloud became. By the time she was within a few streets of Ross' house, she had to slow to a crawl. People were coming out of their houses, standing in the street, pointing at the roll of smoke in growing numbers. Driving became futile. She abandoned the car and continued on foot, making her way through people idly watching the thick smog in the sky.

As she approached the end of the street and saw the police tape cordoning off the area, she gasped. Her chest throbbed. She pushed towards the front of the crowd, squashing between heavy bodies, the smoke in the air making her lungs feel dry.

Her eyes focussed on the house generating the heat, the house the firefighters were striving to battle against.

She fought her way through the remaining people,

lifting the tape. Her heart was in a vice, the grip tightening by the second.

Suddenly, there was a strong pair of hands on her shoulders. The feeling of her body being pulled back.

Instinctively, she struggled, turned to face the tall, uniformed policeman. A reflection of flames danced in his eyes. "That's my boyfriend's house!" she cried. She pulled away from him, shouting, "Rosssss!"

FOURTEEN

THE CALL CAME at half-past nine and took Helen by surprise.

"DCI Lavery, this is DI Connell from the Control Room."

"I'm not the Duty DCI this evening," she replied quickly, lifting the newly poured glass of red wine to her mouth.

"I realise that, ma'am," he said, "but there has been a fire at 21 Castrell Street." She shot forward at this remark, droplets of wine spilling into her lap. "The resident," he hesitated as if he was reading from notes, "a Ross Kendle, is missing, thought to be in the property, and his lodger, an Anna Cottrell, is giving a statement to officers at the scene. When the officer radioed through, both of these names were highlighted as being linked to your Operation Marlon."

"Do we know how the fire started?"

"Not yet, but the firefighters are treating it as suspicious."

"I'll get straight down there. Thank you for letting me know."

When she arrived at Castrell Street, it looked like a scene from a Hollywood movie. Firefighters had extinguished the final flames but were scurrying around, collecting up hoses, putting their equipment together. The street was cordoned off by two marked police cars with flashing lights. Hordes of onlookers, some of whom would have no doubt been evacuated from their nearby homes, looked on avidly. She had been forced to pull out her warrant card in order to fight her way through the crowd.

Helen headed for the first familiar face and held out her hand, "Alison?"

DS Strenson turned to face her. "Hi, ma'am." She smiled, shook her hand. "Control room told me they called you."

Helen smiled back at her. She had worked with Alison Strenson a couple of years back, on a project to centralise the Control Room across the Area, and they retained a good, professional, friendship. "How are you?"

"Fine thanks, and you?"

"Good." Helen nodded, then cast her eyes back across the scene.

"I hear you've got Op Marlon?"

"For my sins." She raised her brows. "That's why I'm here." She pointed towards the smoky street. "What do we know?"

"Not much at the moment. A neighbour was putting some rubbish out at around eight-thirty and noticed the smoke billowing into the back garden of number 21. He called the fire service who alerted us."

"What about Ross Kendle?"

"Not accounted for as yet. His girlfriend, a Miss Cottrell, was staying with him. She went out just after seven."

To meet me, thought Helen.

"She returned around nine o'clock," Strenson continued. "Mr Kendle was at home when she left. She has given us contact details for friends and family, but we can't locate him at the moment."

"Where is Anna now?"

"She made a brief statement but was suffering from shock. Refused to go to hospital, so we took her back to her parents' home."

Helen looked around her. "Who's in charge?" She nodded her head backwards towards the fire engine.

"James Campbell is senior on scene," Strenson said. She pointed to a lean man with a shock of orange hair sticking out from underneath his helmet.

"Thanks, Alison. Good to see you again." She patted her on the shoulder. "Keep me updated will you?"

"Sure."

Helen wandered over to see Campbell who was speaking into his mobile phone, his voice loud. "Get him here as soon as possible."

She arched her forehead and flashed her badge as he ended the call. "Helen Lavery."

He shook her proffered hand. "James Campbell."

"What can you tell me?" she asked.

"We think the fire started around eight o'clock. We got here around eight-thirty. It took us about half an hour to get it under control."

"I understand you are treating it as suspicious?"

"Yes, judging by how quickly it spread and how difficult it was to get under control, I'm pretty sure there's been an accelerant used."

"What about the resident?"

"Can't get in there to check at the moment." Campbell shook his head seriously. "Having said that," his eyes grew grave, "if he *was* there he wouldn't have survived."

"How long before we know?"

"Terrace houses have a timber roof structure which has collapsed. It's not safe for my guys to go in at the moment. I was just on the phone to a Building Structural Engineering Company we deal with and they're sending somebody straight out. He'll be able to advise on safety and help us search the debris." He shook his head. "I don't think we'll have much more news for you before the morning."

TOWNSEND WAS DEEPLY disappointed. Despite leaving home at five this morning, a jack-knifed lorry on the M6 had meant tail-backs which delayed his journey to the West Country considerably. It was nine o'clock before he arrived at the small market town of Ripley. He cursed bad drivers, lorry drivers in particular. Surely spending day and night in a truck would teach you how to handle it properly? Now, most working folk would have left home on their journey to the office, the shop, the bank, the school—whatever their occupation. So much for the early bird...

He sipped his coffee and tucked into the fried bacon, eggs and tomatoes on his plate, the yolk oozing out of his egg as soon as the knife caught it, spilling across the plate. Somehow now the time didn't seem to matter so much. And he needed to eat, didn't he? Placing the last mouthful of bacon in his mouth, he grabbed the corner of buttered bread he'd saved until last and mopped his plate with it.

When he finished, he wiped his fingers on his napkin and leant back in his chair. The waitress was leaning over to clean the table opposite, her black trousers stretched across tight buttocks. *Nice*, he thought. She moved away and he glanced at his mobile phone. There was a missed call from the station. He could live with that. Right now he wanted to concentrate on the task in hand, to make sure that he could find something to back up his gut feeling. The DCI said she thought the clue to solving this murder lay close to the family. Well, he felt sure that the answer was *within* the family and he was about to do everything he could to prove that.

Since the Detective Support Officer had highlighted the name change in Kathleen's history he had worked hard, applying for address details from the Department of Work and Pensions, searching through Births, Deaths and Marriages in the Ripley area. It was laborious work, usually carried out by admin staff, but he didn't want anyone else involved. Not yet.

He licked the last of the tomato ketchup from his lips and narrowed his eyes smugly as he stared at his mobile phone. Yes, he would find the key to this murder. Then the snooty DCI would have to admit what a good detective he was. Maybe he would get a commendation, maybe even promotion? That would teach her.

Anna could feel strong beams of light across her forehead. She tossed her head from side to side and scrunched up her closed eyes. *Leave me alone*, she thought. But the light persisted, forcing her to raise her arm to cover her face.

She was awake now and suddenly aware that her nostrils were raw, compelling her thoughts to return to the night before. The night before… Every muscle in her body ached with a mixture of fatigue and anguish at the thought.

She remembered the feel of the cold, leather seat

in the police car, as she sat next to the uniformed officer, feeding him details of Ross' friends, his family. Anyone Ross may have visited that evening. She'd sat, head in hands whilst the officer made call after call: to Ross' parents; his brother, Phil; his best friend and colleague from school, Mart; each one a negative result. Ross hadn't been there, they hadn't seen him for several hours, days, weeks in some cases. Nobody would know for sure until many hours later if Ross had died in the fire, the flames far too virulent for the firefighters to penetrate and check. So she clung on to hope, like a baby with a comfort blanket, knowing that it was highly likely that his charred body lay amongst the remains of his broken home.

Anna lifted her arm just enough to allow her eyes to open slightly, resting it behind her forehead. As her pupils focused she realised that she was back in her bedroom at her parents' house. The flickers of light she felt were those battling to break through a tiny gap where the curtains weren't drawn together properly at the top. She blinked several times and frowned. She had no idea how she had got there.

Maybe it was all a bad dream. Cold now, she tucked her stray arm back underneath the covers and suddenly jolted, every organ in her body feeling displaced by the shock. She was fully dressed, still wearing her jeans and Ross' top from the night before.

Anna sat up in bed, pushed back the duvet and lifted the blue Helly Hanson sweat top to her nose. She could smell Ross, his Armani Pour Homme aftershave. But there was another smell, battling to drown out all the others. The unmistakable, strong smell of smoke.

She heard the ring tone of her mobile, the same plain

standard ring that she hadn't changed, hadn't amended because it was only temporary. But being only temporary meant that few people had the number—Ross! She reached over and grabbed the phone, her heart immediately descending as she looked at the illuminated screen.

She clicked to answer, raising the phone to ear. "Hello." Her voice was barely a whisper.

"Anna? Is that you?"

"It's me, Rab."

"Sorry, for a moment there I thought I'd dialled the wrong number. It didn't sound like you."

It's not a good time. But she couldn't afford to shut him out now. What was that saying? "Blood is thicker than water"—even if he was practically a stranger. "I'm sorry, Rab, something bad has happened."

"Oh…" A silence followed, as if he was unsure what to say next. "Umm… Can I help?" His light-hearted, friendly tone was replaced with a tight, serious inflection. Anna didn't know what to say, where to start.

"Anna, are you still there?"

"I'm still here." *Come on, spit it out—he'll find out soon enough anyway.* "There was a fire last night." There she'd said it. She closed her eyes and exhaled heavily through her mouth.

"I heard about it on the local News. Other side of town. Someone you know?"

"It was my boyfriend's house. I've been staying with him since…" Her voice faltered.

"Oh my God! Anna? Are you OK?"

"I'm not hurt. I was out at the time."

"That's a relief… I'm sorry. I had no idea."

"How could you have done?"

"What can I do?"

"Nothing, thank you. There is nothing anyone can do."

"Your boyfriend…" He broke off, as if he were afraid of continuing.

"Ross." He had a name and for some reason it seemed important to use it. "I don't know yet. I'm still waiting to hear."

"I'm so sorry." Silence again. "Where are you now?"

"Back at my parents, for the moment anyway."

"Would it help if I came over?"

"I'm not sure they'd appreciate it." She flinched the moment the words left her mouth. "Sorry, I mean… Well, as much as I'd love to see you, it's all a bit awkward isn't it?"

"I guess so." He sounded dejected.

"It's early days. We'll get together soon. Somehow."

"I want to help."

"Thanks, I really appreciate that. Just stay in touch for now. OK?"

"Whatever you want. Call me anytime."

A lump rose in her throat as she ended the call. Talking about it, smelling it and remembering last night's events made it all seem so real. Right at this moment, she had never felt so alone.

BACK IN HER office, Helen read the email marked "urgent priority" over again. Fire officers had assessed heat damage and burn patterns, and their sniffer dog had found traces of petrol at Castrell Street. The fire was started deliberately. They worked through the night sorting through the debris, but no body was found. *No body.*

For the present, the incident was being investigated separately by Area CID. DS Strenson had launched a missing person's enquiry and promised to keep her updated. But she knew that their enquiries would be limited. Ross was a grown man, not a minor, or a vulnerable member of society. If he wanted to take off for a few days—and people did occasionally without telling friends or colleagues—then so be it. Many a missing person or "MISPER" enquiry had cost the police gravely in terms of resources and time, only to find the person, whether due to relationship, financial, work or other pressure, returned in a few days. And these days the police had to prioritise. Budgets were tighter than ever.

The only information they had so far was that a neighbour of Ross' had seen him leave the house with a man around seven-twenty the previous evening. The description at the end of the email was brief: excessively tall, around 6ft 3ins with thin, white-blond hair combed back from his face and blue/grey eyes.

But where was Ross now? Ross' disappearance *had* to be linked with the murder investigation. She was convinced of it.

Helen picked up the phone and dialled urgently.

"DS Strenson?"

"Alison, this is Helen Lavery."

"Oh, hello there. Did you get my email?"

"Yes, thank you. Could you do me a favour?"

"What are you after?"

"Can you get an e-fit done of the man seen with Ross last night please? It's possible there is a link to my murder enquiry." Helen had learnt about e-fits on a recent training course and whilst it was being rolled out throughout the UK, not all forces including Hamptonshire currently had the relevant technology. It was much quicker and cheaper than obtaining an artist's impression, and astonishingly more accurate in most cases.

"I didn't think we had the resources for that."

"We don't, but Berkshire do. If you phone this direct number," she scrabbled around in her briefcase for her notebook and read the number back, "and ask for DS Shaw, he'll sort you out. We have an agreement with them for this sort of thing. Tell him to mark it priority."

"Certainly, ma'am. Umm…"

"What is it, Sergeant?"

"What about the cost?"

Why did finances always have to get in the way? "I would have thought that tracing this man would have been crucial to your investigation. It's also possible that there is a link to my murder inquiry." The line went silent. "Who's your Inspector?"

"DI Wilden." Now Helen understood. Paul Wilden was renowned for being tight with his budget.

"Any problems, get him to ring me."

"Fine." She sounded relieved. "I'll get on to it right away."

There was a knock at the door as she replaced the receiver. "Come in!"

Jessica Keen bit her lip as she walked into Helen's office. Although she'd worked as a support officer for the homicide team on many occasions she had rarely set foot into a DCI's office. And she hardly knew this one.

Helen looked up. "What is it, Jessica?"

"DS Pemberton said you were asking about the checks into Kathleen Cottrell's background?" She spoke nervously, the words rushing out of her mouth.

Helen sat back in her seat and smiled kindly. "Sit down." She gestured at the chair opposite.

Jessica sat down with her hands in her lap, folding

them together time and time again, as if she were wringing out wet washing.

Helen watched her for a brief moment. "Don't worry Jessica. You are not in any trouble," she reassured her.

"I was carrying out the background checks on Anna's parents and discovered that Kathleen changed her surname."

"What, before she got married?"

"Yes, she was born Gravell, but her name was changed to Gardner when she was seven."

"I didn't know that. Did you inform DS Carter and the HOLMES team collators, so that they could cross reference the information and get the right checks done?"

Jessica chewed the side of her lip now. "No. Well you see, Inspector Townsend told me not to. Said it might be nothing. That he would look into it personally and then come to you direct if there was anything in it."

That explains everything. Townsend had not been present at the morning briefing and when Helen asked Pemberton where he was, he'd said that he was on an enquiry in the West Country and would be back later. Nobody seemed to know any details about the enquiry.

"I see. Thank you for letting me know." So that was why he hadn't responded to her call. If there was one thing Helen hated, it was covert by-investigations and secrecy. Whatever the results, they always ended in tears.

TOWNSEND RAPPED THE door hard for the second time and sighed heavily. Why didn't people invest in doorbells or proper knockers? Having spent the last ten minutes banging on the doors of empty houses, his enquiries were proving fruitless. He'd tried number 16 Harwell Street, where the Gravells had lived, then the adjacent houses, before expanding his search. He was desperate now to find somebody at home, let alone somebody that remembered the Gravell family. He sucked his teeth loudly and cursed the lorry driver again.

As he turned and walked back down the path he saw an elderly man struggling with bags of shopping. The old man didn't look at him, but concentrated on heaving his groceries. Wisps of grey hair, from beneath his tweed cap, blew gently in the wind.

"Excuse me?"

The old man looked up, visibly startled by the size of Townsend. But instead of answering he bent his head downwards and ambled along.

"Hey. I'm talking to you." Still no response came. "Please, I'm the police." He was walking behind him now, amazed at the pace he'd suddenly managed to find. Townsend was ferreting through his pocket for his warrant card. He found it as he caught up with the man and stepped in front of him, waving it.

The man looked up with fear in his eyes. "I can't help you," he said gruffly and made to walk on.

"Please?" Townsend blocked his path.

The old man dumped his shopping down now, anger clouding his face. "I haven't done anything and I don't know anything," he said sharply.

"You're out early to do your shopping," Townsend said in what he hoped was a friendly tone. "The shops have barely been open an hour."

"That's the way it is around here, as if *you* didn't know it. You have to get up early, before *they* wake up."

"Who?" he asked, not sure whether or not he really wanted to know the answer.

As he stared up at Townsend his angry expression turned to confusion. "Your accent isn't from these parts, is it?"

"No, I'm just here on some enquiries. Before who wake up?" He lowered his tone to place an emphasis on the word 'who'.

"The yobs. Lazy beggars. Can't be bothered to work. They don't need to when they can live off the State, do they? And if they need a little extra, they hound us. You can't tell me it isn't the same where you come from? You'll see none of my kind out here in the afternoons."

"You should tell someone. Things can be done about this sort of thing you know."

"Hmph! Things can be done? You're definitely not from round here. Half of them have got ASBOs and it makes absolutely no difference. Even the local Bobbies turn a blind eye. ASBOs! Not worth the paper they're written on."

"I'm sorry. You're right, I'm not from around here," Townsend said, as gently as he could. "I'm from the midlands. I've come over to trace an old family that used to live at number 16?"

"Number 16? You'll be lucky. The world and his wife have lived there over the years. Never known a house change hands so much. Wouldn't be surprised to hear that it's haunted or something."

"You've lived here a long time?"

"Fifty-three years. Too long. Now if you'll excuse me I need to be getting back." He bent down and gathered his bags.

"The Gravell family," Townsend said quickly. It was

worth a try. If he had lived here all that time maybe, just maybe, he might remember something.

"Never heard of them." His voice rasped as he started to make off down the street.

Townsend watched after him. His day was rapidly moving from bad to worse.

Then, just as he reached the corner the old man stopped and jerked his head back round to face Townsend. Without putting his bags down he shouted, "You could try Lucy Walker at number 18. She's lived there forever."

Townsend's shoulders drooped. "Tried that. No answer. But thanks anyway."

He was just making a mental note to call back later when the man shouted again, "You have to bang really hard. She's almost deaf." And with that he scuttled off around the corner.

It had started to rain, heavy drops falling from the dark sky. Townsend turned up his collar. Maybe he should just give it one more try? It would only take a couple of minutes. What did he have to lose?

He retraced his footsteps back to number 18. The front garden of the grey semi-detached house was surprisingly well kept. A square patch of lawn was flanked by borders, well stocked with low maintenance shrubs: Lavender, Potentilla, Broom. He thought how pretty it would look in spring and summer.

He knocked at the green, council issue door and stood for a moment. There was no answer. He tried again and, remembering the old man's words, rapped harder and glanced across the garden. There was a weathered, wooden bench underneath the window, in dire need of a paint job with a slat missing. He wondered when somebody had last sat there.

Just as he was about to turn away, he heard a noise in the hallway, a soft shuffling of footsteps that were gradually getting louder, then a cough. Metal clanked together as locks were drawn back; the jingle of a chain sounded. The door juddered as it opened revealing a very small gap, the tension straining the chain, just enough for a pair of deep blue eyes to stare out.

For most of his life Townsend had enjoyed the benefits of his 6ft 5ins. Towering over friends and colleagues, he had become accustomed to looking down on people in the literal sense. However, this was undoubtedly the smallest adult he had ever faced. Well aware that deterioration of bone composition caused people to shrink as part of the natural ageing process, he found himself staring back at an elderly woman who was no taller than Tilly, his ten-year-old niece, and she was small for her age.

"Yes?" There was a rasp to the woman's voice, as if it had been worn almost hoarse over the years.

He spoke as loudly as he felt politeness would allow. "I'm sorry to bother you, ma'am. My name is Detective Inspector Townsend. I've been sent here from Hampton police on some enquiries." He held his warrant card in front of her face.

She narrowed her eyes and scrutinized it carefully. "What do you want?" There was that rasp again, in every word she spoke.

"I'm looking for Lucy Walker."

"That's me."

"An elderly gentleman," Townsend cringed as he realised that he didn't even take his name. He pointed weakly towards the corner, "said you might be able to help."

The pair of eyes studied him for a long moment. "What did he look like?"

She doesn't seem very hard of hearing, thought Townsend. "Who?"

"The elderly gentleman?"

"Flat tweed cap and long beige raincoat." As he spoke he raised his hand to just below his shoulder indicating height.

It seemed to work. Recognition showed in her face, but she didn't mention his name. "How do I know you are who you say?"

"You are most welcome to ring Hampton police station. I can give you the number." *Please don't. That'll really open the hornets' nest.*

She moved away from the door and, just as he thought she was going to take him up on his offer, he heard the sounds of a metal chain being removed before the door was opened wide.

The lace collars of a cream blouse sat over a lilac cardigan that looked hand knitted, which was fastened across her chest. Navy stretch trousers hung off her frail frame and a pair of pink, slip-on slippers covered her tiny feet. Her short, white hair was curled away from her face, in the way hairdressers "set" elderly ladies' hair. "You'd better come in."

"Thank you." He followed her over the swirly, seventies style, hall carpet along to the last door on the right, which led into a small, but tidy, fitted kitchen. White fronted cupboards and drawers, edged with silver handles, were fitted on three sides and at the far end sat a table, half of which was folded down. The grey, Formica work surface and the beige, mock tile effect, linoleum floor were spotless, apart from a few cat biscuits scattered around the edge of a bowl beside the back-door. Townsend stopped and looked around the room. He hated cats. For some reason they sensed his dislike and always made a beeline for him. But he could relax. There was no sign of moggy today.

"Sit down." She pointed at one of the chairs beside the table.

"Thank you."

"Can I get you a tea or coffee?"

"I'll have a tea, please."

She shuffled over to a white, jug kettle and flicked the switch. Although she moved reasonably quickly, he noticed that one of her feet seemed to be almost dragged across the floor. "So, Ernie said I could help you, did he?" she said with her back to him, pulling two flow-ered mugs off a wooden mug tree.

Townsend reached into his inside pocket for his note-book and pen and jotted down the name "Ernie". "Yes, he said that you'd lived here a long time."

"Sixty-two years next month," she replied, as if it was such an achievement that she should be nominated for an OBE. She continued to prepare the tea, grabbing a metal teapot and placing tea bags in carefully.

"That is a long time. I bet you've seen lots of changes."

She turned to face him. "You can say that again. 1948 I moved in. Of course Larry was still alive then." She glanced across at a photo on the windowsill of a grey-haired man sitting in an easy chair, a yellow bird on his shoulder.

Townsend rose and walked over to take a closer look at the photo. He could see now that the bird was a bud-gie. "Is that your husband?"

"That's Larry," she replied, "been dead for twelve years now. Never a better man walked this Earth."

"How long were you married for?"

"It'd be sixty-four years this year. Are you married?" she asked as she placed the teapot, mugs and a closed sugar bowl on to a small tray and carried them carefully over to the table.

Townsend thought about his answer for a moment. "No, not anymore."

"Hmm. That's the modern way. Folks don't stay married these days." She poured out the tea as she spoke. "Sugar?"

"No, thank you."

She passed him a mug of darkly stewed tea and sat down opposite him. "Still, I expect you haven't come here to ask me about my marriage have you?"

"No. I was wondering if you could tell me anything about the Gravell family that lived at number 16?"

"The Gravells?" She looked up, surprised. "My, that was years ago. What do you want with them?"

"There's a possibility that a member of their family can help with a case I'm working on."

"What sort of case?" she asked suspiciously.

"I can't say too much at this stage. We're just carrying out routine background checks. Do you remember them?"

"Yes, I remember them very well. They had a lovely little girl with blonde ringlets." She broke off for a moment, digging deep into the archives of her memory. "Kath, Kathryn…" She placed her fingers over her mouth and patted gently. "Kathleen, that was it. She was a real cutie."

"Can you remember when they moved in?"

She looked up into mid-air for a moment. "The summer of 1958. Couldn't forget it. My sister Maud moved to New Zealand that year, married a Kiwi."

"How long were they here for?"

"Five years."

"You seem sure of that."

Her face froze and she stared into space, recalling the memories. "Absolutely sure. You see they moved out in very tragic circumstances."

"Oh?"

"I can't see why it would interest you now," she said, "but anyway, I don't suppose it would make much difference. They'll be all grown up now."

"How well did you know them?"

"I guess you could say that we were friends," she hesitated, adding, "in a neighbourly sort of way. I babysat for Kathleen a couple of times. Held their spare key in case they got locked out… But I didn't approve of what they did to her. That was just plain cruel."

"What do you mean?"

"The way they went off and left her on her own like that. Just five years old. It was me that found her, me that called her aunt. And they never came back for her, did they? No heart. That poor child. So beautiful and all. To be deserted by her own parents."

"Are you saying they left her alone in the house?"

"Left her alone, deserted her, however you want to word it. They packed their things and didn't come back. It was only because I heard her crying through the wall that I found her, poor little mite. Shut in there, all on her own. My Larry said, 'Folks like that didn't deserve the blessing of children.'"

"So you called her aunt?"

"Yes, I had met Aunt Kate many times when she visited. My Larry said she liked the men, bit of a floozy like, but I thought she was just a working woman. Not married. She came to get her and took her to live with her by all accounts. I had a couple of Christmas cards from them, they seemed to move around a lot, then nothing. Another family moved in and we all moved on."

"So you lost contact?"

"Yes."

"Did you inform the police?"

"Sorry?"

"When she was left alone in the house?"

"No. Larry said we shouldn't get involved. It was for the family to sort out. We just called her aunt and she arranged everything. Even spoke to the Council about the house. Seems like they were behind with the rent as well."

They sat in cold silence for a moment. She looked up at him. "Things were different in those days," she added, as if she read the astonishment in his face.

Townsend sighed inwardly. It would be unlikely that there would be any police records.

"One thing always puzzled me about the whole affair," she said, looking away absently, her face folding in confusion.

He looked across at her and she was gazing at the net curtain which covered the back door. "What's that?"

"Why they left *her* and took the son."

Townsend started. "Pardon?"

She looked into his eyes.

"Mind, he was only a baby at the time, not even walking. But it seemed strange that they should leave one child behind, but take the other."

FIFTEEN

HELEN PORED OVER Operation Marlon's policy log. In accordance with police procedure all major incident managers were required to keep a log in which they recorded all their decisions, the strategies they set and their reasoning behind it. The books were numbered and confidential to the force, providing an explanation of the investigation at every point.

In view of the Super's threats she wanted to make sure that there were no gaps, nothing screamingly obvious that she had missed, that a colleague may notice immediately—leading to a quick arrest. She looked at her watch. It read two o'clock. She was desperate. She had just over a day to solve this case before another senior officer muscled in.

Helen was not labouring under any illusions. The introduction of an assistant at this point in the investigation would blight her career, whatever the outcome. In an organisation where strong characters and competition at all levels was rife, it would be seen as a weakness in her professional ability by her seniors and a failure in her role as an incident manager by her team.

A single knock at the door caught her attention. Without awaiting invitation, a dishevelled looking Townsend strode into her office. "Ma'am," he said.

She pointed at the chair opposite her. "I gather you've been busy."

He nodded briefly. "I've been to Ripley..."

"I'm quite aware of where you've been," she said tightly.

He faced her, eyes burning, head held high. She stared back at him fiercely. She could see that he was waiting for a tirade of abuse and, yes, inwardly she was seething, intent on verbally ripping him from limb to limb. But Helen needed something, she needed a result urgently, and at the moment, with a blurred CCTV image all that she had to offer for a potential suspect, she needed to know what Townsend had gleaned.

When she spoke her voice was calm, calculated. "Right. Out with it."

He looked up at her, surprised. "Ma'am, I..."

"I'm not interested in your explanations, Simon. I'm sure you are well aware of the tenuous nature of your position on this team, and I'm positive I don't need to remind you about the dangerous consequences of covert investigations." She fought to keep her voice even. "I just hope that your journey has not been completely wasted."

He reached into his pocket for his notebook and spent the next ten minutes summarising his findings. As he finished he looked up at Helen. She didn't miss the twinkle in his eye. He was obviously pleased with himself.

"Thank you," she said, keeping her face deadpan. "I think we need to get Kathleen Cottrell in immediately, don't you?" The twinkle disappeared. He nodded gingerly. She guessed he was struggling to read her this time. *Now you know what it feels like.* "And ask the team to instigate an urgent trace on the son. We have a starting point with the name, rough date of birth and address in Ripley—DWP should be able to help with the rest."

"Right."

"And no more secrets. In future if you have a hunch, an idea, a feeling, even a premonition, then you come to me straightaway. Is that clear?" He looked her straight in the eye and nodded.

"Right, that will be all." A wave of compassion reached her as he rose to leave the office. Perhaps this was his attempt at an olive branch? Keeping her face expressionless she called after him, "Simon?" He turned back to face her. "Well done."

ANNA SAT IN the kitchen picking at a bowl of cornflakes, pushing the sprinkles of sugar off each individual flake. She sighed, put the spoon down, closed her eyes and tried to picture Ross in her mind. Ever since they'd met she had retained this picture of him in her head: he was wearing a white t-shirt and blue cut off cycling trousers, his brown hair in dire need of a cut, flopping over his face. He was smiling, that boyish, next-door smile that made his eyes shine and hinted mischievous acts were afoot. This is how she always remembered him.

But today she could see nothing. She pulled her phone out of her pocket and instantly her heart dropped into the pit of her stomach. It was the new phone. There were no photos on this one yet. She closed her eyes again and prayed. She had never been a religious person, never quite sure whether she believed or not, but right now she wanted to believe. She wanted to believe that somebody or something out there would listen to her, and bring Ross back.

Something made her open her eyes and stare back

at the screen. And then she saw it, the little symbol indicating that she had a voicemail message. A bolt of lightning shot through her body.

She pressed call and lifted the phone urgently to her ear. It was from a DS Strenson, asking her to call back urgently. As she pressed the call button she could feel her chest tighten.

"DS Strenson."

"Hello, this is Anna Cottrell. I have a message to call you?"

"Yes, Anna. Thanks for calling back. I just wanted to let you know that the fire service found no body at your boyfriend's house."

"So, he's alive?" Relief gushed out of her lungs.

"All we know is that he wasn't killed in the fire at his home."

"So, where is he?"

"We've launched a missing person enquiry and we're doing all we can to find him. We'll keep you informed."

Her momentary elation was flattened. "Missing person? What does that mean?"

"At the moment I think it would be a good idea to keep an open mind. Are you absolutely sure that there isn't anyone he might have gone to visit?"

"No, I told the officer this last night." She scratched her head irritably.

"Has he ever wandered off before, perhaps for some time on his own?"

"Never. He'd never do this to the kids. He was due at work this morning."

"Are you aware of any financial or professional problems he may have?"

"No. He'd have told me," she said sharply. *What is*

the point of these stupid questions? Just find him. "Do they know how the fire started?"

"The fire officers have confirmed it was arson. That's all I can tell you at the moment."

Arson. Anna gulped. "Surely… Surely, you don't think that he started the fire himself?"

"I didn't say that. But we do have to investigate every option."

"It's not true."

The detective ignored her comment. "You have my number now, Anna. Call me if you think of anything?"

"OK. Errr…detective?"

"Yes?"

"Do you think this is linked to the murder in my flat?"

"We have no reason to think that at this stage. We are treating it as a separate incident." A short silence followed. "Anna?"

"I'm still here."

"Call me straightaway if he contacts you."

Anna swallowed. "OK."

"I'll be in touch." The line clicked as DS Strenson ended the call.

Ross, where are you?

She could hear footsteps behind her, feel the weight of her mother's eyes. "Good news?" Kathleen asked gently.

Anna twisted around to face her. "Ross didn't die in the fire."

Kathleen moved to sit opposite her daughter. "That's wonderful."

"Is it?" Anna said, her voice brittle. "So, where is he?"

"I'm sure the police are doing everything they can."

They sat in awkward silence. Anna picked up the spoon and stared at the cereal in her bowl. "Come on love, you have to eat something," Kathleen said softly.

I don't have to eat anything. She wanted to shout, but didn't trust her voice. Her brain was too numb to argue anyway.

"Would it help to talk about it?" Kathleen said.

She looked up at her mother, met her eyes momentarily before looking away. Anger flared through Anna's chest. Talk about it? They never talked about anything. What about *her* childhood? Did she know that Anna knew her secret? Would she confide in her daughter anyway?

The constant secrecy was beginning to suffocate Anna. "There's nothing to talk about," she answered, "Ross has gone. That's it."

"I just want to help." *Stop it. One moment, I'm ungrateful for being adopted and you've done me a big favour, the next you want to help.* She started to wonder whether her mother genuinely wanted to help or she was merely appeasing her own guilt. But Anna's brain was incapable of giving this much consideration. Her head was full. And it didn't matter now anyway. What mattered was finding Ross.

She rubbed her hands vigorously up and down her face and thought of Ross again but still nothing came to her. He was becoming a memory. There was only one place where she could go to get a proper reminder.

"I'm going out," she said, pushing the bowl away and standing up.

"Where?"

Anna ignored her, grabbed her jacket and made her way out of the back door. "Do you want me to come with you?" But Anna never heard the end of the sentence. She'd marched to the end of the drive and was now well on her way down the street. She was going to find Ross, even if nobody else could be bothered to do so.

LATER THAT DAY, Kathleen Cottrell sat perfectly still, back straight, hands folded together in her lap. Her appearance was almost fastidious. Short, grey hair was softly curled away from her face. She wore a red sweater with a medium length, gold chain around her neck, from which a heart-shaped locket hung. Matching heart-shaped studs decorated her ear lobes. A gold bracelet peeped out from beneath her cuff. Townsend guessed that she was one of those women who would walk through the woods on a wet, muddy day and come out in a clean wax cotton jacket and shiny Wellington boots.

He was furious. Helen had insisted that they interview Kathleen as a *witness*, in one of the suites usually preserved for rape or child abuse victims, rather than a suspect. Her reasons behind this were simple: being interviewed as a witness negated the need for a solicitor; the interviews were recorded by DVD and later admissible in Court, should the need arise; the interview rooms were more casual and comfortable than a formal room in the custody block, which may help to draw the requisite information out of her. But Townsend didn't get it. *Why should she get such special attention? She had withheld information, hadn't she?*

He couldn't be doing with the soft leather sofas, the coffee table and box of tissues, the carpeted floors, the Monet—Water Lilies—print on the wall. As far as he was concerned they needed to come down on her hard. But he wasn't in charge. Yet.

Kathleen's eyes flickered from Detective Dark, who sat opposite her, to Townsend and then back again. "Would you mind telling me what all of this is about?" she said sternly, focusing her attention now on Townsend, rightly guessing his seniority in rank.

"For the purposes of the recording, could you tell us your maiden name?" Detective Dark asked.

She turned to face her, head raised in a disapproving manner at this woman who looked young enough to be her daughter, as if she hadn't given her permission to speak. "Gardner," she replied confidently. "Now what…"

"Have you ever been known by any other names?"

Kathleen's displeasure at the interruption was obvious, "Cottrell," she replied tightly.

"*Before* your marriage," Dark continued, ignoring the attempt at sarcasm.

"I don't know what you mean?"

"What is the name that appears on your birth certificate?"

Kathleen gave her a hard stare, betraying her annoyance at the intrusion into her personal life. She unclasped her hands, folding her left arm across her stomach. For a moment Townsend thought she was going to cross her arms defensively across her chest, but instead she rested her right elbow on her left wrist, holding her right hand up and out beside her shoulder, as if it held a cigarette. "I don't see what relevance that has to your enquiries," she finally remarked, stiffly.

"This is a murder investigation, Mrs Cottrell," Detective Dark said. "Everything is of interest."

"I cannot see how my family…"

"Let us be the judge of that," Townsend cut in. "Just answer the question." She glared at him. The forefinger on her raised hand started to gently pick away at the skin around her thumbnail, a habit that could appear vulgar on some people. However she almost carried it off demurely, appearing not to damage the painted nail.

Townsend stared back at her. She reminded him of his (soon-to-be) ex-wife. They shared the same air of self-importance, scratchiness. *Bet her house is like a show home too. Just like Judy.* He was glad to be rid of her. Glad to be back in Hampton, on home ground. Soon the Super would recognise his talents, realise that he had turned the investigation around. Not like Lavery. *Making DCI in ten years on the accelerated promotion scheme. Didn't compare to real police work.*

Kathleen sat tall in her chair. "Gravell," she answered finally, "but I'm sure you know that already."

"Why were you reluctant to tell us?" Dark asked.

"It is a part of my life I choose to forget," Kathleen said. She had regained her composure now. The picking had stopped, although the arm still sat there suspended, the long nails folded delicately.

"Where were you born?"

"16 Harwell Street, Ripley," she replied. She sighed dejectedly. "I lived there with my parents for five years, before I was adopted by my aunt, Kate Gardner. She raised me. A few years later she changed my name over to hers. Now I…"

"Where are you parents now?" Dark cut in.

She glared at her again. "Dead."

"Did you see your parents again, after you went to live with your aunt?"

"No. They decided that they couldn't cope with me. So we made a clean break. Aunt Kate became a mother to me."

"And where is your aunt now?"

"She died two years ago. But I don't see what relevance…"

"Were there any other members in your immediate family?" Townsend interrupted.

Kathleen shot him a suspicious stare. The picking started again, a faint sound of a nail working away at the skin could be heard which she appeared to ignore. "No, just my aunt and myself. She didn't have any children of her own. And she never married. We moved around a bit—with her work, you know." She gave a small nod.

"What about when you lived with your parents at," he hesitated to look at his notes, although the address was ingrained in his mind, "16 Harwell Street, Ripley?"

She picked away at the skin, harder now. "I had a brother," she admitted finally. "He was a baby when I went to live with my aunt."

"What is his name?"

"Aaron."

"His full name?"

"Aaron Gravell." She coughed, the words sticking in her throat.

"Did you see him again?"

"Not whilst I was growing up. No."

"What about recently?"

"What…" Kathleen hesitated. Her nostrils flared. "What is all this about?" she asked. "I had a difficult time in my early childhood and I have undergone years of therapy to help me recover and put it behind me. Why rake it all up now?"

"I'm sorry if this is difficult," Dark said, "but I need you to answer the question."

"I've seen him once," she snapped. "You can check with Edward. He was there."

"Your husband?"

"Yes."

"And when was this?" Townsend cut in.

"I can't remember the date exactly," she tossed her head, "earlier this year."

"Can you be more specific?"

"A few months ago—August maybe. He sent a letter saying that he wanted to meet up, have a reunion. How he found me, I'll never know." She shook her head dismissively. "There are no secrets these days."

"What did you do with the letter?"

"Ignored it, obviously," she said, rolling her eyes. "Then he turned up on the doorstep."

"When?"

"A couple of months ago."

"September?"

"Yes, around the middle of September. Said he wanted to get together, meet my family. I turned him down flat, explained it was a painful part of my life that I wish to forget. I have made my own life and it doesn't include him." Describing her resolve appeared to relax Kathleen and she sat perfectly still staring back at Detective Dark.

"How did he react?"

"I'm not sure really. He seemed a bit taken aback." She looked away and wrinkled her forehead. "He actually seemed quite nice. In different circumstances..." She broke off, staring into space for a moment. "Then he noticed a photo of Anna on the side."

"Oh?"

"He asked who she was and when I explained she was my daughter he said he would like to contact her. Seemed to think he had a right to see her, that she was his niece, his own flesh and blood. He demanded that I tell her about him and gave her the choice of whether or not to meet him." The picking started again, more vigorously this time.

"And did you?"

"Tell Anna—absolutely not! She has no knowledge of my early life and I prefer to keep it that way."

"So how was it left?"

"I told him he had no rights to Anna, that she didn't share his blood because we adopted her. He seemed to lose interest then."

"Did you hear from him again?"

"No, nothing. And I don't expect to either." A muscle twitched in her jaw.

"Kathleen. Do you still have the letter?" Townsend asked.

She looked across at him. "No, I ripped it up and put it in the recycling bin."

"You don't happen to remember the address do you?"

"Why would I? As I have explained to you, I have absolutely no intention of either myself or my family being in contact with him again," she said tightly.

As Townsend stared at Kathleen Cottrell, he noticed a smudge of blood on the skin beside her nail. It was as if her past had clung obstinately to her for all these years, sitting just beneath the surface, inexorable to all the therapy a purse could buy. Counselling had provided some respite but nothing could make the pain disappear completely.

SIXTEEN

ANNA WASN'T SURE how long she had been walking. She reached the end of her parents' street before turning sharply right and climbing a stile, then making her way over the fields behind her parents' house, down to the river. *Ross loved it down here*, she thought to herself. A rope was still hanging from the large Aspen beside the water. The same rope that she had played on as a child, that Ross always swung on when they walked this way. She ambled along the riverbank for a while, looking longingly at the areas where they had picnicked last summer. All those long, balmy afternoons filled with sausage rolls, crisps, wine, before paddling in the river, then falling asleep on the clear areas of the bank. But today there was no sunshine, just bare branches moving mournfully around in the cold, November wind. It seemed the trees shared her desolate mood.

She reached a large, weeping willow, its bare branches hanging to the ground, climbed underneath and leant up against the gnarled trunk. This was where they had made love, invigorated by the warm summer sunshine, the tree in bloom providing the perfect curtain, blocking out the rest of the world.

With a heavy heart she headed back towards the main road. Whilst waiting to cross she looked down into a large puddle. A small streak of oil had leaked into it and was sitting on the surface. It reminded her of Ross' battered old escort, just the sort of car that would leak oil. Had Ross been here? She looked up and down the street as cars zoomed past. They always drove too fast on this stretch. For many years the residents of Worthington campaigned for speed cameras, but all they had been offered was the odd speed revelation dial and a couple of mornings with traffic cops and speed guns. A gust of wind blew, cutting into her face, forcing her to blink and move on. She would be warmer if she walked.

As she made her way out of Hampton's leafy suburbs and into the country, her phone started to ring. She dug deep into her pocket, looked at the screen, sighed disappointedly and answered.

"Hi, Anna. How are you feeling?" Rab's voice was flooded with concern.

"Like my heart has been ripped out of my chest. How about you?"

A momentary silence followed, as if he wasn't quite sure how to answer. "You sound distant."

"I'm on my way into town."

"Oh, want to meet?"

"Not at the moment, thanks. I'm just heading back to the flat, wanted to pick up a few things."

"By foot?"

"I need the exercise." *And I need to look for Ross*.

"Are you sure there's nothing I can do?"

"No, I'm fine really. I need to clear my head. I'll call you later."

"Take care."

She rang off without saying goodbye. It was good of Rab to be concerned, but right now she just wanted to be alone.

Anna continued on into the country, walking past empty houses with bare drives, the owners out at work. Every now and then she would see movement in a house and her head would turn instantly. Was Ross in there? Every time a car passed she scrutinized the driver, the passenger too if there was one, but her search proved fruitless. She was grasping at straws and she knew it.

Why Ross? Why now? It didn't make sense. She felt like she knew him better than anyone, maybe even his parents right now—it just wasn't like him to run away.

What is it that thing that animals tune into? When they won't enter a home because it's haunted? Anna didn't believe in ghosts, but she didn't disbelieve either. She just hadn't seen one to confirm the theory so the door was left open. Like with religion, she had seen no evidence yet to show that God existed—she was still waiting for her own miracle to convince her inner jury that he was real. *Sixth sense—that's it.* Anna did believe in a kind of sixth sense, in trusting one's own intuition. And now her own gut was crying out to her. Ross hadn't disappeared, gone off somewhere of his own free will. He had to have been taken. But by whom? Why? And she just hoped with all her might that he was still alive.

The light was starting to fade as she reached the sign for Little Hampstead. She suddenly felt cold, as if the temperature had dropped dramatically. Her legs were beginning to ache, but the familiar sight of her home village was welcoming, encouraging her to pick up speed. More than anything now, she needed to get back to the flat. Even if she couldn't see Ross in person, couldn't touch his face, she could look at an image of him.

Anna turned the corner of Flax Street warily, looking around for signs of the press. Relief filled her veins when she found it deserted.

She could smell fresh wood as she made her way into the flat, the new lock working like a charm. She left the front door open behind her. The sense of quiet which she used to revel in made her feel uneasy and she crossed into the kitchen and flicked the switch on the radio. *Chasing Cars* by Snow Patrol blared out. Anna closed her eyes and swallowed. Typical—it was one of her favourites, one of *their* favourites. Only last week they were checking the tour dates on the Internet. Last week, before this nightmare began.

Leaving the radio on, she forced herself to walk through the open door into the lounge and switch the light on. It looked clinical, just as it had the previous day, the absence of pictures and soft furnishings removing its soul. She moved on to the bedroom. Gary Lightbody sang out, the words softly filtering through the open doors.

At least her bedroom still felt personal. She sat on the edge of the bed and looked around at the wine-red drapes that framed the window against a background of white walls, the mock red chandelier that hung from the ceiling over the top of her black wrought iron bed, the black and white photos of Audrey Hepburn and Marilyn Monroe on the walls.

She had read somewhere that a woman's house was like a window into her soul and it wasn't until she had placed her individual and special mark on it, that it really felt like home. In contrast, a man regarded his house as a practical base where renovations and maintenance may be required, but not decorating for the sake of changing a colour scheme.

She thought about Ross. He hated this room. He

teased her, calling it a boudoir. He disliked the gothic, fringed drapes over the window most of all. Right now she promised herself that if she got through this, if she got Ross back, she would compromise and change them. Her small concession to him.

Anna felt uncomfortable, as if her organs were twisted into a mess inside her like a tangled ball of string. Her gut told her that everything led to her. Somebody was punishing her, but she didn't know who or why.

She considered the people close to her. The kindness in her father made him incapable of committing an act as brutal as murder. Her mother? Mentally unstable, yes, but a killer? She couldn't comprehend it.

Then there was Ross. The man with a zest for life that she had practically lived with for the past two years. He was missing. But he couldn't harm a human any more than Cookie could.

What about Rab? She had only known him for two days. Such a short time, although it felt much longer. Could Rab be a manipulative killer? A psychopathic murderer? Was he charming her, biding his time before she became his ultimate victim? Was he playing a game, enjoying the chase? But DCI Lavery had said he wasn't a suspect. And why would he want to kill her after spending all this time trying to find her again? It didn't make any sense. None of it did.

Anna sat down on the edge of the bed and picked up the photo that sat on her bedside table. It had been taken last year on a trip to Venice, both of them standing on the Rialto Bridge. He was behind her, his arms encasing her as if she may try to get away, his head resting on her shoulder. And there it was, that boyish grin.

She pressed her lips together, expecting tears which

didn't come. The effects of the last week felt like some-one slowly letting the air out of her lungs, so much so that now she was almost completely deflated.

She picked the other photo up of her parents and thought back to when she had been a child. She had hated going to bed before them, being the only one upstairs, insisting on all of the doors being left open.

"What if something happens?" she would say.

And her father would try to reassure her, "I'm only seconds away. You only have to call and I'll be there."

"But what if you don't hear me?"

"Of course I will. If you shout loud enough, people will always hear you."

A thought struck her. Standing up and placing her hands around her mouth for maximum effect, she hol-lered at the top of her voice, "Ross!"

The silence was almost deafening. Nobody moved, nobody came running. *He lied.* Sometimes you can shout as loud as you like but nobody paid any atten-tion. She sat back down on the bed.

And then she heard it, a scratching noise, the sound of a door swinging slightly; footsteps.

Anna caught her breath in her throat and jumped up again staring at the door. *Ross!* Her heart was racing as a head appeared around the doorframe. Then it sank rapidly.

"What are *you* doing here?"

"I was worried about you. Was that you shouting?"

"Ummm. Yeah."

"Are you OK?" Rab's forehead creased in concern.

"I think so." She looked up at him. "How did you know I was here?"

"You told me, remember? On the phone." He smiled comfortingly.

They stood in silence for a moment. "How did you get here?"

"I borrowed a friend's car. I can give you a lift home if you like?"

She nodded nonchalantly and looked around the room. It was so familiar. She wasn't ready to go back to Worthington, back to her parents' meticulously tidy house. Not yet.

He seemed to sense her mood and sat down on the edge of the bed, opposite her. "Did you know that you left the front door open?" She nodded, watched as his eyes darted about. "Great room."

"Thanks." She gave a watery smile, sat back down on the bed and swung her legs around, tucking them underneath, so that she was sitting cross-legged, facing him.

He leant over and picked up the photo, which lay next to her. "This Ross?"

She nodded.

"He looks nice, decent."

Anna looked at him and wondered how you could tell that from a photo. But it was true. Ross was sound. "You'd really like him," she said.

Another silence followed. She stared at him for a moment. Once again, he seemed to sense her curiosity. "What?" he asked.

"I was just thinking that I hardly know anything about you."

"What do you want to know?" His face looked like an open book and slowly her body started to relax.

"What happened to you when our mother died?"

"I was put with a family on the West side of Hampton. The Roxleys." He gave a small grunt as he remembered.

"You didn't like them?"

"No. Well, yes. They were actually very nice. They already had two boys. Richard was two years older than me—really academic. Strange lad, always in his room listening to music with his nose in a book."

"Not like you then?"

"You could say that. Oh, I liked books, don't get me wrong. But I was also eight years old and into anything as long as it included a ball. I don't think he even noticed I was there; until I took his Walkman to pieces."

She glanced askance at him and he grinned. "I put it together again afterwards," he said, "just wanted to see how it was made."

She couldn't help but smile. "What about the other boy?"

"Charlie?" His eyes widened. "He was only four, sweet really."

"What were their parents like?"

"When I think of them now, I realise how nice they really were, how much they tried…" Rab's words trailed off. He was lost in thought.

"What happened back then?"

"Then? I hated them. I hated the world. I had lost my mum, my dad, you, moved across town so I couldn't see my friends and started a new school. My world had turned upside down and I blamed everyone for it."

"What did you do?"

He rolled his shoulders. "I can't remember much—just that it was a nightmare… I broke things, was rude to everyone, missed school. They tried for six months until they let me go." He stopped for a moment, staring into space. "She cried on the day I left."

"Who?"

"Mrs Roxley." He shook his head, "In spite of everything. I couldn't work out whether her tears were due to fondness or failure..."

"Where did you go then?"

"I was moved around a bit for a few years, then went to the Taylors in Weston. Janet and Ron. Landed on my feet there."

"Back on home turf?"

He smiled, happy memories. "Exactly. And Janet and Ron were...different."

"How do you mean?"

"They seemed to kind of understand. However angry I got, however frustrated, they'd sit me down and talk to me. And they really listened. Nobody had done that before." They sat in silence for a moment before he continued, "Strange really. They never had any children of their own. Don't know why. But they'd fostered loads over the years. There were always adults coming back to see them that they had cared for at some stage. Janet made you feel part of a family, her family, and everyone mattered."

He looked across at her. "They worked tirelessly at helping me to get in contact with you." He shook his head. "But we always came up against a brick wall."

Anna pressed her lips together sympathetically before she said, "They sound like amazing people."

"They are. It was them that got me into go karting."

"At Worthington?"

He nodded. "We practised there every Sunday, but they drove me all over the country to competitions. I was really good," he gave a cheeky smile, "even though I say so myself." He fidgeted with his feet, kicked off his trainers, swung his legs on to the bed and laid back. He looked as though he was perched on a shrink's couch.

Rab sighed in happiness. "All those years of karting made me a top notch driver. Passed my driving test after four lessons." He glanced at her smugly.

"Wow!"

His face clouded over. "That was my downfall. That was why they wanted *me* to drive eight years ago." She remained silent as he continued, "I didn't even know what I was there for. I mean I knew it was a bit dodgy, but I didn't know what the job was. It was all top secret. It wasn't until I saw the guns…"

Anna froze. She tried her hardest not to look shocked. "What happened?" she asked gently.

"Armed robbery. They'd planned it for months. Only it went wrong and they shot a guy." He sat up and looked at her. She could see the hurt in his eyes.

"Did he die?" Her voice was a whisper.

"No, thank goodness."

Anna nodded, relief flowing through her.

Rab flinched. "The worst part about it was Janet's face in court, the day I was sentenced. Her disappointment sliced through me like a knife."

"Do you still see them, Janet and Ron?"

"They visited me a few times, but I was a long way away so we wrote to each other. It was them that got me into plumbing. I can't believe they still believed in me." He nodded slowly to himself. "I'll always be grateful for that."

So now she knew. "Why plumbing?" Anna asked,

keen to lighten the atmosphere. "Why not engineering, or computers?"

He thought about this for a while. "Didn't want to be stuck behind a desk all day long, web designing, drawing specs for machinery, or in a factory building something. I like to be out and about. Anyway," he added, "people will always need homes, heating, water. And there's always a shortage of plumbers."

She nodded. You couldn't disagree with that. "Are you allowed computers in prison?" she asked, slightly abashed.

"Computers, yes." He nodded. "We can use the Internet, although it's regulated and heavily monitored. Very frustrating... I used to set up everyone's mobile phones for them though. Loved doing that."

"Are you allowed mobile phones?"

"Not officially. They are banned, but they still get through."

"How?"

"Wives, girlfriends..." He shrugged. "Where there's a will there's a way, I guess."

There was a question niggling away at Anna, a question she could no longer avoid. "Why did you do it?" she asked quietly.

As he looked across at her, she could see the same intense expression spreading across his face. "I owed someone a favour."

"What favour could be worth that?" She regretted the words as soon as they'd left her mouth.

Rab's face hardened. "You have no idea."

"Sorry."

He continued as if he hadn't heard her apology. "Everyone knew how much I wanted to trace my sister.

Jonny's girlfriend worked for the DSS. She used their main computer to find you. I remember it was called the 'Departmental Central Index'—it contains details of everyone living in the UK. She looked through the records for you, traced your new name. Once I had that information it wasn't difficult to find changes of address. She went out on a limb for me, could have lost her job if she had been found out."

Anna's heart sank. "A big favour."

"You could say that. I was asked to drive for them in return." He shook his head. "Shouldn't have agreed to it. I always knew Jonny was a mad bastard, but I was desperate."

She looked across at him, racked with remorse. She couldn't imagine how anyone could want to go to such lengths to get to know *her*.

Rab jumped off the bed and reached down for his trainers. "That's it. My life history," he said, re-tying his laces. "Now come on, let's get you home."

It was like closing a book before finishing the story. Anna wanted to reflect on it, discuss it, but he clearly wished to move on. "OK," she said, "I'll just pop to the loo first."

When she walked back into the bedroom Rab was sitting back on the side of her bed with her mobile phone in hand, looking at the lit screen. She shot him a puzzled look. "What are you doing?"

"You left it on the bed," he said, jumping up, "didn't want you to forget it." And with that he handed it to her and headed out the door.

She stared after him for a moment as the light slowly went out, then grabbed the photo and followed him out of the flat.

HE WATCHED THEM leave from behind the parked cars, across the street. Both of them, together now. He crouched down as they climbed into the car opposite, careful not to be seen. Rab was talking, he must have said something amusing because she laughed, a chuckling laugh that one shares with close friends, family... They seemed to be getting to know each other well.

As hatred flushed through him, his mouth curled into an evil grin. *Good. Enjoy it while it lasts. It will make the pain all the more difficult to bear.*

THERE WAS A pungent smell of alcohol in the air as Anna walked through her parents' back door that evening. She smiled to herself. Her father often enjoyed a glass of whisky in the evenings. Perhaps it made her mother's company more palatable?

The first thing she saw was a brown, padded envelope, curled in one corner, sitting on the kitchen table. Curious, she went over and examined it. As she lifted it, she looked at the addressee: Miss Anna Cottrell 12 Worley Close, Worthington, Hampton, in the large, scrawling letters of a thick, black marker pen. There was no postmark.

"Dad!" she called through to the lounge.

Moments later she heard footsteps and he appeared in the doorway. His face was tinged with red from the heat of the whisky. "You're back. Any news?" he asked gingerly.

"Nothing, I'm afraid."

"Sorry."

"When did this arrive?" She held up the package.

"No idea. You mother found it posted through the

letterbox this evening. Looks like it was hand delivered. You expecting something?"

Anna squeezed it. "Not that I'm aware of."

"Oh." He watched her turn it over in her hands. "Well, aren't you going to open it?"

"I guess so." She pulled down the paper catch on the underside which ripped open the package revealing a clear plastic bag with what looked like a piece of crumpled, hard material inside. She searched back through the packet. There was no note. Puzzled, Anna turned it over. What she saw made her take a sharp intake of breath. And the scream that followed pierced her father right through to the bone.

SEVENTEEN

HELEN OPENED THE new message from DS Strenson and quickly clicked on the attachment. A man with fair, almost white, hair, gelled back from his face, and pale grey eyes stared back at her. Her cheeks flushed with adrenalin. *Could this be Aaron Gravell?*

The image flicked a switch in her memory. She screwed up her eyes and thought for a moment before reaching for her policy log, turning back the pages urgently until she found what she was looking for. Her stomach flipped. She grabbed the phone.

She watched Pemberton lift the receiver in the incident room and place it to his ear through the open venetian blinds which covered the windows to her office. As soon as he heard her voice he looked back at her. "Ma'am?"

"Could you get me a copy of the description of the man seen with Jim McCafferty on the day of the murder?"

"Certainly."

"And find out if there's any news on the CCTV footage enhancements would you?" She lifted her wrist and pointed at her watch.

"OK." He nodded in that animated way that people do when they want to show understanding from a distance.

"Thank you." As she replaced the receiver, it rang immediately.

"DCI Lavery?"

"Inspector, it's Alison Strenson. Did you get the e-fit?"

"Yes, thank you. Any leads yet?"

"Not yet. We plan to circulate the image. We'll keep you informed."

"Thank you."

"Actually, I've just had a phone call from Anna Cottrell. Apparently, she's been trying to contact you."

Helen screwed up her forehead, reached in her bag for her mobile and clicked the screen open. "I have no missed calls. I'll check with the incident room. What did she want?"

"She's been sent a package, believes it to be her boyfriend's tattoo."

Helen jolted forward. "Has she been interviewed?"

"Not yet. We only just took the call. I wanted to speak with you first."

"Thank you, I appreciate that. Where is she now?"

"At her parents' home in Worthington."

"I think I'll go out and see her myself." She thought back to the piece of skin removed from Jim McCafferty's arm. "This could be a direct link with the MO on our murder."

"No problem. I thought you might say that. Let me know how you wish to take it forward?"

"Sure. Thanks, Alison."

Helen replaced the receiver, walked over to the window and looked out into the car park below. A man in a black suit was removing a large briefcase from the boot of his car. But she didn't pay him much attention. Instead she stared over the car rooftops, gathering her thoughts. She remembered the Super's concern— "Removal of the tattoo bothers me." Nobody knew about the piece of skin removed from Jim McCafferty's arm apart from those working on the investigation. It hadn't been released to the press. Her scalp prickled.

A brief knock at the door drew her attention away from the window and she turned to face Sean Pemberton. "Here is the description you asked for." He leant over the desk to hand her the paperwork. "And I've checked with Pluto Digital and they are still working on the footage. But they said they're making good progress and should be able to forward us some enhanced stills by first thing tomorrow."

"Thank you," Helen said. "Are there any other messages? I've been told Anna Cottrell has been trying to contact me?"

"Not that I'm aware of. I'll check with the others."

"Thank you." Helen was only half listening as he turned and left the room. Her eyes flashed over the shopkeeper's description of the man who was seen with Jim McCafferty.

"Yes!" she exclaimed, her left hand clenched into a fist, as he re-joined her, a slip of paper in his hand.

He stared at her confounded.

"We have a match!"

"Pardon?" She ignored his remark, instead re-reading the description, as if it were too good to be true. He continued to wrinkle his forehead, then pushed the piece of paper forward. "Found this on Townsend's desk, came in about an hour ago."

"What is it?"

"A message from Edward Cottrell, asking to speak to you."

She shook her head dismissively, but even Townsend couldn't spoil the exhilaration she felt at this moment. "Get your coat!" she said, jumping up.

Pemberton thrust his head back and stared at her. "Where're we going?" He was looking at her as if she were quite mad.

"I'll explain in the car. We need to get out to Anna Cottrell's parents' house, and quick!"

"Give me two minutes…"

IT WAS EDWARD Cottrell who answered the door. Helen thought how he had visibly aged in the few days since she had last seen him. Dark shadows had crept underneath his eyes and the creases on his balding forehead seemed deeper than ever.

There were no greetings, no polite insignificant comments. "Thank you for coming," was all he said quietly. He held up his hand once they had joined him in the hallway to halt them in their tracks. "She's taken this very badly," he said gesturing his head towards the door to the kitchen which was slightly ajar.

Helen nodded and deliberately lowered her voice. "What time was the parcel delivered?" she asked.

He looked blank and shook his head. "I'm not sure exactly. My wife found it when she returned from the shops." Helen shot Pemberton a quick glance. *So Kathleen hadn't shared her visit to the police station that afternoon with her husband.* Edward scratched his head above the left ear. "Must have been about three o'clock. It certainly wasn't there when I went out for the newspaper this morning."

"Was it hand delivered?" Pemberton asked. He pulled open his notebook and started scribbling.

"Definitely, I would say. There doesn't appear to be any postmark on it."

"May we see it?" Helen asked. Edward was standing in the middle of the hallway awkwardly, blocking their way.

"Errr. Certainly." He cringed, causing the wrinkles in his face to deepen around the eyes.

"Where is it, Mr Cottrell?"

"It's in the kitchen—with Anna. She hasn't let go of it since she opened it."

They followed Edward into the kitchen. Anna was seated at the small breakfast table in the centre of the room. Helen thought how chillingly cold she looked, despite her parents' warm central heating. Almost ghost-like. She didn't acknowledge their presence as they walked in, but sat in the chair rocking backwards and forwards in slow motion, her eyes frozen on the package in front of her.

Helen lifted the chair next to Anna and tilted it sideways before sitting down to face her. "Anna." She spoke quietly, leaning in towards her. If Anna was aware of her presence she certainly didn't acknowledge it.

"Anna?" Still nothing. Helen looked up at the others.

Kathleen appeared at the doorway. "Anna, its Detective Chief Inspector Lavery and Sergeant Pemberton, love," Kathleen said.

For several seconds nothing happened. Slowly the rocking ceased and Anna lifted her eyes. They looked completely empty. "I know who they are," she said.

Helen spoke gently, "Anna, you've had quite a shock. Can we get you some water or something?"

"No, thank you." She blinked.

"I'm going to need to ask you some questions. Is that OK?"

"More questions. All everyone does is ask questions." She started to shake her head. "Asking questions won't bring Ross back."

Helen's eyes flicked sideways at the package, then back to Anna. "May I take a look?"

A glint of life appeared to return to Anna's face. "Why?"

"Anna, I can't help you if you won't let me."

She looked away and seemed to be churning over this comment. Finally she looked back, blinked again and nodded silently.

"Thank you," Helen said. She pulled some green, latex gloves out of her pocket and stretched them over her hands, before lifting the packaging and turning it over slowly. The lack of postage and postmark confirmed Edward's theory that it had been hand-delivered. She picked up the piece of shrivelled material which was secured in a plastic bag, the bag sticking to its contents. It felt surprising stiff and slightly wrinkled in places. However, despite the wrinkles Helen could clearly see an outline, about three inches in diameter, which looked like a figure of eight, staring back at her.

"Anna?" she asked, placing the contents back on the outer packaging. "Have you seen this before?" She pointed at the tattoo.

"It's Ross'," muttered Anna.

"Are you absolutely sure?"

Anna looked up at her. "Definitely. It's from the top of his right arm. The sign of infinity. He had it done in college, on a whim. He's regretted it ever since. He keeps it covered up these days." She swallowed and pointed. "Look, you can still see the scar from his bike crash last year."

Helen reached back for the bag and looked more closely at the piece of skin. Sure enough a faint, pink line could be seen across the centre of the tattoo. "Anna," she said as calmly as she could, "We are going to need to take this away to be examined. Is that OK?"

Anna didn't reply for some time. Silence filled the kitchen. All eyes were on an oblivious Anna who was staring into space. When she finally spoke up, her voice croaked, "He's dead, isn't he?" She lifted her gaze to meet Helen's.

"We don't know that," Helen said. "All we know is that we need to find him urgently. Are you sure you can't think of anywhere he might be, any other friends, acquaintances even, that he may have visited?"

"Nothing." Anna shook her head. Her body started to rock again, almost of its own volition. "Nothing," she repeated. "I've been racking my brains." She continued to stare at the detective when she suddenly froze, a light appearing in her eyes. But it wasn't a bright shining light, more opaque, as if frosted in fear. "They're taking them down one by one, aren't they?"

Helen frowned. "What do you mean?"

"Whoever is doing this to me? They're taking them out—people close to me—one by one."

"Anna, we don't know that," replied Helen in a desperate attempt to reassure her.

"Yes they are," said Anna staring at her wide-eyed.

"I'm the only link to each of these incidents. And sooner or later they're going to come looking for me…"

HELEN TOSSED AND turned that night. Thoughts of the investigation kept seeping into her mind. It was known that serial killers sometimes liked to remove something from their victim, like a keepsake, a trophy. But a piece of tattooed skin? And why send it to Anna? It didn't make sense.

She had also read that serial killers often adopted a pattern to their killings: knots being tied in the same way, or victims being arranged in a certain manner. However, research suggested that some violent criminals had a higher than average IQ, enabling them to adapt their behaviour to lessen the chance of being caught. Maybe the skinning wasn't for a trophy. Maybe it was for another purpose? *Maybe it was to scare the hell out of his ultimate victim?*

Helen shifted again. She could feel the blood pulsing through her veins. The previous twenty-four hours had been manic: the fire, Ross' disappearance, the removal of his tattoo, all represented a turning point. Her investigation had stepped up a gear. She now knew that these crimes were not only linked but calculated incidents. And Anna was right, she was the direct link between the two. She needed to protect Anna and find Ross fast.

Personal protection was no mean feat and certainly not something which was easy to instigate. Since the introduction of the Human Rights Act, police officers had to demonstrate they had reasonable grounds to believe a person's safety was in danger and obtain their full agreement, otherwise it was an invasion of their rights. Usually used as part of a witness protection programme it was also very expensive, meant lots of paperwork and authorisation at the highest levels.

After her conversation with Anna, Helen had left Pemberton to take a full statement and gone out into the Cottrell's cold back garden. She needed time to think. She was starting to understand why her father had called the role of Senior Investigating Officer on a murder enquiry the most responsible and important job in the police force. This was a judgement call and she knew that the decisions she made at this moment could make the difference between life and death.

Her immediate priority was to protect the Cottrells. If she was right and the killer was someone known to the family, then sooner or later they would have to surface. Once resolved on this, she finally reached for her phone and called Superintendent Jenkins. She couldn't authorise protection at this level, bureaucracy demanded his stripes behind her.

He had sounded irritated at first, the noise in the background betraying that he was out in public. She guessed maybe in a restaurant with friends. But once updated, he had proved surprisingly helpful. He agreed to allocate a Family Liaison Officer to spend as much time as possible with the Cottrells in their home over the next few days, a specially trained police officer who would provide a dual role by supporting the family, updating them on developments in the case *and* support the investigation by asking questions and observing behaviour, feeding back any information which may drive the investigation forward. Although she didn't think of the Cottrells as direct suspects, it was always possible that one of them may be involved in some small way. With a police officer close by at all times they may pick up on something, one little comment that may lead them to the killer. Helen's thoughts concentrated mainly on Kathleen who appeared to be the most unstable of the three.

Jenkins had agreed that an alarm should be provided to the Cottrell family, with a direct link to the control room so that they could contact them should anything suspicious occur. He also approved her request to have the Armed Response Vehicle to be stationed outside the Cottrell's property for the next twenty-four hours (when its presence would be reviewed and continued if necessary), unless they were deployed elsewhere, when a marked police car would take over.

As they neared the end of the phone call, just when Helen thought she had made a breakthrough with Jenkins, he delivered the sting in his tail. DCI Sawford would be arriving on Friday to assist with the investigation. He was giving evidence on a case in Court first thing, and would join them after lunch. *I hope they keep him all day*, Helen had thought to herself. But realistically she knew that wouldn't happen. The Courts never finished late on a Friday.

Later, she'd delivered the news to the Cottrells. What had followed was a diplomatic discussion with Anna and her parents where Helen had painstakingly explained that, in view of recent events, their safety needed to be a priority. They were to stay at the property, if at all possible. They had readily agreed to the alarm, but Kathleen was wary of the police presence. She'd taken some persuading, but finally agreed.

Arrangements, completion of all the relevant paperwork, making other agencies aware, had taken hours. It had been almost two o'clock in the morning by the time she'd got home, peeled her clothes off and jumped straight into bed but, in spite of this, she still couldn't sleep.

Helen shifted again and closed her eyes firmly. The pressure was increasing. There was not only the expense to consider. A large, visible police presence would almost certainly increase public interest again. Jenkins was expecting an arrest—and fast.

EIGHTEEN

AARON GRAVELL COCKED his head as he watched the detectives unwrap the new tapes and place them in the recorders. Having waived his right to legal representation, he sat alone, wide eyes watching their every movement as they prepared him for interview. When it came to the point where he had to identify himself for the tape, Helen leant closer into the computer screen, from where she was watching the interview remotely. Was that a glint of excitement in his eye?

She was also surprised to see how little resemblance he bore to his sister. The fastidiously smart Kathleen would have been disgusted at how her brother's blue and white striped shirt sat loosely over a rotund stomach, his grey trousers stretched across his large thighs. Aaron was stocky with wide shoulders and a round face, littered with broken veins. His hair still showed signs of blond, although what was left was razored to a number one making him appear almost bald, but he did not look severe like Kathleen—quite the opposite. His blue eyes shone and he had one of those faces that almost always looked cheerful, in spite of his mood. His appearance disappointed Helen. Although Aaron shared the fair hair and pale eyes, the witness descriptions had indicated a slimmer, taller suspect.

He had no previous police record, but had been easy enough to find. A quick trace at the General Records

Office confirmed his birth in the Ripley area, along with the names of his parents. DWP had then assisted with the rest, tracing through child benefit and national insurance records they tracked him down to an address in the Birmingham area.

Pemberton and Dark had both been surprised when they picked him up that morning. He hadn't seemed fazed at all, more inquisitive. Pemberton said that he had never witnessed an interviewee who had come along to the station so amiably—particularly when he'd been told that he was to be interviewed in connection with a murder enquiry.

In Helen's experience, novices usually fell into two groups—those nervous at what was going to happen and those angry about the intrusion into their time. But he displayed neither of these emotions. Either it was her imagination or he was actually amused and interested by the whole event, as if he couldn't wait to get home and relay the experience as anecdotes to friends over dinner. Plus his wife, Jenny, of twenty-six years, had come along for the ride and was sitting in reception waiting for him. Did they think this was a family outing?

Once introductions were over, DC Dark started the questioning. "Could you tell us where you were on the afternoon and evening of Friday 20th November?"

"Last Friday?" Aaron looked across at the bare wall, deep in thought. He scratched the back of his neck, "I was down the road at number 33. I'm building a conservatory for my neighbour. Was there most of the day."

"Number 33?"

"Yes, 33 Winchester Road."

"Can anyone verify that?"

"Sheila York is the owner. She was there most of the day, only popped out for a bit in the afternoon to walk the dog."

"What time would this be?"

"Around three o'clock. But she wasn't gone for long. Bubbles, her Great Dane, caught her dew claw in a wire fence. They came back about a quarter of an hour later and she took her to the vet's." Aaron screwed up his face. "Poor girl—covered in blood she was."

"And did you stay at the property?"

"I packed up around half-three, just after she left, and went home. Like to leave early on a Friday."

"And where did you go then?"

"Home. Jenny and I are re-decorating. I helped her peel off the wallpaper in the back bedroom."

"Did you go out again that evening?"

He stared at the desk as he thought for a moment. "No. We stayed in and watched *Goodfellas* on DVD with a few beers. It's one of my favourite films."

Helen nodded across to DC Spencer at this point, who went into the incident room to detail officers to get the alibi checked urgently.

"Thank you," continued Dark. "Do you know a man called Jim or James McCafferty?"

"Never heard of him. Is that who was murdered?" He looked from one detective to another. Neither responded. "It is, isn't it?"

Helen watched as they sat in silence for a moment, a tactic often used in interview to induce the interviewee to talk. Most people hated silence. "Well I'm sorry I can't help you," he said eventually. "I never knew the man."

"Thank you. Would you like to tell us about your family, Aaron?"

He looked surprised at the change of tack. "Yes, I have a wife named Jenny, whom you've met, and a daughter named Ellie. Is this something to do with them? Because I'm sure they don't know him either."

Dark ignored the question. "How old is your daughter?"

"Twenty-one years old." He sat tall, every inch the proud father. "She is at Northampton University reading criminology." *Is that it?* thought Helen. Is he using this as research on police procedures for his daughter's course? Ready to report back on a real life police interview.

"Anyone else?"

"Not on my side," Aaron replied succinctly. "My parents are dead and I have no siblings or aunts and uncles still alive."

"When did your parents pass on?"

He cocked his head again, then straightened it before he rubbed his chin. "Let's see. Dad died... It must be three years ago now. Mum died last year."

"Were you close?"

He frowned, blinked and nodded slowly. "Suppose so. I was an only one and they lived in the same village. Jenny and I nursed Mum through her cancer, until she was too ill and went into Cranfield Hospice."

"You had no siblings?"

Again, that head cocked but this time it was joined by narrowing of the eyes—as if he'd figured out where the questioning was going. "Not that I see, no."

"How do you mean?"

"Well, I have a sister named Kathleen but we are...

What's the word? Estranged. Don't tell me this is something to do with her?"

"How did you find out that you had a sister?"

He exhaled loudly through an open mouth. "It's rather odd actually. I grew up believing I was an only child and it wasn't until last year that I heard."

"Can you explain to us how you found out?"

"Mum told me. She called me to the hospice one day, about a week before she died, said she had something important to tell me." He paused, stared into space, as if he were recalling those moments.

"Go on."

"She said that she had been *'expecting'* when she met Dad, with someone else's baby. They got married quickly and he took the child on as his own. Mum said she was beautiful—people used to remark on her blue eyes and blonde, curly hair. But he couldn't warm to her. Every time he looked at her, every time people remarked how lovely she was, all he could see was my mother with another man. They almost broke up over it."

"What happened?"

"I came along and she was sent to live with Aunt Kate, Mum's sister. We never saw her, never even visited. Mum said it broke her heart, but it would have made it all the more difficult to see her, watch her grow up from afar. So she cut ties with her and Aunt Kate for good."

"Why do you think she told you?"

He stared at the table for a moment, lost in thought. "I think she was thinking of Ellie," he said finally.

"Your daughter?"

"Yes. You see she's an only child too. We couldn't

have any more. My wife's parents passed away many years ago and she only has one brother who lives in Scotland. Mum used to worry about Ellie being lonely in her old age. I genuinely think that she meant us to look her up and try to establish a relationship, for Ellie's sake."

"What did you do?"

"At the time? Nothing." He shook his head. "I told Jenny, of course, but Mum's condition was deteriorating and we were back and forth to the hospice twice a day. We decided not to think about it again until after she'd gone."

"How did it make you feel?"

He turned down the corners of his mouth. "Not sure really. I was a bit shocked I suppose."

"Were you angry?"

He thought for a moment. "No, not angry. I just felt a bit…numb, and disappointed maybe. She's not dead as well is she?"

Dark shook her head. "You were disappointed?" she said trying to steer him back round.

"Yeah. I mean it would have been great to have had a big sister to play with at home."

"Would you say you felt agitated?"

"To be honest, I didn't give it a lot of thought. Mum was really poorly, and I was working on a barn conversion that we had a penalty clause on if we didn't finish it by the deadline. So, I didn't have a lot of time to dwell on it. I must admit, when I found the photos in the loft I felt a bit… Well sad. Of what might have been…" He stared at the table again, mesmerised in thought. "I say," he said looking up, "I'm sure her family wouldn't be involved with anything like murder. They just don't seem the type."

"What happened after your mother died?" Dark said, determined to continue on track.

"Nothing at first. We were busy tying everything up, arranging the funeral, wake and all that. It wasn't until afterwards when I was clearing the house that I found some old papers in the loft. There was a birth certificate, a picture—you know, those colourful splodge ones that young children do that don't look like anything in particular, and some baby photos. It wasn't until then that I found out her name was Kathleen."

"What did you do?"

"We decided to try to trace her. Spoke to the Salvation Army at first. Someone at Jen's work told her that they can help to trace long-lost relatives. But after a couple of months, when we didn't hear anything, we decided to give it a shot ourselves."

"How did you find her?"

"My wife has a friend who's into genealogy. We used the Internet mostly, then sent off for certificates and things. It was quite exciting actually. We felt a bit like detectives."

"And what did you find?"

"That she is alive and married to an Edward Cottrell. They even live in Hamptonshire. Worthington to be specific. I can give you the address if you are interested? I think I still have it at home."

"That would be helpful. Have you made contact with her?"

"I wrote to her. She didn't reply. I was going to leave it at that, but Jenny insisted we try again, so we called around to her home one Sunday afternoon, a couple of months ago."

"What happened?"

He snorted, dismissively. "Once I introduced myself I was made to feel very unwelcome. Her husband was polite, but she was rude. Asked us to leave and never contact her again. Jenny was quite upset."

"And did you?"

"What?"

"Leave?"

"Absolutely. There wasn't any point hanging around. Shame though," he added.

"Why?"

"Well she has a daughter only slightly older than Ellie. They could have been great friends."

HELEN WAS IN a stinking mood by the time she arrived home that evening. Aaron Gravell's alibi was confirmed and, in the absence of any relevant evidence, they had been forced to release him. Just when she thought they were at the brink of a breakthrough, just when she thought they were getting somewhere, they were nowhere. And all the time the clock was ticking...

Finding Ross was a priority now and she had taken the unusual step of arranging an urgent press conference early that morning, with his family present, seeking out witnesses to record his last movements. But, as the public face of Operation Marlon, she hadn't been able to chair it. Helen decided not to release the removal of the tattoo, not to include Anna, not to give the public any indication that Ross' disappearance and the murder inquiry were linked. The last thing that Helen wanted was to increase any press attention directed at Anna, or encourage speculation that she was involved in two potential murders. Such attention may frighten the killer away and do irreparable damage to Anna.

Instead, Superintendent Jenkins had stepped up and taken over. She had watched it remotely and he had done a good job. The parents had been tearful, Ross' father appealing for witnesses, sightings, anything. But so far, apart from the odd crank call which often occurred when they set up public appeals, they'd received nothing new to go on.

Helen had been so sure that the killer was someone close to the family. But what if they weren't? What if she'd been wrong all along? It was almost as if someone, somewhere was playing a game, but she wasn't party to the rules. A week down the line and the investigation was going nowhere and, with Sawford looming on the horizon, it felt like the lowest point in her career.

As she unlocked the front door she was taken aback by the sound of a soft bark. She walked into the hallway tentatively. Was that coming from her lounge? She stood still for a moment and listened quietly. Nothing. "Hello!" she called out. And there it was again, the unmistakeable sound of a deep, gruff, bark, and scampering footsteps getting closer by the minute.

She placed her briefcase on the floor, removed her coat. There was a strange smell in the air that she couldn't identify. Helen rubbed the back of her neck as she crossed the hallway to the kitchen.

As soon as she opened the door she felt the blow to her face. Instinctively, she raised her hand to her lip in pain as a huge tongue lapped across her face.

"Boomer! No!" Matthew rushed into the room from the conservatory, followed quickly by Jane Lavery.

Helen sat up and stared at the cream Labrador which had turned to face her son and was now whacking its tail against her head, a movement that seemed to make its whole back end waggle.

She looked up into the face of her mother. "What's going on?"

HE LICKED HIS lips as he sharpened his instruments, one by one. Slowly does it. He was working up to his crescendo. Everything had to be just perfect. Last night he had been prowling around the field behind Anna's parents' house, watching the furore. He paused, closed his eyes and felt the blood still fizzing through his veins. Three months of meticulous planning, now coming together. And, after tomorrow, he would regain the respect he deserved. *Nobody* would dare cross him again.

It was like a game of chess and he was making all the vital moves. He had already annihilated the pawns, defeated the bishops, removed the knights and rooks. Tomorrow he would face his queen. And everybody knows that once the queen is lost, the game is inevitably over.

NINETEEN

ANNA STARED AT the digits on the bedside clock. It was six o'clock. She had barely slept a wink. It clearly wasn't bad enough that she had discovered a murdered body in her flat, her boyfriend had disappeared and she had been forced to move back in with her parents. Now, with the presence of the police permanently fixed in her mother's lounge downstairs, she felt that she was under house arrest.

Someone must hate me very much.

She pondered the extraordinary events of the last week. Bizarrely, in some ways things were starting to make sense for Anna. She had been cared for and supported during her upbringing. Her mother had always been controlling, but maybe, considering what she had learnt about her background, with the best possible intentions. During her teacher training she had read about children that experienced such abnormalities in their formative years. They either repeated them or fought against them. Her mother had fought against them, just fought a bit too hard.

But Anna had never really felt like she fitted in. She had never been able to put her finger on it, but something was not quite right. Now that the paradoxical life she had lived for so many years had been shattered in a matter of days, that part of her life was starting to make sense, whilst the other side—her relationship with Ross, her future—was falling apart at the seams.

She felt suffocated. She needed to get out of there. It was just a matter of how…

HELEN OPENED THE curtains and stared out at the early morning darkness. The weatherman on the radio was promising a morning frost which would clear the skies to provide brilliant sunshine, the only kind of winter's day that could be described as pleasant in her book. The case drifted into her mind. George Sawford was joining them today, on a sunny day, when they had no significant leads. The weather was probably the only good news she was going to get. She grabbed her bathrobe and made her way downstairs. That same thick, damp smell hung in the air, like clothes that hadn't dried properly. She could hear a noise—thump, thump, thump as she approached the kitchen and opened the door, gingerly this time.

The lapse in time had done nothing to curb the dog's enthusiasm. It came rushing towards her, but this time she was ready. She stood firm and pushed it gently away. It responded by licking her fingers and she couldn't help but smile inwardly at the happiness of the friendly creature.

"Boomy, that's enough now," warned Jane Lavery. She looked up at her daughter. "I think you've found a new friend."

"How long is she here for?" Helen asked. She side-stepped the animal, leaned over and flicked the switch for the kettle.

"Only a week. Susan flies back on Thursday."

"Good."

"Oh, don't be such a spoil sport. She's lovely really, just a little exuberant." Her mother leant down and stroked the animal's soft head.

"Yes. I discovered that last night. I'm nursing a bruise on my thigh," she raised a hand to her head and touched it lightly, "and I've got a lovely one on my forehead too. All in all, I think I did well to escape a black eye."

"Well, she's just a puppy really, only fourteen months. She'll calm down."

"I'm sure," Helen said.

"Anyway, I think it'll be good for the boys."

"So you said last night."

"Don't you think so?" Helen shrugged back at her mother in response. "It'll give them a bit of a focus," she continued, "just what Matty needs right now."

"If you say so. How was he yesterday?"

"Oh, the same really."

Helen sighed and pointed across at the side. "I've picked up a couple of leaflets on the Air Cadets." The words *Air Cadets* caught in the back of her throat.

Jane Lavery's face brightened. "I'm sure he'll be really pleased." They stood in silence for a moment. "You are doing the right thing you know," her mother added softly.

"Yeah?" Helen's voice broke as she said it. "Then why does it feel so wrong?"

Helen pressed her forehead again in an effort to relieve the ache that was rising in intensity. The dog was now chasing a ball around the kitchen, a ball which was clattering against the bottom of the cupboards. "Can't she do that outside?"

Jane Lavery gave her daughter a disapproving glance.

"Come on, Boomy. Somebody got out of bed the wrong side this morning. Come and have a treat in my lounge."

There were days when Helen loathed her mother's intrusion into her adult life. Days when she resented the ridiculous notion that a thirty-something woman still lived with her mother, and it wasn't as if she was caring for her in her old age: *she* was actually looking after her. Days when she wanted her independence, to look after her own family, her own way—bring back a partner and have mad, passionate impromptu sex on the dining room table when the boys were in bed, drink bottles of wine and sleep-in until lunchtime the following day. This was one of those days. And the guilt sucked away at her, draining her of emotion, oxygen, life itself.

HELEN ARRIVED AT the station just before eight. Pemberton followed her into her office.

"Morning, ma'am."

"Morning, Sean. What's up?"

"Rab McCafferty is downstairs. He's been here for over half an hour. Says he won't leave until he's spoken to you."

Helen dropped her bag and briefcase on her desk and turned to face him. She pushed her tongue against the teeth at the side of her mouth and thought for a moment.

"OK. Can you get me the CCTV stills and the e-fit of the suspect?"

"Sure." He disappeared and left her pondering as she unpacked her briefcase. *What could Rab McCafferty want to see me about so urgently?* She was just pulling the last file out when Pemberton returned with the pictures covered in a buff file. He had read her mind.

"Shall I come with you?"

"Not for the moment, Sergeant." She hesitated and looked over his shoulder into the incident room. "No news on the Inspector?"

Pemberton followed her gaze. "I saw him first thing."

Very diplomatic. Her patience with Townsend was now running very thin. "What is his problem?" she asked.

"Same as it's always been. He's got some inflated opinion of himself."

This outburst from Pemberton surprised her. "Clearly, you've worked together before."

"Not *together*, as such. I don't think he works *with* anyone. We were on an Auto-theft Operation about two years before he left Hampton. He was just the same then."

Helen shook her head in disbelief. It was amazing how, in such a large organisation, this sort of behaviour still got swept under the carpet. Not this time...

She looked up at Pemberton. "Thank you, Sean. I appreciate your frankness."

"No problem."

"If you see the Acting Inspector, could you tell him I would like a word?"

"OK."

Helen sighed. Right now, she had more important matters to attend to. "In the meantime, can you do the briefing for me?"

"Sure."

"Thanks. Do interrupt me if anything of interest comes to light, please?"

"Of course."

Helen picked up the stills and moved out of the office. As she made her way into the back of the main station to the interview rooms, she thought of her family.

A twinge of guilt jabbed at her. Perhaps she had been a bit hard on her mother this morning? After all, she was only helping out a friend. And maybe the dog would be good for the boys? Perhaps she should make an effort and take the dog for a walk with them all later? Rab had lost his father. He couldn't spend quality time with him anymore: open a birthday card, share a beer, laugh, have fun. She could and she resolved to do something with her own family at the earliest opportunity, even if it had to include the dog.

"GOOD MORNING, RAB." SHE SHOOK his hand and settled herself opposite him. "What brings you here so early?"

"Couldn't sleep." He scratched his right temple.

"Must be catching."

"Pardon?"

"Nothing," she said, shaking her head. "Is there something I can do for you?"

"I'm not sure. I keep going over everything again and again in my mind. Why would anyone want to hurt Anna? It doesn't make sense."

"We're doing everything we can to try and find out. Are you sure there isn't anything else you can tell us? Your dad was killed and Anna's boyfriend has disappeared. It seems to me that you two are linked together in this case somehow."

He sighed. "I've been racking my brains, gone through all Dad's friends, acquaintances. I'd say enemies but he didn't really have any. As long as he had his beer and his fags he was happy."

Helen tilted her head to one side. "And if he didn't?"

"He wouldn't hurt anyone. Might have stolen a few

things, but he would never have rubbed anyone up the wrong way like this. He didn't have it in him."

"What about you?"

"Me?" He looked up at her, surprised by the change in direction. "Well, I'm sure you'll have checked my prison records. I was clean, kept my head down. I just wanted to get out and get a life. I never wanted to end up like my dad."

"What about outside of prison?"

"I don't have those sorts of friends."

"What about the guys you did the robbery with? Maybe someone has a grudge against you? Or your family?"

"They're all still inside. And they were only friends of a friend. I did my time. I only got out before them because I wasn't linked to a gun. I was just the driver." He twisted his head to one side. "But I never shopped anyone. I'm not a snitch."

"Maybe they don't know that. Maybe they've organised something on the outside?"

Rab shook his head. "Don't think that I haven't considered that. No... They might rough you up a bit if you pissed them off, but murder? No, that's not their thing. They're just thieves..."

"Thieves that shot someone..."

"It was a mistake. The gun went off. It was never meant to happen."

Helen opened the file of photo stills and e-fits of their potential suspect and laid them out on the table one by one. There was a still of the man with Jim McCafferty in the newsagents at Weston on the day of the murder, a side profile of the same man and another of their backs as they left. It was surprising how the digital imaging company had managed to enhance them, sharpen up the blurred edges.

When Helen looked up, the colour had completely drained from Rab's face. He stared at them, wide-eyed in horror. She was expecting some distress—he was looking at his dead father and the date and time was clearly noted on the still. But was that a flicker of recognition in his eyes? A shot of adrenalin rushed through her.

"Rab, these are images taken from the newsagents in Weston on the morning your father was killed." She pointed at them one by one. He opened his mouth, appeared to be trying to say something, but closed it again. "And this is an artist's impression," she pointed to the e-fit, "based on witness descriptions of the man who was seen with Ross on the night he disappeared."

Rab looked like he had seen a ghost. "Have you seen him before?"

He nodded silently.

"Do you know his name?"

Rab nodded, then placed his head in his hands. "I don't believe this…"

PEMBERTON MET HELEN on the stairs on her way back up to the incident room. "The Super wants to see you in his office."

"He can wait," she said rushing past him. "Get everyone together, now!"

Helen was buzzing and by the time she had relayed the story to her team each one had contracted her excitement.

"I want the suspect located as a matter of urgency, but don't do anything rash. We are dealing with a potentially deranged, possibly psychopathic, but certainly very dangerous man. I want everyone on it. This is our priority."

It was with renewed vigour that she climbed the stairs to the Super's office. Finally, they had turned a corner. It was only a matter of time now before they had a result, she was sure of it, and she couldn't wait to share the news.

June, Superintendent Jenkins' secretary, was securing stray strands of hair back into a loose bun at the back of her head. She looked up as Helen approached her desk. Her kind face showed remnants of prettiness in younger years but sagged with age. "Go straight in. They're expecting you," she said briskly.

They, thought Helen. When Pemberton had told her that the Super wanted to see her he hadn't mentioned company. *Don't tell me Sawford has arrived early, after all?* Her heart dipped. She knocked briefly at the door and entered before receiving invitation.

"Ahhh... Helen. Thanks for coming." Jenkins was seated behind his desk, a nonchalant look on his face. As she closed the door, she was surprised to see that it was Townsend standing at the far side of the office.

Townsend gave a fleeting nod before fixing his eyes on the Super. The knowing look that they appeared to share did not escape her attention.

"You asked to see me?"

"Yes, Helen. Take a seat." He pointed with an open hand at the chair opposite his desk.

"Thank you." She approached the chair and moved it out slightly, placing it at an angle so that she could see Townsend in her peripheral vision. Something about the cool atmosphere made her suspicious. She sat herself down, taking time to arrange her suit jacket, before resting her hands in her lap and lifting her head to face the Super, in an attempt to feign confidence. Her nose twitched at the faint smell of furniture polish that filled the air.

"Helen, Townsend here has just been updating me on your case," Jenkins said, nodding briefly in his direction before slowly pressing his hands flat together and lifting them up so that the point of his fingers touched his chin.

"Good," she replied with as much confidence as she could muster. She wasn't going to give them any help at all. *What is Townsend up to?*

The room went very quiet, as if he were expecting her to say more. Instead, Helen allowed her eyes to wander to the window. All traces of sunshine had now disappeared as the day had subsided into a dank, grey fog.

"I understand that you have released Aaron Gravell?" Jenkins continued eventually, lacing his fingers in and out of each other. "Can you explain your reasoning behind this decision?"

Surely Townsend wasn't out to undermine her? *He wouldn't, would he?* She sat upright in her chair, opening up her diaphragm. "Certainly, sir. He was interviewed and has an alibi, which has been substantiated. We have no evidence to hold him." She looked directly at Townsend who, it seemed, was deliberately avoiding eye contact. Well, she was not going to make this easy for him.

Jenkins looked across at Townsend. "Inspector Townsend here," he briefly inclined his head towards the Inspector, "believes he was released too early." He gave a backwards nod. "Perhaps you would enlighten us, Townsend."

There was the first body blow. Helen could feel her nostrils flare. *How dare he?*

"Yes, sir," Townsend said. "Interviews with the Gravell's family neighbour in Ripley, and with Kathleen Cottrell, show that he knew about the set up in the Cottrell household. He was rejected when he tried to establish a relationship with them. He had shown a particular interest in Anna and knew that she was adopted. It wouldn't have been too difficult to trace her natural father."

Helen pictured Aaron Gravell in her mind. The family man who was so completely comfortable in his own skin that he almost appeared to enjoy being interviewed in connection with a murder case. She couldn't help herself. "What about his alibi? Motive?" she cut in.

Townsend finally looked across at her, narrowing his eyes contemptuously. "His wife is his alibi. She's lying. It's obvious."

The Super shifted in his chair.

Townsend raised his voice a decibel. "Christ, he's the best suspect we've had so far. We just need a bit more time—to match up the witness profiles, unravel his motive."

Helen turned to face the Super. "Sir, I can see no reason why I should pay my detectives overtime to work through the night to find a case when there is absolutely no evidence. We are continuing routine enquiries into Aaron Gravell's background as part of the wider investigation, but I do not see him as a suspect at this time."

"That's because *you* didn't find him," Townsend hissed.

Helen could feel the heat of the blood, rushing through

her brain cells. *How dare he?* She fought to keep herself calm. "On the contrary, Inspector, it was excellent police work—you discovering the Gravell family background." Duelling for a fight, her compliment clearly startled him. Helen ignored him and ploughed on, "But we actually have a clearer suspect in our sights that matches both our witness profiles."

She was aware of Townsend's head jolting, his face clouding over, but it was Jenkins who spoke first, "Why wasn't I informed of this?"

"It's only just been confirmed. This morning Rab McCafferty identified the CCTV still of the man who was seen with Jim McCafferty on the day of his murder. The still shares the same characteristics as the man seen with Ross on the night of his disappearance." She paused for a moment, glancing sideways to watch the colour drain from Townsend's face. Strangely, it didn't give her any pleasure.

"His name is Kane Edwards. He was a prison guard at Lardell, one of the prisons where Rab was detained. Rab describes him as a nasty piece of work, a bit of a social inadequate who supplied the prison heavies with drugs and sim cards for their illegal mobile phones. In return, they made his life comfortable through their contacts on the outside—cash, women on tap, that sort of thing. Basically he was on their payroll." She couldn't hide the excitement in her voice. "Rab and he never got on. Three months ago he was shopped and suspended—just at the time when Rab was moved to an open prison. Rab wasn't involved but his cellmate gave a statement incriminating Edwards." She paused for a moment. "Apparently Kane vowed to avenge the person who shopped him. Due to their mutual dislike, Rab believes that he blames him, instead of his cellmate, and this is his revenge."

The Super raised his eyebrows. "Why his sister? Why not go after him?" he asked.

"Maybe that would have been too obvious. But he knew about Rab's desire to meet up with Anna after his release. He had access to his cell in prison to obtain personal details, addresses and the like, and clearly has a motive to upset Rab's family."

"Have we located him?"

"My team are tracing him as we speak."

The ring of his phone interrupted them briefly. The call lasted less than a minute. Finally, Jenkins nodded several times, finishing up with a, "Certainly." He replaced the receiver, checked his watch and stood. He looked over at Townsend, who glanced away, then turned to Helen. "Well, that's resolved the issue. This seems to be a case of misunderstanding. I'll leave you two to sort it out. I've been called up to see the Chief, so I'll brief him on the latest developments whilst I'm there. Let me know as soon as you find this Edwards." Helen nodded. He stopped and turned as he reached the door. "What about this Rab McCafferty?" he asked. "Have we put anyone with him?"

"An undercover. I'll make sure we watch him twenty-four hours."

"Right, well, ring the moment you have something. And don't forget, Sawford is joining you today. Maybe he can assist with the search." And with that he left the room with the haste of a man consumed by ambition. She didn't miss Townsend widen his eyes at this remark. *Just like a scorpion*, Helen thought to herself, *the sting is always in the tail.*

The room hushed. She turned slowly to face Townsend who appeared to have lost his composure, his head hung like a naughty schoolboy. When she finally spoke she kept her voice calm and even. "In future, if you have any concerns about the investigation, I'd be grateful if you would come to me instead of trying to take my legs."

Those final words got his attention. "Taking legs" was a phrase used in the force when another police officer went behind a colleague's back, seeking to undermine them. He shot her an icy glare. "Not a very nice feeling is it?"

She felt her teeth clench, but maintained her steely reserve. "What?"

"You've side-lined me ever since we began this investigation."

She could feel her anger rising. "Simon, it was you who was smoking in the car park, missing important details through the first briefing, you who went off and carried out your own covert investigation…"

"You didn't even want to speak to me on the phone that first evening," he interrupted.

Helen rolled her eyes. This was like dealing with a child. "It doesn't take an inspector to secure a crime scene. Your skills were far more valuable to me in setting up an incident room, arranging for resources, so that we could get started at the earliest opportunity."

Townsend screwed up his own face. "You think you are so high and mighty, don't you? Better than the rest of us…" His voice was acidic.

"I beg your pardon?" she asked.

"Can't bear anyone else taking the glory, can you? You felt threatened by me right from the beginning, by my experience, so you cut me out."

She fought hard to keep her reserve. "Frankly, Simon, this inquiry has been dogged by your lack of support and negativity throughout. You're supposed to be my deputy."

"There you go again. *'Supposed'*. You think you can come here with your flashy degree, take some exams and step straight into your father's shoes."

The mention of her father caught her slightly. It was a low ball. "Let's remember who is in charge here, Simon. I give the orders. You obey them. If you're not able to do that, then you're in the wrong job."

"My record speaks for itself. Good police work. That's what counts. I got a result in the West Country."

His sheer arrogance flabbergasted Helen. "What counts is obeying orders. Have I not made myself clear enough? God, Simon, I shouldn't need to explain force discipline to an officer of your service, or rank for that matter."

Townsend's face turned to stone as he ignored her comments and continued, "It was obvious from the first time I spoke to you on this case. I could hear the contempt in your voice. The same contempt as when I left Hampton. You people, you don't care whose toes you tread on, how many careers you ruin, to get to the top."

The truth was that Helen had no idea why Townsend had left the Area all those years ago. Of course, his sudden departure had fuelled all sorts of rumours. The most popular assumption was that the bosses had engineered the move due to his laziness. He wasn't nicknamed "Cuff" for his diligence in investigating jobs that was for sure. Then there was the incident with PC Bland…

But she had heard enough. She leant forward, spoke

loudly. "Simon, I honestly had no idea why you left the Area eight years ago, but I can assure you it had nothing to do with me."

"Yeah, right..."

"That is right!" The decibels in her voice rose with each syllable. He shook his head as she continued, "I suggest that you check out your facts before you go around accusing people in future."

She straightened. "I refuse to continue with this conversation, other than to repeat that you are seriously mistaken about your accusations." She made to go, but turned as she reached the door. "I'm going back to the incident room. You have two choices—either put this behind you, come down and do your job properly, or leave. Because if you give me any reason, any reason at all, to think that you are not following orders in future I'll throw the book at you. How *dare* you undermine me, go behind my back and question my abilities!" With that she turned on her heels.

Helen marched down the stairs angrily. Had he really harboured this misconceived grudge against her for all these years? More likely, it was a mixture of jealousy and guilt. The question was, how did an officer with his track record and inability to work in a team, manage to make Acting Inspector?

TWENTY

"HE'S DONE A RUNNER."

Helen stared at a frustrated Pemberton and then looked around the room at her weary team. While she was in the Super's office they had all been on phones, searching computers, speaking to neighbouring forces, in an attempt to locate their suspect. "What do you mean?" Helen asked. "Somebody must know where he is?"

"We've checked with Lardell force and the prison," Pemberton said. "Edwards was arrested for possession with intent to supply cannabis at Lardell prison, but they only caught him with 1oz altogether, so he was released on bail pending enquiries. That's when he did a moonlight flit. They didn't realise until he failed to answer his bail four weeks ago."

"What about his car, bank accounts, credit cards? He must have used his phone?"

"It seems he planned out his escape very carefully. He withdrew the last £800 from his bank account two days before he was due to appear. There has been no activity on his mobile. We can't trace his car—good chance he's trashed it if he's planned this—and there has been no activity on his credit card, although he has left rather a large debt outstanding. It seems our Mr Edwards was intent on not going to prison." That wasn't surprising. Nobody liked a bent prison guard, not police, other guards or prisoners, no matter how many of the latter owed him favours.

"So what is he doing for money? Somebody must be looking after him?"

"Best case scenario is that the group he was working for in the prison have taken him under their wing, put him up in some shithole and he'll be selling drugs for them. Probably even lent him a car, too. That way he can just work in cash which is untraceable."

"What have Lardell done to try to find him?"

Pemberton shrugged. "He's not high priority for them. Just a 'fail to answer bail'. With resources pushed as they are, he'll be another open case file for an overloaded Area detective."

Helen sighed loudly. "Well he's high priority to us. Look, we know he was in Hampton last week. The chances are that he is still in the locality. Get our own detectives to check their contacts in the field. Someone must either know him or know of him. Try the drugs team too. If your theory is right then a new face on the block would not go unnoticed."

Heads nodded as Helen continued, "Make sure that we circulate the stills throughout our force, particularly to the instant response team. We need all our people to keep their ears and eyes open. And circulate them to neighbouring forces too. Oh, and get me Jack Coulson on the phone please?" she barked at Pemberton. "We'll see if we can get his image on to the front page of the tomorrow's *Hampton Herald*."

IT WAS ALMOST four when Helen heard somebody holler, "Afternoon!"

She looked up from her desk to see a short, wiry man

standing at the entrance to the incident room. Her team looked back at him, a few nodded, others just stared. It wasn't surprising really, as she hadn't shared the new arrangement with them yet. She had needed them focused on finding their suspect.

George Sawford strode through the incident room and entered her office without knocking.

"Afternoon, Helen," he said.

"George." She shook his proffered hand.

He was no taller than 5ft 2ins, with fox-like features and a clump of light, brown hair on his head which permanently stuck up around the crown area. George had joined Hamptonshire force in the early 1990s (when they had dropped the height restrictions). Rising quickly through the ranks, he was known for his ambitious nature and attention to detail. For the last nine years he had served as a Senior Investigating Officer, managing murder investigations, cold case reviews and sitting on review panels. But he was also well known for the cunning chip on his shoulder. He was driven to find something, to get a result at whatever cost. It was almost as if he had something to prove to the world.

"Sorry I'm late, but you know what Judge Tallins is like."

She nodded back at him and watched as he sat himself down opposite her.

"Would you like me to give you a brief overview of the case?" she asked.

He rubbed his chin briefly, eyes searching across her desk. "Errr… No, thank you. I think I'll start with your policy log and we'll see where we go from there."

Helen could feel her hackles rising. He wasn't going to make this easy. Although outwardly he appeared calm and collected, inwardly she could see that he couldn't wait to get his teeth stuck in. It was no secret that he played golf with the Super, the Chief Constable, and many other influential people in Hamptonshire including the Mayor. And he was craftily astute, seeking out big, high profile cases that caught the public eye. *Celebrity Cop.* There could be no doubt that, with Central Government introducing the election of Police Commissioners, this was his ultimate aim. And he didn't care who got in his way. He was gunning for her blood. Well, she wasn't going to bring herself down to his level.

"As you wish," she said, lifting it from her desk and passing it across to him.

"Thank you. He placed it on the edge of the desk and moved to unpack his briefcase.

Oh no you don't. "I've arranged for you to have your own office down the corridor," she said. "You won't be disturbed there." She watched him hide his surprise. He was also an excellent actor. *You didn't think I was going to let you loose in here?* "Why don't you follow me and we'll get you settled?"

"Of course." He shoved a notebook back into his briefcase, picked up her policy log and followed her out of her office, back through the incident room and along the corridor.

Helen opened the door to the old, windowless store cupboard and switched on the light. It had been used on a number of occasions as an overflow office when they were particularly busy in the incident room, or they had a review team in. It felt cold today and very bare. Apart from a few lonely boxes stored in the corner, it housed a desk and a couple of chairs, one either side. There wasn't much room for anything else.

"There you go," Helen said, opening her arm to escort him in, as if he were getting the Super's office.

"Right." If he was cross or felt marginalised, he was careful not to show it. But Helen had seen him in practise before, and underneath the blank expression, there was a knowing acknowledgement. The parameters had been set.

"I should know what your current priorities are?" he asked, turning to face her.

"We are looking into a potential suspect," Helen replied, deliberately playing it down. "It's all in the log. Give me a shout if you need clarification on anything."

"Will do, thank you."

As she nodded and turned to go, a thought suddenly gripped her. "Coffee, George?"

"That would be great," he replied, and this time there was an air of surprise to his voice.

"The machine is just next door. Do help yourself." And with that she marched back down the corridor.

"WHAT IS HE doing here?" Dark whispered loudly, jerking her head in the direction of the corridor as they begun the afternoon round up. George Sawford's presence in the former store cupboard had not gone unnoticed.

"The Super feels that we might benefit from some expertise on the investigation," Helen said, her face impassive.

"More like putting us on trial." Helen was surprised by Pemberton's remark. He was usually always one to toe the line. General mumblings spread around the room.

"Whatever we think," Helen continued, as the voices gradually hushed, "we are stuck with him. So, let's make the best of it."

"Is he joining us for briefing?" Helen was surprised to see Townsend at the back, speaking up for a change.

"He's just familiarising himself with the investigation so far. I'm sure he'll join us when he's ready. Now what do we have?"

"He's a haemophiliac." Helen stared at DC Spencer. He had travelled over an hour, earlier that day, to interview Mrs Edwards and was feeding his findings back to the team.

"His mother says it has blighted his life. He hated being different from the other kids, having to avoid confrontation in case it went too far. Didn't have many friends, she puts it down to him moving schools twice due to bullying. He always wanted to join the Army, but failed the medical." He paused to look down at his notes. "He was an only child, she brought him up by herself and wouldn't be drawn on his father—said they haven't seen him for years. She still calls him by his real name, Kevin, although these days he prefers to be known as 'Kane'. Apparently, he re-named himself after the fictional Kung Fu character."

"Wasn't that spelt C-a-i-n-e?" Pemberton interjected. Everybody laughed. "It was one of my favourite shows as a kid," he admitted.

"Well he wasn't the brightest button at school by all accounts. Anyway, he discovered bodybuilding when he reached his late teens and his mother reckoned he almost doubled in size. Did a variety of jobs before he joined the prison service: car valet; taxi driver; worked in the Army surplus store, bouncer."

"Bouncer!" exclaimed Dark, "Great job for a haemophiliac." Everyone laughed.

"She seemed proud of him, keen to talk," Spencer continued, "really pleased that he joined the prison service. Last saw him two months ago and he seemed happy. He phoned her last Sunday, was talking about settling down, said he'd met someone. Was going to bring her over to meet her. She was ecstatic about this. It's the first time he's ever mentioned a girlfriend. Apparently, he's very private about that part of his life. Needless to say, she doesn't appear to know anything about the suspension or the drugs charge."

"Why did she think you were asking about him?" Helen asked.

"I just said there had been an incident in the prison and we were investigating. I didn't mention it had anything to do with him."

"Good work. We don't want her warning him that we're getting close."

"Oh, she wasn't surprised. She said he had alerted her that the police may get in contact. He fed her some dross about working undercover in the prison on a confidential case."

"She'll get a shock when this comes out," Dark said, shaking her head.

"Right," Helen interjected, keen to move on. "Thanks Steve. Anything from Intelligence?"

Pemberton shook his head. "We've circulated his image. Spoken to Area CID, Drugs Squad. Nothing at the moment. But they're on the look out."

Helen sighed. "OK. What else have we got?"

Dark raised her hand. "I spoke to the Prison Governor at Lardell."

"And?"

"Governor Wheelen remembered Edwards well. Apparently, his personal file makes for very interesting reading."

"Good," Helen said, "Details?"

Dark stood up. "His first post was A Wing," she said, consulting her notes. "Initially, they were very pleased with his progress. He seemed to build a rapport with the prisoners, easily diffuse situations, that sort of thing. But then a number of incidents gave rise to rumours that his relationship with some prisoners," she hesitated, looking for the right words, "lacked a certain professionalism, should we say?"

"Like?"

"The other guard that partnered him on A wing expressed concern that Kane was becoming lax in enforcing prison policy, extending privileges for some inmates like association time out of the cell, letting them spend time in the library on their own, that sort of thing." She extended her arm in an animated fashion.

"Then one day he walked into a cell, surprised to see Kane deep in conversation with a prisoner. They stopped talking as soon as they saw him, but he overheard part of the conversation which was enough to make him suspect that Kane might be passing messages, on behalf of the prisoner, to associates on the outside." She paused for a moment, as she turned the page, "The problem was they lacked evidence. He only overheard a few odd words. So, after six months, the Governor decided to move Kane to another wing under the pretence of a developmental move."

Helen nodded. "What happened then?"

Dark ran her eyes back over her notes. "He moved

to D Wing, where Rab was held, and he was a model officer for a while. It was several months before the other guard on D wing put in reports of Kane showing over-familiarity with certain prominent prisoners, one in particular from an organised crime background, a leading figure in drugs supply."

"Someone who would be still running their operation from the inside, and looking to manipulate anyone who could make that happen," Helen said. The role of a prison officer was notoriously low paid, a fact that did not escape inmates who were always on the look out for those who may be prone to corruption. "So, do we have a name?"

Dark nodded. "Carl Peacock was the key figure, based in Birmingham, doing twelve years for conspiracy to supply cocaine."

"I remember that one breaking," Pemberton interjected. "It was a huge haul at the time and a lengthy trial if my memory serves me right. He was a tricky customer with links all over the country."

"Get me everything you can on him. And speak to the Drugs Squad. See what they can give you on any links with our Area," Helen said.

"No problem."

"OK, Rosa, please continue."

"His association with Peacock and his friends reinforced their suspicion. Also, prison intelligence indicated that drugs were being brought on to the wing." She rubbed the back of her neck, turned the page again.

"Then, one day, after a routine search of the wing, the other officer doubled back, did another search of some of the cells. He found two sim cards in Peacock's and three small packets of cocaine in another that Kane had missed."

"So he was befriending particular inmates, those who could extend privileges to him on the outside?" Helen said.

Dark nodded. "Lardell is a Cat B prison-worst kind for manipulation. Wheelen suspected that Edwards had been bringing in drugs and sim cards for some time, it was just a matter of catching him in the act. But even this wasn't enough to dismiss him. He seemed relieved when they actually found a legitimate reason to get rid of him."

"How did they catch him?" Helen asked.

"They have routine checks in and out and then do spot checks on their cars regularly. It's all a bit honoured in the breach though, often there's a leak and they all seem to know when and where the spot checks will be. Well, this time they kept it quiet. Edwards was found with 1/2oz in his locker in four wrappers, along with three sim cards. But in his car they found another 1/2oz distributed amongst another four wrappers and twenty sim cards. He was cute though, he used 'quality street' sweet papers for wrappers. Actually the Governor was a bit disappointed. They were pretty convinced that he was supplying the harder stuff, heroin and cocaine, but didn't find anything near him that day."

Helen nodded. Since the relaxation in the cannabis laws, that quantity of the drug could be explained away for personal use. Although folding it into multiple separate wrappers was a strong indication of possession with intent to supply. "How was he receiving payment?" she asked.

"They found a notebook in his car, with many of the

inmates' girlfriends, siblings, friends, contacts details. When they raided these inmates' cells they found mobile phones and drugs wrapped in the same coloured papers."

Helen furrowed her brow. "How could Kane's charges not have come to light earlier?"

Pemberton cut in, "Lardell prison is one of the modern, privately owned ones. The Governor was away on holiday when we made our initial enquiries and they were very cagey with their information. It took all of my powers of persuasion to get Rab's personal records. And if he didn't give direct evidence and wasn't named on Kane's case, they probably felt it wasn't relevant."

"Fair enough. Might be worth getting the names of all of his associates in D Wing and running them through the normal checks? I guess Peacock was probably in charge, but it's possible some of the other prisoners may also have links to Hamptonshire." Helen thought for a moment. "So we have a man who struggled to make friends, no girlfriends either that we know of until recently, supplying drugs and sim cards to prisoners in return for payment and favours through their contacts on the outside? Free entrance to clubs, I'm assuming, women, the lot."

"He finally got the popularity he must have craved for years," Spencer said.

"Then someone shops him and bursts his bubble. He doesn't only lose his job, but more importantly the lifestyle," Pemberton said.

"Well we've put his face out there," Helen said. "Surely someone will know him, come forward? An address is all we need." She looked at her watch. "Tomorrow is Saturday. The papers will be out in the morning.

Are we all set up to man the phones?" Heads nodded back at her.

"OK everyone. Let's hope that we get a stroke of luck." As she turned to go a phone rang in the distance, a normal everyday occurrence in the incident room, but for some reason it turned her head.

The mumbles and movements of everybody moving back to work suddenly stopped too.

"Yes. Yes. Great. I'll pass that on. Thank you." DC Spencer put the receiver down and looked up curiously.

"What is it, Steve?"

"The tattooed skin that was sent to Anna Cottrell? That was forensics. They've found a short, grey/black hair attached to the back."

"Oh?"

"It's not human. It belongs to a dog—probably a German shepherd."

AN HOUR LATER, Helen wandered down to the little office, surprised to see the door closed and even more surprised when she opened it to find the room dark. George Sawford had obviously gone home for the evening. She switched on the light and glanced at the desk which was completely empty. Her policy log had gone with him.

TWENTY-ONE

THE GENTLE HUM of her phone woke Anna early. It was still dark outside. She stuck an arm out from underneath the duvet and dragged it off the bedside table to her ear.

"Anna?"

She didn't recognise the gravelly voice. "Yes."

"I wonder if you can help me?"

She peeled her eyes apart and looked at the screen, it was number withheld. "Who is this?" Sleep filled her voice.

"I'm a friend of a friend. I have some news about Ross."

She jolted up to a seated position. "Who is this?" she repeated.

"I can't discuss this on the phone."

Her scalp pricked, goose bumps tumbling down her neck, through her shoulders, spreading into her back. "Is he alive?" she breathed.

"Yes."

Her whole body tensed. "I'll get the police, they are here, they can help..."

"No!" he interrupted urgently. "No, Anna. No police."

Anna sat in silence for a moment. *No police.* A wave of nausea flew over her. This man clearly had some connection to Ross' disappearance. "What do you want with Ross?"

"Look, I'm doing a favour for a friend. They need some assistance. If you help me, Anna, then I'll help you. How does that sound?"

She sat in silence again, unsure of what to say. "What do I have to do?"

"I can't discuss it on the phone. Can you meet me, Anna, on your own?"

Anna froze. "Why?"

"So we can discuss it further?"

"How do I know you won't kidnap me?"

"Come on, Anna. Nobody is kidnapping anyone. I won't hurt you, I promise. I'm just passing on a message." He kept repeating her name over and over again, like somebody vying for her undivided attention. Well he had got it.

"And if I help you, I get Ross back?"

"Yes."

"Alive?"

"Yes."

Anna turned this over in her mind for a moment. "Prove to me that he is still alive."

The line went dead. Anna could feel panic making the hairs stand up on the back of her neck. Had she gone too far? Was he telling her the truth? What if this was the one opportunity she would have, the one chance to save Ross and she had messed it up?

She was just about to speak when she heard another voice at the end of the phone.

"Anna." It was barely a whisper.

"Ross!"

The gravelly voice returned. "Convinced?"

Her heart sank deep into her chest. "What have you done to him?" she asked.

"He's fine. Now, are we going to meet up?"

"Please don't hurt him."

He ignored her response. "Do you know Bracken Way?"

Bracken Way was a disused railway line that ran through Hampton. It was often used by dog-walkers, families and cyclists over the summer months. "Yes," she replied faintly. It was very secluded at this time of year. *The perfect place for a murder.*

"If you join it at the Keys Trading Estate entrance, walk up about half a mile, you'll see a bench in memorial to an Alan Thomas, who died in 1998. It's about twenty yards before the tunnel entrance. I'll meet you there at three o'clock."

Anna shuddered. She remembered cycling through the tunnels with Ross in summertime, perfectly dark apart from the odd glint of light through the old ventilation shafts—a surreal experience. She thought for a moment, feeling brow-beaten into submission. It was as if her strength were seeping out through the pores of her skin. Well if she couldn't save herself, she would try to help Ross. She owed him that much. "OK."

"You must be on your own. The people I work for are very wary. If there is any inkling that you have informed the police, or brought somebody with you, then you will never see Ross again."

"How do I know that you'll do what you say?" she asked, edgily.

"You just have to trust me. See you at three o'clock, prompt. I won't wait around." He rang off and she sat on the bed staring into space for a moment, not really sure what to do next. Had she done the right thing? Should she tell the police?

HELEN WALKED IN through the front of the house and carefully opened the kitchen door. It was empty. The house was unusually quiet. There was no TV blaring out, no music coming from upstairs, not even the sound of voices. She fixed her head on to one side. *Where is everyone?*

Suddenly, she heard a crash and the sound of laughter coming from the garden. She crossed the kitchen and looked out of the window to see her mother, Matthew and Robert throwing a ball to each other in the garden. The dog, who clearly hadn't noticed her arrival, was racing round and round them in circles, madly trying to catch the ball at each throw. Helen stood there a moment watching her family, a goofy grin tickling her lips. They looked so happy.

Robert noticed her first. He put his hand up and waved. Matthew followed his gaze and stuck up his thumb in greeting. Helen raised her own hand in utter amazement. *That is the first time Matthew has smiled in, well…* She wasn't sure how long.

The group were gathering together now and racing towards the door, Jane Lavery trailing behind, lifting a couple of terracotta pots that the hound had knocked over in its excitement. Helen braced herself for a grand greeting from the dog, but none came. She ran down the garden and into the kitchen alongside Robert, wagging her tail, adoring eyes not leaving his face. It seemed that he was much more interesting than she was.

"Hi, Mum." Robert said, his cheeks flushed from the exercise.

"Hi there. You all look to be enjoying yourself."

"We are." He looked down at the dog and rubbed her head lovingly. "Boomer's great, isn't she?"

Helen smiled.

"We're just going for a walk. Wanna come?" She looked over at Matthew as he spoke. His own pink cheeks made him look younger.

"I just popped home to pick up some papers…"

"Please!" Robert shouted. His face looked so angelic she couldn't find it in herself to say no.

She glanced at the station clock on the wall. It was twelve o'clock. She could call it her lunch hour. And there was nothing they could do but wait until there was a sighting of their suspect. Intelligence had been very poor on Hamptonshire links with both Carl Peacock and the other inmates on D Wing. The Drugs Squad had come up with a few possible names but nothing that had led them to Kane. Not surprising really, prominent figures in organised crime usually kept their tracks well covered. Plus the phones had been depressingly quiet all morning.

Helen was totally fed up with Sawford. Having probably been up for the best part of the night, pouring over her policy log, picking holes in her investigation, he had come in that morning loaded with questions. She had meticulously answered them one by one but, despite attending the morning briefing and being informed that Edwards was their number one suspect, he had said that he felt there were still unanswered questions from the Cottrell family background. Perhaps he could pursue this line whilst her team were busy tracing Kane? In the end, Helen had sent Townsend down to brief him, as the resident "expert" on the Cottrell family. They deserved each other. *That'll keep them both out of my hair for a while*, she had thought.

"I'm sure I can spare an hour." She winked. "I'll just make a quick call."

"Yeah!" Both boys grinned at her. *This is like the old days*, she thought to herself as she walked into the lounge to call the office, *when I was the most important thing in their world*. It might have been a nostalgic moment, probably short-lived, but it felt good.

Jane Lavery, having tidied the garden, walked through the back door as Helen re-entered kitchen. The dog immediately rushed over to her and she petted her head. "Good girl," she muttered, then turned to her daughter. "How are things?" she asked.

"Mum's coming for a walk with us," Robert said.

Jane Lavery looked at her daughter and smiled knowingly. "What a lovely idea. Why don't you go and get changed and I'll make you a quick cuppa before we go?"

As Helen walked back out into the hallway, she could see the local paper had landed on the doorstep. It always came early on a Saturday. She rushed towards it and opened it out. As promised, Kane Edwards stared back at her from the front page, his pale eyes more striking than ever. She took a deep breath and slowly exhaled through her mouth as she read the piece appealing for anyone who had seen this man to come forward. She checked her watch, bit her lip. Hopefully it was just a matter of time.

By the time she had hastily phoned Pemberton and told him she would be out for an hour, but to ring her immediately if there was any news at all, and walked back into the kitchen her family were all dressed up in coats and hats ready for their walk. She lifted her coffee mug to her lips and poured it down as quickly as the heat would allow.

"Where are we off to?" she asked, as they stepped out of the back door. The modern housing estate they lived on was at the edge of town. If you turned left at the main road at the bottom you headed back into town, turning right led you past a grassy field which had recently lost its herd of cows, alongside a working fir tree mill and then out to open countryside.

"The park," Robert said, running on ahead with the dog, Matthew close at his heels.

Helen sighed and Jane Lavery smiled at her. "No matter how much they grow, they still love the park."

Helen nodded.

"How are things at the office?"

"We've had a bit of a breakthrough."

"Great."

"Well, kind of. We have a fairly firm suspect but can't locate him at the moment. He seems to have disappeared off the face of the Earth."

"So you're playing the waiting game?"

"You've got it. Photo's out there, we're just hoping and praying someone will come forward."

"I'm sure they will."

"Me too. I have a good feeling about this one." They continued in silence, making their way back towards the town. They passed a newsagent with a stand of *Hampton Herald* newspapers outside. Helen crossed her fingers in her pocket. They just needed a little nudge.

After walking about a mile up the road they reached Oakwall Park, a large grassy area which included two football pitches, a tennis court and a stretch of river at the far side. Despite the chilling wind, the November sun had attracted many people. A group of lads were playing one goal football at the end of the footy pitch, the young children's play area was teeming with toddlers and small children climbing, swinging, racing down slides. A couple in the distance were walking a spaniel. It was a family afternoon in the park. Helen couldn't remember the last time she had done such a thing.

Robert and Matthew ran on ahead and Boomer followed them, clearly enjoying her exercise. Jane and Helen wandered along together behind, watching them. The dog ran over to the spaniel and they jumped around and rolled on the grass together, playing for a while. Helen smiled. Boomer was clearly a very friendly animal.

They made their way right across to the other side of the park towards the river. It was much quieter on this side. Robert had found a stick underneath one of the large oak trees and was throwing it for Boomer who was happily retrieving it. His grandmother went over to join him.

All of a sudden she felt a presence nearby and turned to see Matthew, running across the field to catch up with her. "Hi, Mum!"

"Hi there. OK?"

"Yeah. Listen, thanks for the leaflets. It looks really cool. Can I join?" His face looked flushed, happy.

Helen summoned up all her courage. And when she spoke the words, despite the Royal Air Force Cadets, or any force for that matter, being against her better judgement, she sounded positive, optimistic. "I think that would be a great idea."

"Thanks!" And then he took her completely by surprise by giving her a huge hug right in the middle of the park. She stood still in astonishment as he hurtled off across the field towards Robert and her mother who were now walking back in her direction.

She waited until they all reached her before moving on. A jogger passed them in a hooded jacket, the wire of an iPod just visible. Then no one—it was as if they had this part of the park to themselves. The sun felt deliciously warm and Helen undid her jacket.

Matthew and Robert were now attempting to climb a tree in the distance and Boomer ran back towards Helen and Jane and circled them. They had reached the river now and walked along its grassy bank. The dog went down for a drink.

"Boomy," Jane called, when she didn't re-appear. Nothing. "Boomer!" Still nothing. "Oh, where has she gone?"

"Don't worry, Mum, I'll run on ahead, maybe she's gone further down the riverbank." Helen snatched the lead and ran off, enjoying the feeling of the chilling wind on her face. She dropped down the bank and stopped, looking in both directions. Nothing.

"Boomer!" She followed the contour of the river around a bend and could just make out something in the distance. As she got closer she could see that it was Boomer, jumping around with a German shepherd. She started to jog. The dog saw her now and wagged her tail.

"Boomer, come!" The dog didn't respond to her call and stood wagging its tail beside a man sitting on a bench. He reached out to stroke her head. He looked vaguely familiar. Helen screwed her eyes up. He looked *very* familiar. Her heart skipped a beat.

She was almost upon them now. "Boomer!" she called. The dog ignored her. Helen looked at the man and he looked back at her. There was mutual recognition in their faces.

He got up quickly, towering above her. "Come on, Sam," he growled, and made up the bank. Helen scrambled to get the dog on a lead and raced off after him, trying to reach into her pocket for her mobile phone at the same time. But, by the time she reached the top of the bank, she could no longer see him.

Her boys rushed over and grabbed Boomer. "Guys can you take Boomy back to Granny please," Helen asked, her eyes darting back and forwards. "I need to get back to work now."

"Aren't you coming home to get changed first?" Robert asked.

Helen was looking about furiously. He couldn't disappear into thin air, surely not? And then she caught a glimpse of the tall figure in the distance with the dog. Jane Lavery had joined them now. "Mum, I need to get back to work *now*," she said to her mother. "I'll leave the boys with you."

"No problem. Come on lads." And with a quick hug to Robert she moved on into a quick jog, trying to remain as inconspicuous as possible. She could see that he had reached the far end of the park and was waiting to cross the main road. She peered around from behind a tree trunk and quickly removed her jacket, tying it around her waist inside out and tucked her hair behind her ears. It was a small concession at looking different, but worth a chance. The road was busy with Saturday afternoon shoppers making their way out of town. He stood still for a while, waiting for a gap in the traffic.

Helen took her chance and lifted her mobile phone, racing through the options. She selected the wrong number in her haste. *Come on!* Cancelled and re-selected. Eventually Pemberton answered.

He was crossing the road. She would have to talk and go. "Sean, it's me. I don't have much time. I'm in Oakwall Park and I'm heading towards Birch Road. I've located Kane Edwards and I'm following him. I need backup here, now."

"Are you OK?"

"Yes, fine. Quickly please!"

"Stay on the line." She could hear him fire instructions into the background. It was less than a minute before he responded, "IRT will be there in three minutes. ETA eight minutes for the armed response car. Are you still OK?"

Helen was out of breath. She had nipped in and out of the traffic and was desperately trying to stay on the trail of her suspect. "Yes, I'm in Groves End. I can see him, he's just turned a corner into Lime Street." Lime Street was lined with large old Victorian terraces, many of which had been converted into apartments and flats. Those in the job called it "bedsit land". It was also the centre of the red light district of Hampton.

Helen crossed Groves End and clung to the parked cars as she approached the entrance to Lime Street. A Toyota Hiace camper van was parked directly opposite the junction. She peered through its windows. *Damn.* He had gone again. Then, she just caught sight of the dark tail wagging as it entered a house, before it disappeared and a door banged shut.

Helen glanced along the road. It was the house on the end. From her position here, she could watch the front entrance and the side gate, which was the rear access. She ran across the road, glimpsed the number and crossed back quickly. "Number 84 Lime Street, on the corner of Lime Street and Groves End. He's inside…"

ANNA LOOKED OUT of her bedroom window for the ump-teenth time and shot another glance at her watch. It was half-past one. Her father was still in the garden. The garden was her only hope of escape. As a teen-ager she'd climbed out of her bedroom side window a couple of times, down on to the extension of the garage roof which swept below. From there she had shimmied down the drainpipe and out into the garden. Of course she was convinced that her father knew what she was up to, but he never told her mother. It was their shared, unspoken secret. This way she was able to go out to some of the parties that her mother would never have approved of. She'd even mastered the art of climbing up, back then. She stared down at the garage roof below, estimating it was only about a three-metre drop. She was a few pounds heavier these days, but surely she could still manage it?

A knock at the door broke her concentration. She jumped back like a naughty child up to mischief. "Yes?"

Kathleen Cottrell put her head around the door. "I've made a late lunch. A selection of sandwiches mostly." *A selection of sandwiches, anyone would think she was entertaining the Queen.* Anna glanced across at her. This was typical of her Kathleen, initially arguing against a police presence "intruding into her home". As soon as PC Emma Cole arrived she automatically treated her as the house-guest.

DCI Lavery had explained that Family Liaison Of-ficers were very specially trained to be unobtrusive to family life, providing a supporting link between the police and the family. Anna guessed that the police woman was in her late thirties, a round woman of me-dium height, with dark, curly hair that danced on her shoulders and dimples that appeared in both cheeks when she smiled. Dressed in a calf length black skirt and lilac blouse, Anna thought she looked more like a health visitor than a police officer.

But she had to admit that PC ("Call me Emma") Cole had certainly settled in very well. She had an easy way about her and seemed to affect just the right mannerisms and say just the right words to impress Kathleen. Anna had caught them laughing together in the kitchen that morning, Emma with a cup of tea in her hand, tea contained in Kathleen's Royal Doulton—a service preserved for only *special* visitors.

"I'm not hungry, thank you."

"You ought to eat something."

Not wishing to alarm her mother or give any clues as to her plan, Anna thought fast. "I know, I'm sorry," she said in the most convincing voice she could muster. "I'm just tired. Perhaps I could come down and have some a bit later?"

Kathleen angled her head. "Oh, OK dear, if you wish." She turned and left the room.

Anna listened to the footsteps disappearing down the stairs. Then, to her delight, Kathleen called her father in from the garden. This was her chance. She watched her dad disappear from sight and slowly opened the largest of her windows. The chill rushed in and caught her in the chest, forcing a shiver. *Quick now.* She reached over and grabbed an old, red hooded fleece from the chair beside her bed. Her face creased at its colour. She would have to put it on when she was safely away over the fields. Then she wound her legs out of the window, reaching down as far as possible, and jumped.

A slight thud left her in a crouched position. She

stayed still for several seconds, until convinced that the noise hadn't caused alarm, rubbing her legs. They felt OK, so she shifted over to the edge. Shimmying down the drainpipe which navigated the side of the garage and into a water butt at the bottom proved to be more difficult than she had remembered. The fittings had decayed over the years becoming loose in the wall. She slipped a couple of times, grazing both her knees, dropping the fleece jacket. But eventually her feet found the water butt and she was down. The fleece landed in a soft pile next to her.

Anna looked around. She couldn't slip out through the side and past the front of the house, like she had done years ago, in case there were any police officers out there. No, this time she had to pass through the garden, climb the fence at the bottom and circumvent the field beyond to take her back to the main road. This was the most dangerous part.

Anna froze and listened carefully. The absence of voices from the kitchen indicated that her mother had served lunch in the dining room. She really was in entertainment mode. And without a backward glance she ran, as fast as she could, down the 200-yard garden and clambered over the four-foot fence at the bottom. For a while she stayed put, on the other side of the fence, catching her breath and listening hard. Then, for the first time in days, a smile actually spread across her face. She was free.

THE RAPID RESPONSE vehicles arrived first, but covertly as Helen had insisted. No blues and twos, no sirens. She didn't want to alert Edwards until they were ready, until everything was in place. This was belt and braces. The last thing they wanted was an escape on their hands. They parked secretly in the road parallel to Lime Street, communicating with her through Pemberton whom she remained connected to on her mobile phone the whole time.

Then came the firearms team, looking like a bunch of prima donna actors, trussed up in bullet-proof vests that over exaggerated their biceps. Helen guessed that every one of them, even the women, harboured child-hood desires to be James Bond. They quietly spread through the area.

Helen had been required to wait for the tactical advisor for the firearms team to contain the area, liaise with force intelligence to find out who was registered as living at the address, made sure that it was as safe as possible for his officers to enter the property. She understood the need for these provisions. If intelligence suggested that a family with children lived at this address, it would be wrong to enter en masse—they may have a hostage situation on their hands, or worst still create one, putting officers in undue danger. But right now the clock was ticking away...

As soon as he gave her the signal, she, still hidden behind the campervan on the opposite side of the road, raised her mobile to her ear. She gave the command, "3-2-1-Go, go, go!"

Armed officers flew from their positions behind cars, tucked around corners, low behind fences.

Bang! The door was pushed in with the battering ram. Body after body of heavily armoured officers streamed into the house. The noise became a din, as tumultuous voices, banging of doors, thunder of footsteps all merged together. Helen heard a dog barking, more shouting, doors slamming… *Come on*, she thought, *bring him out.*

An officer came out holding the German shepherd's collar. "It's only a pup," he called out laughing. It was animated, geared up by all the excitement. *Where is he?* thought Helen. Uniformed bodies started piling out of the house. Helen walked over to the front door. "What's going on?"

"He's not here," PS Bates, head of the Armed Unit, said.

"What do you mean, not here? We've been watching both the front door and the rear exit. How can he have left?"

"No idea, but he's gone. You'll want to get in there and take a look though—he's one twisted geezer."

TWENTY-TWO

KANE EDWARDS' FLAT occupied the whole first floor of the end terraced house. The front door led directly into the lounge. Furnishings were limited to a brown three-seater sofa and a television in one corner. The room was dominated by three elements. Firstly, Anna. The wall behind the television was plastered with photographs of her: Anna in the café with Rab, Anna on her bicycle, Anna's rear as she made her way through a crowd outside her flat, Anna in her parents' garden; side profiles, full frontals, pictures taken from every angle. There was even a photo of Anna in the police-issue, navy jogging suit she had worn home from the station, the Saturday before.

As if the photographs weren't chilling enough, the opposite wall was covered with computer printouts, posters, pages torn from books of the armed forces—soldiers at war. As Helen's eyes flicked over the pieces she picked up a theme, a focus. The photos showed soldiers from different disciplines, cultures, countries and backgrounds. She could clearly see the Italian Army parading in all their finery, the Russian Red Army marching, the British RAF saluting and pictures of warships, tanks, aeroplanes.

As she scanned down she noticed that the pieces were becoming more specific. There were printouts of means of torture—water boarding in the Iraq war, amputation in Sierra Leone. Goose bumps formed on her arms. DC Spencer's words flashed in her mind, "...haemophiliac...blighted his life... Always wanted to join the military, but failed the medical..." Was it possible for someone's thwarted ambition to turn so ugly? The majority of articles and printouts appeared to focus on the Russian/Afghan war in the 1980s and in particular the Mujahedeen tactic of slicing the skin off Soviet soldiers. Helen shivered. He was studying his art. Just as a bird watcher may gather books, articles, photos about his hobby, Kane Edwards was doing the same. Was slicing tattoos from his victims just the beginning?

Strangely, that wasn't the thing that bothered Helen most. What really worried her, what really turned her blood to ice, was the number of weapons he had accrued. A samurai sword hung off the wall alongside a bayonet and above a couple of sabre claw knives. The carpet underneath the window was strewn with nun chucks. She walked into the kitchen again and caught sight of a baseball bat, leaning neatly against the wall beside the back door.

Helen's stomach churned as she pulled out her mobile phone and dialled Pemberton's number urgently. He answered on the second ring.

"Sean, get hold of the liaison officer at the Cottrells, will you? Make sure that she locks all the doors and keeps all family members inside."

"No problem."

"And make sure the armed car's down there will you?"

"Will do. I take it he's given you the slip?"

"Yes," she sighed, "but we need to catch him and

quick. By the looks of his flat he's working up to something. And there's no telling what will happen if we don't get him off the streets now."

ANNA WAS ANGRY, angry at the intrusion into her personal life, her home, her belongings, her relationships. Angry at the emotional pain and suffering inflicted on her family and those close to her over the past eight days. Angry with the lies, secrets, deception she had unknowingly faced over the years. And the anger fired her up as she trudged through the fields towards Cross Keys.

She could hear her phone ringing and pulled it out of her pocket. Recognising DCI Lavery's number she scowled at it and rejected the call. A text message also flashed in the inbox and she clicked to see who it was— Rab. She sighed and put it back into her pocket without even reading the message. *Leave me alone.*

The ring road roundabout at Cross Keys was busy with shoppers heading in and out of Hampton city centre, families travelling to and from their destinations, people on their way home from work. She had to wait several minutes before she could get across and take the third exit into Keys Trading Estate.

In stark contrast the trading estate was quiet. She passed a car workshop with a few vehicles parked outside, a printing company, which looked deserted, two engineering companies and a couple of brick buildings which looked like offices. One was called "Angel Sportswear" but the A was hanging off the sign. They all showed little sign of life. Anna guessed that many of them either didn't work Saturdays or opted for an early finish. Only a few die-hards were left to finish up. As she progressed into the trading estate the noise of the traffic eventually subsided. She left it all behind her and it felt strangely peaceful.

Her thoughts turned back to Ross. She knew now that she would sacrifice herself for him if necessary. Dying would be easy compared to the life she had lived this past week. It would feel like someone switching off the light, taking away all the pain, the confusion, the distress to those around her. This wasn't living. It was more like living hell. She continued on her path deeper into the estate.

The entrance to Bracken Way was set back from the road, surrounded by a small car park, marked with the sign of a white bicycle on the blue background for the "National Cycle Network". Formerly a railway line, it had fallen victim to the mass cull of the railways in the 1960s and lay stagnant for many years. Around thirty years ago the neighbouring councils clubbed together and invested in a development programme which transformed it into a cycle and walking route, placing several small car parks and picnic areas at intervals along the route so that people could decide how far they wished to travel.

Anna thought back to when she had last used this route with Ross. The track ran for almost twenty-two miles, but not many people covered the whole route, apart from the seriously determined cyclists. They had packed a picnic and cycled the whole length and back, on that warm August afternoon, encountering walkers, cyclists, runners, families, couples, people walking dogs, on the way. It had been a hive of activity, families jostling for a safe area to take the children and a flat ride on their bikes. There had even been an ice-cream van parked at this entrance.

But there was no ice-cream van today, no crowds to be seen. Even the car park was empty. *Perfect place for a murder.*

Anna stepped on to the track uneasily, eyes darting around. She could smell damp wood, the branches on the trees not recovering from the recent rain. The silence was eerie.

Paradoxically this disused railway track lay only a mile from the busy Cross Keys roundabout. But even at this time of year, when their leaves had disappeared, the mature, broad leaf trees and high vegetation managed to block any noise.

Nervous doubts crept into her mind. *Should I tell someone where I am? Just in case?* She forced one foot in front of the other, towards the tunnel entrance. Her pace slowed slightly, but she wouldn't allow herself to stop. If she stopped she would turn back, she knew it. *And then what would happen to Ross?* Apprehension flooded her veins.

The sudden buzz of her phone made her jump. *Calm down.* She stopped, retrieved it from her pocket—another message from Rab. She sighed and stared at his name for a long moment. This was her chance. A quick text was all it would take. *Perhaps this is a trap? If I just...*

At that moment she felt a strange sensation. The hairs on the back of her neck stood on end. Somebody, somewhere was watching her.

Anna looked up. The tunnel was now in sight in the distance. Was that movement down at the bottom? She scrunched up her eyes. She wasn't sure if it was a figure or the bare branch of a tree hanging down. Hastily, she put her phone back in her pocket, not quite summoning the courage to turn it off. *Perfect place for a murder.*

She started walking again and soon realised, about two hundred yards from the cavernous tunnel entrance that it was a huge tree branch, belonging to an old oak tree. It looked like it had been hit by lightning, hanging awkwardly away from the main part of the trunk. She breathed a sigh of relief and carried on walking.

It was just as she reached the bench that she heard it. A soft crunch, followed by a gravelly voice behind her, "You can stop right there…"

As HELEN ENDED the call to Pemberton, she felt crushed. Anna had disappeared from her parents' home, slipped out without anyone knowing. How could that have happened? Her mind was buzzing. Now they had lost Kane and Anna. This was a recipe for disaster.

Her father had told her that heading a murder investigation was like a drug. He should know. He had carried the job for almost fifteen years, right up to his retirement. He had said, when you worked a case, caught your killer, you made a huge difference to everybody's lives. This was the big time, catching the real bad guys—there was no other job that offered the same rush.

Except right now Helen didn't feel any rush. It was all going belly up. And with *Celebrity Cop* Sawford breathing down her neck, this was all she needed. She could just imagine his insidious mind working overtime now, plotting how he could turn this around to suit his own ends. She reached for her phone, selected Rab McCafferty's name and actually crossed her fingers as she pressed dial.

ANNA SWUNG AROUND, then froze. The man behind her froze too. He didn't say anything for what seemed like several minutes, just stood, like a waxwork statue, staring back at her. A familiar statue.

Anna cast her eyes behind him in confusion, then found her voice at last, "I wasn't expecting…"

His eyes pierced her skin. He seemed to read her mind. "Had to make sure you weren't being followed."

"Where's Ross?" Anna stared back at him defiantly, using all of the bravado she could find, battling to get the words out evenly. *Where have I seen you before?* She thought inwardly.

Kane Edwards stared back at her, his eyes open rather too wide for her liking. Then he tilted his head to one side as a mischievous, evil smile crept on to his lips. "All in good time."

This is wrong. Get out of here.

Kane held his head back, took a long, deep breath through his nose and looked around him. "It's lovely here, isn't it?" he said, finally resting his eyes upon her again. They were so pale, so menacing.

Who are you? She tried to stand tall. "You said you have some information about Ross?"

He looked her up and down and she felt as though a large spider was crawling up her neck.

"I did, didn't I?"

"Look, if you've lied to me…"

"Do you like blond men, Anna?"

Her stomach churned.

"I like brunettes. I like you." He took a step closer and she instinctively stepped back, stumbling in her wake.

Fear crept through her veins. *Keep him talking.* "Let Ross go. Please?"

His face clouded slightly. "We can talk about Ross later. Let's get to know each other first, eh?" He reached forward and attempted to run his index finger down the side of her face, but she ducked out of the way defiantly.

"Come on, Anna, we're just being friendly."

Her stomach turned upside down. He was much taller than her, well over a foot, and he wore combat trousers and a combat gilet, the pockets bulging. His arms were bare, in spite of the cold weather. She looked at his yellow teeth, his thinning white-blond hair scraped away from his face. He lifted an equally yellow, tobacco tinged finger and rubbed it along his jaw line. All the time he stared straight into her eyes, a gesture she found disconcerting. If he did blink, she didn't notice.

"What do you want from me?" Anna asked finally.

"Just to get to know you a bit better," he said, his piercing eyes looking deep into her.

"What do you mean? I don't even know who you are," she said confounded.

He reached into one of the top pockets and pulled out something.

Anna gasped. Her address book. The one she couldn't find in her flat. That meant...

"I feel I know you quite well myself," Kane responded, a cruel smile on his lips.

She wanted to turn, to run, but her feet were rooted to the floor. He was much taller than her, maybe even fitter. No doubt, he would be much quicker. She managed a swift glance over her shoulder.

Again, he tilted his head to one side. "Looking for someone?"

She shook her head, small jerking movements, but said nothing. The truth of the matter was that nobody knew she was here. All those chances... Rab had tried to contact her. But no. She did nothing. And now she was here, all alone.

"Leave me alone."

He put the book back in a pocket. "Don't be like that. Come on, we have a lot in common you and I. We both like Muse."

"W-What?"

"And I love the intermezzo too. *Raging Bull* is one of my favourite films." She looked back at him puzzled, feeling completely at a disadvantage. "And I listen to *'Eyes Open'* all the time. Just like you..."

The penny dropped. He hadn't only taken her address book, he also had her iPod. "Where's Ross?" She struggled to keep her voice even.

He stood still and raised his eyes to the sky. Perhaps now she could run, turn, quick, if she just...

And then he put his hand into another of the pockets on his jacket, and pulled out the knife. And she knew it was too late...

The blood rushing through her veins turned icy cold. She felt trapped. She turned to run, but he was quick, too quick. He grabbed hold of her by the lapel of her fleece, pointing the knife at her throat. Struggle would be useless, the tip pressing against her skin.

She peered down her nose at the knife. "What do you want from me?" she cried, her palms sweating despite the rapidly declining temperatures. The sun's light was just starting to fade, open skies leading the way to a frosty night.

He ignored her question. She looked up to see his

grey eyes filled with malice, spittle in the corner of his mouth. He looked like a wild animal, preparing for the kill. Or a supernatural character in a film. She shivered, physically repulsed.

He laughed bitterly. He was enjoying himself.

Behind him she saw a movement in the distance. *Yes.* It was a person she was convinced of it. *Don't focus on them. Don't draw attention.* Short glances. It was a man. He was within thirty yards now. Her stomach bounced briefly, then confusion set in…

"Get your hands away from her, Edwards!"

Kane jumped. Anna moved back, lashed out with her leg. But he was too quick for her. She felt a sharp sting as the knife scratched the first layer of skin. Then he tossed her around so that she had her back to him, his thick arms tightening their grip around her.

"Well, well, well. If it isn't McCafferty," he said. "I wondered if you'd show up."

Anna's mind was in a spin. How did Rab know they were here? Unless… Were Rab and Edwards in this together? Some kind of deranged feud against her?

Suddenly, a light switch flicked in her brain. At that moment she finally realised why Kane looked familiar. She *had* seen his face before. He looked like, no he was, the man who she had crashed into on her bike at the end of Ross' road. The day Ross went missing. The day she went to meet Rab. And he was the man who had stared at her from across the road, when she had been in the coffee house with Rab. How many other times had he been there? Stuck at the back of a crowd, hidden behind a parked car, secluded down an alleyway, watching her. Stalking her… She gulped as if there wasn't enough oxygen in the air. What was Rab's role in all of this?

"I'm serious Edwards, get away from her," Rab continued.

"Where do you get off telling me what to do?" he hissed back.

"She's done nothing wrong."

"No, but you have." Anna was sure she could feel his face sneering. He sniffed at her hair and she shivered.

"I don't know what you're talking about."

"No?" He lifted the knife.

"You've got the wrong guy," Rab said. There was desperation in his voice. "It wasn't me. I might not have approved of what you did, but I'm not a snitch."

"It's too late. I know it was you. Estrange told me."

Rab blew a quick, short breath out of his nose. Estrange had been Rab's cell-mate. He had bought heroin off Kane, but Kane couldn't keep up with his demand. "It was Estrange who shopped you. He's done the double bluff."

"I don't believe you. You've ruined my life. Now I'm going to wreck yours."

Rab held his hands in the air. "I'm telling the truth. Honest."

"Ha—an ex con telling the truth. How do you expect me to believe you?"

"Think about it." Nobody spoke for a moment. Time stood still.

Anna wished she could see Kane's face. Work out what he was thinking.

"Let her go!" The voice came from behind them. Kane jolted and turned around. Anna kicked out again. He lost his balance. She slipped out of his grip, ran towards Rab.

She heard a loud crack and then felt a sharp pain as

something heavy hit her. Everything seemed to move in slow motion, like in a car crash. You see yourself rolling into the back of another car, your foot is fixed on the brake but it's too late, too late to stop. Dream and reality mixed together. For a moment she was numb, then she could smell grass by her nose, taste mud in her mouth. Then, pain. Severe, excruciating pain slicing through her stomach. Anna tried to open her eyes but they were glued shut. Voices in the distance were blurring together as a wave of fatigue and pain flew over her. *If this is dying, it's almost easy*, she thought to herself. Just give in to the tiredness, let it sweep you up and take all the pain and complications of the last eight days away. Suddenly, she could hear someone calling her in the background. It sounded like Ross' voice. And then it went all black.

TWENTY-THREE

"Ross?" Anna looked up towards the eyes of a blurred image. Her mouth felt dry. Speech was an effort.

"It's all over now," a voice replied. There was a hint of an Irish accent.

That's not Ross. She blinked, her vision sharpening. She could see the white interior, feel a blanket over her. There was an oxygen mask, wrapped dressings, a man in green overalls—*an ambulance.* She tried to sit up, but felt a hand on her shoulder.

"Lie down, you need to stay calm."

Anna swallowed, but continued to push against his hand. For a moment, when she had thought she was dead, she had imagined herself joining Ross, being re-united in a kind of heaven together. Now it haunted her. *No, this isn't right. It was supposed to be me.* "Ross!" she yelped.

"Come on. It's over. They've got him. You're safe now." The voice was soothing.

Got who? She wanted to say. Instead, she felt a stab of pain in her arm. And then more darkness.

Helen checked the final words to her report, before she clicked the print key. There was still heaps of work to be done. Files would need to be put together. CSI were still gathering evidence from Kane Edwards' flat. They had found footprints in the backyard beside the fence—it looked as though he had jumped the fence and escaped across the other gardens. These footprints would be measured, examined along with all the other evidence that would need to be bagged up, labelled, sorted and filed in readiness for court. She guessed they would go for trial. Edwards had gone "no comment" throughout his interview—popular advice from solicitors who thought their clients were banged to rights. No problem, they would be ready for him. And, until then, he would be remanded in custody.

Helen thought of his home: the pictures of Anna, the obsession with the military, the numerous weapons. Her mind moved on to Ross. When they had reached the trio on the Bracken Way, they had carried out a search of the surrounding area, discovering a farm track that ran along in front of the tunnel entrance, connecting the two fields either side. On the left side, 300 yards up the track, her officers had found a motorcycle, beside a small thicket.

Through the bare branches, they found an old, disused pump station. In summer months it would have been engulfed in the undergrowth, hidden away from the road. And this time of year, with the surrounding fields containing only arable farming, nobody, not even the farmer, would have any need to come down the track. A perfectly secluded location on private land—close enough to the Bracken Way to walk up and meet Anna, far enough away so that nobody, even the odd dog-walker that may use the Way at this time of year, would hear Ross' muffled cries for help. Kane had been careful to remove the boards at the back, using the rear entrance, again out of view from the track. She wondered how long he had searched for such a place?

Ross had been found, only just alive, prostrate on the floor, arms by his side. He was strapped at both ankles and both wrists, with a mixture of duct tape and plastic gardens ties, to a five bar, metal gate. More duct tape was wound around his waist and fastened over his mouth. There had been a black hood over his head and a make-shift noose was tied around his neck out of white nylon rope. She imagined Kane seeking out something to tie him to, contemplating what he should use to secure his prisoner. He would have been pleased with his choice. The gate would have been taken from a nearby field and provided the opportunity to secure Ross firmly, against a heavy, unwieldy object, preventing movement or escape.

They had found other items in the pump station, too. A plethora of weapons, knives (hunting and sabre tooth), laid out neatly like a surgeon's table by the door, alongside a video camera. *What had he been planning to do with that?* A shiver ran down her spine. It didn't do to dwell on the madness of killers.

George Sawford had appeared outwardly magnanimous, shaking her hand, patting her on the back. But she could see that he was inwardly seething. With her Super seeking promotion, he obviously had his eye on his job. It would be a great short term move for him, Superintendent on the Homicide Team was just about the most high profile job you could get at that level. Well, this was one result that wouldn't go on his CV.

She thought of her family. She had barely spent any real time with them the last week or so. That was something that needed addressing, and sooner rather than later.

ANNA SAT ON the corner of Ross' bed, stroking his hand gently. The thought that he was here because of her, his relationship with her had put him through the torture of the last few days, stupefied her.

On the floor below, her brother was in bed with a bullet wound. A bullet that had been meant for her. She rubbed her stomach which still bore the bruises caused by him leaping at her when Kane had brandished the gun, rugby tackling her to the ground, where she hit her head and lost consciousness. It wasn't until she came around in the hospital that she discovered that her injuries were minor. They kept her in for observations in case of brain trauma, but it was more shock than anything else.

Rab had taken the bullet in his shoulder, but would live. Luckily. She found it hard to believe that the root of the revenge, the attacks on her, her family, her boyfriend had derived from him. It stuck in the back of her throat. On the one side she felt as if she didn't see him again, it would be too soon. On the other—well he took a bullet for her, he saved her life. And it wasn't his fault that a deranged monster sought revenge on him for something he didn't even do, torturing his family to get at him. It was all such a mess. A mess that was now untangling, the threat of danger ceased. And could she blame Rab for trying to find his sister, for unconditionally loving her in spite of the empty years that had passed between them?

When he had suddenly arrived on the Bracken Way, half of her was grateful to see him, the other half suspicious. How had he found her? It was the DCI who told her that, fearing for her safety, he had put a tracker on her mobile phone. *"Techy". That's what he was doing with my phone in the flat.* She remembered how suspicious she'd felt at the time. But without that tracker he wouldn't have been able to locate her, or alert the police to her whereabouts. And who knows what would have happened? She shuddered.

When she had finally awoken it had been light outside. She'd been allowed to sit up, eat half a bowl of cornflakes, drink strong milky tea. DCI Lavery had come to see her, explaining how Rab had told her that the tracker showed that Anna had joined Bracken Way. He had been following the signal himself, arriving only a few minutes before they did. Armed police had surrounded the area, just at the moment when Rab was confronting Kane. It had been PS Bates' voice that had called out to Kane, taking him by surprise, disorientating him for a split second. Kane had stood still as Anna ran towards Rab then, just as she reached him, he had drawn the Glock from his pocket and taken a shot in Anna and Rab's direction, before dropping the gun and being tussled to the ground. A search of the surrounding area then discovered Ross, tucked away in a nearby disused pump station, less than 300 yards from the entrance to the tunnel. It was amazing he was still alive.

Anna touched his hand gently and he stirred in his sleep, turning his head slightly. She stroked the red marks around his wrist where the ties had cut into his skin, then looked over at the fresh dressing on his arm where his tattoo had once been. She had been told that Kane had washed and dressed the wound, to avoid infection, covered him in a blanket to keep him warm. Kept alive, no doubt, in case he needed to be used as bait. But the cold weather had induced mild hypothermia and there were now tubes entering his body at every visible orifice.

She would make it up to him. And her parents. The events of the last nine days had taught her that blood alone doesn't make a relationship. There are more important things like loyalty, friendship, support. Even her mother... Right now her family felt like the most important people in her world and she would make sure that they knew it.

"MY ROUND THEN. What are we having?" Pemberton said, standing and stretching his back before grabbing his glass for a refill. Every member of the incident team (apart from Sawford who had excused himself under the guise of an important dinner party) had gathered in the pub to celebrate and they were in good spirits.

"Excuse me for a moment, will you?" Helen asked. "I just need to make a quick call." It was a lame excuse. Phone home and then make a sharp exit. Right now she needed to give time to her family, support Matthew, help Robert with his homework, give her mother some adult company.

She stood in the small pub entrance outside the men's toilets, curling her nose at the smell of the urine. The phone was engaged. She rung off and stared back into the pub through the open door. Her eyes fell on Townsend at the far end of the bar, chatting up one of the custody suite assistants. She stared at him for a while. They hadn't spoken properly since the argument in the Super's office. She had been aware of his continuing presence in the incident room, but he had shrunk to the background, rarely speaking up or drawing attention to himself, just working behind the scenes. Was he ashamed of himself? It didn't look like it at the moment.

It's a shame really, she thought. He had shown that he was capable of good work. But he couldn't work as part of a team. And all those negative vibes... She rolled her shoulders backwards. His clock was ticking. He may have weathered these sorts of storms at the Met, but this behaviour wouldn't be tolerated in the smaller forces of the provinces. It was just a matter of time.

She sighed and tried home again. It rang several times before she heard a voice.

"Hello?"

"Mum, it's me."

"Oh. Hi, darling. You OK?" There was the sound of laughter in the background.

"Yeah, you?"

"Fine thanks." The dog started to bark, a deep drone, lifted from the pit of its stomach.

Helen hesitated, waited for it to pause. "Mum, just wanted to say..." Her voice was drowned out by more excited barking. It sounded like somebody was playing a game with her.

"Sorry dear, I can't hear you. Quiet Boomy." More laughing in the background as the barking subsided.

"Sounds like you're all having a good time?"

Her mother giggled. "The boys are playing 'Just Dance' on the Wii and Boomy is trying to join in."

Helen smiled to herself, imagining the scene. The dog barked again. "OK, as long as everyone is all right?" She raised her voice to beat the background noise.

"We're fine, thank you."

"I should be back in a couple of hours."

"Great, see you then." Helen clicked to end the call,

the corners of her mouth turning up slightly. Just at that moment a rush of excitement hit her by surprise, almost knocking her sideways. She had never felt so exhilarated. This must be what her father had referred to. *It should be accompanied by a health warning.*

She bit her lip for a moment, pocketed her phone and marched back into the bar. Pemberton was still at the counter, waving a note in front of the busy bar staff.

She stood next to him. "I'll have a vodka and coke," she said smiling. *Plenty of time later for homework...*

The End

* * * * *

ACKNOWLEDGEMENTS

This was my first novel, originally published by US based Rainstorm Press in 2012, and will always be special as it marked the start of my journey in this crazily addictive publishing world.

Special thanks go to all the police officers who helped with procedural research (you know who you are) and also to Chris Lowe, former Divisional Officer of Northants Fire Service, who assisted in house fire research. Any deviations or errors in the book are purely my own.

There were many people who read parts of the script and gave feedback in the early days: Esther Newton, Tim Glister, Joanna Lambton, my dear friend Jean Bouch; my dad and stepmother, David and Lynne. Thanks so much for believing in the book and giving up your precious time to read it and help me to develop my ideas. Gratitude also goes to Rainstorm Press for launching the novel first time around.

I have been blessed with wonderful support by readers, book clubs, book bloggers and reviewers who championed the novel and helped to spread the word when it was originally published. In particular I'd like to thank Dingley book club, Broughton book club, Marvellous Readers, Liz Barnsley at LizLovesBooks, Christine at NorthernCrime and Bernadette Davies. So many more and far too many to mention here—I really appreciate you all. This year I joined 'Book Connectors', 'Crime Book Club' and 'The Book Club' on Facebook and am hugely grateful to all the wonderful readers there who have supported my later work.

Since the rights of this novel reverted to me and the idea to release it myself grew, so many friends rallied around to guide me through the self-publishing process. Huge thanks go to Ian Patrick for his unrelenting support and friendship, Rebecca Bradley for always being at the end of the phone line and Linda Huber for answering all my silly questions and providing a shoulder of support. Once again, far too many others to mention here—I'm truly grateful to you all.

Most importantly, love and thanks to my wonderful husband, David, for painstakingly reading all my scripts in their infancies, and my daughter Ella, who is always cooking me up something to nibble on while I'm at the screen for hours on end.